Shujoy Dutta did a Masters in Philosophy from St Stephen's College, Delhi and entered the world of advertising in 1997. He spent the next ten years in the Creative departments of some of Delhi's leading advertising agencies and the next nine in Strategic Planning, winning awards for both his Creative work and his Planning.

While growing up, he spent a lot of his summer vacations in Haridwar, in the company of many strange and spiritually-minded people. Some of the conversations he had then and the ideas they threw up, made their way to this novel. He is also an amateur palmist and an Internet enabled novice astrologer.

Shujoy enjoys reading about the occult and hopes that one day he will be a Masterchef and chess Grandmaster, but in the meantime, spends his time frying eggs and playing on a chess app set at home. He also dreams of setting up a commune, somewhere near the sea, where artists and writers can live, create, farm, work and eat together. He lives in Gurgaon with his wife.

Like a Pinprick to the Heart

Shujoy Dutta

SPEAKING
TIGER

SPEAKING TIGER PUBLISHING PVT. LTD
4381/4, Ansari Road, Daryaganj,
New Delhi–110002, India

First published in India by Speaking Tiger in paperback 2016

ISBN: 978-93-85288-80-7
eISBN: 978-93-85288-78-4

10 9 8 7 6 5 4 3 2 1

The moral right of the author has been asserted

Typeset in Adobe Caslon Pro by SÜRYA, New Delhi

For my gurus, big and small

One

My father could smell death. He describes it as an overpowering odour, a festering rot. My grandmother had more abilities than I can describe in a line. My sister can communicate with the dead or, let's just say, with other dimensions. My uncle can see spirits, my aunts, well my father's cousins really, get a lot of déjà vu and my mother, I think, just has feminine intuition. What I'm leading up to is this: we have a streak in the family, a strong psychic streak. Perhaps it comes from the fact that we are always praying or something. A typical breakfast conversation in my home is about the nature of God—'Is God the sum total of all consciousness or is God the quality that pervades all consciousness?'—while we butter our toasts.

I kid you not.

Or perhaps we just have some genetic material. More links in the corpus callosum or hippocampus or whatever. Whatever it is, it's there in different degrees and since I came after many decades of praying or because I'm the youngest or further down in the evolutionary chain, my gift is special.

Yes, there's going to be some mumbo-jumbo, so decide whether you want to stay with this and whether you want to believe, because quite frankly I can't be bothered with your scientific temper and need for empirical proof. I've spent my whole life displaying my abilities as proof and it's precisely why I'm ranting in the first place. It's my word against all the 'mysteries-debunked' lot. Your tastes may be more 'Top Fifty Scientific Proofs of the World', I won't stop you from moving on.

If you're still on the page, now to see whether you've also been paying attention.

My father could smell death. Not can. I used the present tense after that, 'he describes it as', that means he's around to tell you what the Grim Reaper uses as a deodorant. Why can't he smell it anymore? He was scared of it, he didn't want the gift. He chose to give it away. Don't judge him yet, you may have done just as he did, once you've heard him tell his bit.

My father's memory, sometime in the late 60s, verbatim:

It must have been Wednesday or Thursday, because it was my turn to supervise the factory or perhaps I was doing Dev a favour, we often covered for each other. There wasn't much for me to do given that the unit was set and functioning. I just had to make the usual rounds, make sure that the workers were doing their shift, that the moulds were all right and that they were producing enough castings. So that when the order came through we'd be all set to produce enough parts. Yes, and keep an eye open for union trouble. But there was nothing really to keep me there after four in the afternoon. Those were different days, no one worked quite as long people do today, so I decided to visit Tulinda.

I had heard he was sick. He was a dear friend of my father's, just a few years younger, maybe five or seven years. I should have called him Tulin Kaku but he was Tulinda. Everyone in the old days, the regulars at the Kali Bari, was a -da or a -di. Tituda, Purnimadi, even I was a 'Tubaida' for many. Khokon, his son, and I had practically grown up together and when he told me that his father had been unwell for about a fortnight, I had decided that I must visit them soon. With how little there was to do that day, it seemed like a good time to pay them a visit.

I left the Wheaton Wires factory and came down Mathura Road, turning right at Nizamuddin, instead of taking the left and going home and came down past Daryaganj, Jama Masjid and after a quick halt at the Bengali Mithai shop in Chandni Chowk, that was bought over in the 70s by the Aggarwals, I reached Tulinda's. Now that area has changed entirely with the metro and a whole lot of new construction, but then you could walk across from their place to where I had parked, near the old St Stephen's building.

I was in a good mood, it had been an easy day. I could smell the fresh roshogollas in the packet that I was carrying, and I was hoping they'd open the packet and offer me one or two. Tulinda's wife, Channi Pishi, was sure to make me something nice for tea and Tulinda would be happy to have some company. (Another of those strange Bengali relationships, Channi Pishi should have been 'di', if you go by the fact that I called her husband Tulinda, or at least

Channi Kakima, but she was a pishima, thus like a sister to my father.) Khokon, I guessed, would still be at the hospital. Even then, we knew he'd be a great doctor, a real healer. So all in all, I was expecting a fairly leisurely session of tea, snacks and chit-chat.

I rang the bell and waited for Channi Pishi to open the doors. They were green-coloured doors in the old style. You know the kind you see in havelis or in the British bungalows. Three horizontal planks on each door and board between them in a very solid old wooden frame. It took a while but finally I heard footsteps approaching, so I knew that they were home. I could hear the jingle of bangles, the shankha and pola and a bunch of keys. Pishi opened the door and I was glad to see her but before I could even smile and say 'Pronaam, Pishi', it hit me. This overpowering smell. It made me sick to the stomach. The nausea welled up and I almost vomited right there at the doorstep.

I held out the packet of roshogollas for Pishi, who had turned a little white on seeing me bending over and wheezing like that. The nausea passed in a few seconds and so I went in, with Pishi enquiring whether I was all right.

'I'm fine,' I lied to her. In reality, I was finding it difficult not to bring up lunch, I completely forgot all small talk. All I was conscious of was this smell. I thought of asking Channi Pishi what it was but then I thought it wouldn't be very polite. So I asked where Tulinda was, 'Tulinda kothay, Pishi?'

Pishi pointed to his room upstairs, smiling weakly. Then as expected she ducked into the kitchen to make something for me to have with my tea. I walked up the wooden stairs which were on one side of the central courtyard and reached the first floor veranda. Tulinda's room door was the second one in front of me but I was having trouble walking upright now. I could scarcely breathe, my stomach was churning, but curiosity about the nature and source of this peculiar stench was also growing. I held onto the railing that ran around the veranda and somehow dragged my way to his room.

It was a large room, full of shadows. A dark rosewood almirah and an old chest of drawers occupied most of one wall and an open window the adjoining one. Tulinda lay sleeping on a high four-poster bed under mosquito netting, covered by a thin printed blanket, looking very weak and small. But the smell in the room was so intense I couldn't bear to stay there any longer. Backing out of the door, I glanced around to see if anything was causing this foul odour, but everything seemed to be in order. I said a hurried bye to Pishi, making some excuse about a sudden turn in my health and then I drove home. I think I could smell that odour in my clothes for the next day or so.

That's as much as Baba told me. I couldn't get any more details out of him. What was in the room? A dead rat perhaps? Did he check whether they were burning things outside or not? Since it was Old Delhi, everything reeks anyway, and the house was near a tannery. So big deal. I did do some digging to get the facts, to establish that these things can happen, that someone can smell death coming. But his memory wasn't aces when he told me this story and anyway he was recreating the scene. He wasn't really recording the details of what happened before—it was just a normal day and afterwards all he could think about was the smell. Well, he didn't know it then but that was the first time Baba smelt Death.

Two days later Tulinda, Tulin Dadu it should be for me, died. Baba got a call from his friend Khokon and he rushed across. He accompanied the body to the cremation grounds and after spending more time than is considered normal these days, came home, touched some iron, chewed something bitter, threw his clothes in a pile in the corner of the room and had a bath. Then, without eating, not because of anything ritualistic but because he wasn't hungry, he went to sleep. Everyone thought he was just upset by Tulinda's death. If I was around then I would've been able to tell him what bothered him. The way it is with these abilities, the first time they dawn on you, the first time they wake up, you know you have it. Almost like when you see a rash and you know it's no ordinary rash, this bitch is gonorrhoea. You have that feeling, called 'sinking' usually, there is a weight to it, it's heavy in your heart and feels different, but it's not sinking. So my father realised something within him had changed and he was quite uncomfortable.

In complete contrast, the first time I came to use my gift, it felt certain, and it didn't bother me a bit.

One of our family friends, Ashima Sarkar, or Bulu Pishi, as I called her, had come to the flat for lunch or mid-morning tea or whatever it is that you were allowed to pop in for those days. I must've been seven or so. I had picked up a book on palmistry just that morning. These books lay around the house, so it was easy to pick one up. I was quite fond of Bulu Pishi. She always made a very dramatic entry when she came home. It was different from the way my family was, so it was exciting and sunny. And she was warm and affectionate as well, giving me a tight hug, smothering my face with kisses and speaking to me in a saucy flirty way. Maybe not quite flirty, but like she would speak to an attractive man. I was seven, so she was play-acting and I knew it. But it was a nice charade, nonetheless.

She pushed the door open, it wasn't locked in those days during the day, and pranced in, in a rustle of nylon and went straight to the kitchen where Ma and Thamma were making lunch. I heard her squeal with delight on seeing the preparations. It must have been a traditional meal but for Bulu Pishi that was a luxury. She was after all a modern working woman, with little time for elaborate Bong dishes and ten-course meals.

I just remained in the drawing room, lounging on the sofa by the window, reading Cheiro's book on practical palmistry. The way I liked to, with my head on one of the arms and my legs on the other. I guess I could fit into the breadth of that sofa then. It made no sense to take a break and go see Bulu Pishi, she would come around and pamper me and I could say my Hi.

Once her squealing was done and she'd invited herself for lunch I guess she asked about the rest of the family and subsequently found me in my holiday wear: tiger shorts and vest, reading. After the hug and kiss she noticed the book I was reading and like any encouraging aunt, asked,

'So darling, what do you see in my palm? You can tell me anything, huh, no secrets between us.'

I was keen to test my skills, and to indulge Bulu Pishi. I kept the Cheiro aside and looked at her palms, concentrating hard. She continued prompting like the indulgent aunt that she was, 'Left hand or right? Aren't you supposed to read the left hand of a woman…oh, this is the head line, and isn't this the line of fate? So what does it say?'

From all that I had read or picked up from dining table conversation on palmistry, I couldn't make out anything. After staring at her hands for a while when I continued to remain silent, I guess she thought I needed more specific prompting. 'So,' she enquired helpfully, 'when will I go abroad?'

It may seem a little weird but I guess in the early 80s after one's marriage, kids and career, a trip abroad was the thing most desired. Given that her husband had landed a bank job in Dubai, it was only a matter of time before she went too. Really when I think back now, she was just being kind. But that was not for me. I frowned and said, 'There's no trip abroad, Bulu P.'

She smiled, not happy but disbelieving the little boy she so loved to cuddle. Who couldn't yet be hated for being negative. 'Really?' she said withdrawing her hand, 'But little master, your uncle's there already and I'm in the process of wrapping things up.' Then she shook her head, dismissing my prediction, 'Look again, maybe you missed something. See, there's a faint line here.'

I shook my head, I really couldn't see anything else.

That's when my grandmother (Thamma for my sister

and me) walked into the little consultation, dishcloth and plate in hand. She may have overheard my prediction but I hadn't heard or seen her come in. She heard Bulu Pishi's polite cajoling, the encouragement to be a better palmist, and got into the act of convincing me to say something positive. It was supposed to be an education in good manners, but I was adamant and seven. So I stuck to my initial reading, albeit with a slightly weaker, weaselly but more or less the same, 'I can't see any trip abroad.'

They shook their heads, dismissing my poor manners as childish stubbornness and returned to more grown-up matters. Lunch was had soon after. I don't think Bulu Pishi asked any more questions that afternoon. Not even for Thamma's special shukto recipe. Nor did I get scolded for poor manners. In Thamma's eyes, I hadn't done anything wrong. I had just read what I saw.

Bulu Pishi's husband was back in a month or thereabouts, so she didn't get to go to Dubai, after all. What her husband had been offered wasn't really a manager's position, it was more support or something. So he, with his offended middle class intellectual pride, returned to his motherland and his kind. That was my first reading and I was sure when I did it, that what I had said was pretty much the way it was going to turn out.

Two

~~~~~~~~~~

After Tulinda's death, if Baba heard someone was suffering, he would go visit. To both verify that he had this sense and to diagnose the fatality of the affliction. He was right more often than not. For many years, well into my childhood, he sniffed around like a bloodhound. He suffered and introspected and all but he went through the whole hog to test that he had this ability. It became a bit of a joke at home. Thamma said half seriously that he'd make more money as an agent with the Life Insurance Corporation of India than he would with his new business. (He had started a plastics company with two of his colleagues at Wheaton Wires.) Ma used to nag him about the amount of time he spent at cremation ghats, worrying that he'd become impure or mad or fall down the class ladder. And my sister Abira—Didi—and I would just prod and poke asking him stupid questions.

'So you say it smells like shit, like diarrhoea shit or normal?'

'It should smell when people aren't sick either, I mean everyone's going to die right, so when do they start stinking?'

'Couldn't it be their clothes or some fungus?'

'How is it you can only smell this and not other things like accidents, drugs or bad luck?'

'You think it is their souls leaking out? How funny if our souls stink? Are souls like soles, huh, huh?'

It may have been his mild-mannered demeanour or just how he carried it, but no one really thought much of it and he himself played it down. Till the night in Neeraj Uncle's room. That was the one time I've seen him go somewhat nutty about it. See, Neeraj Uncle and Baba had been roommates in college, joined the same company, toured west India together, shared alcohol and perhaps women in their single years, then married nine months apart. Sooraj Bhaiya, his son, too was more or less Didi's age. So, they were close—Neeraj Uncle and Baba, that is.

When Neeraj Uncle came visiting from Bombay (it hadn't become Mumbai yet) he usually stayed at the Hyatt Regency in Delhi. It was an occasion for us to do a five-star meal.

I was twelve and unable to find anything decent to wear. I had my jeans on, a tailored pair. Ma had given me the money on my birthday and taken me to get them stitched. Navy-blue and what qualifies as comfort fit today, but just the regular thing then. I was tossing T-shirts around. They were no good, they were the kind of clothes one wore to play in the evening. Stained and torn, not the stuff you wear out to dinner. Two other T-shirts I had outgrown. The only shirt that made the cut was this cotswool thing and it was too warm for that. My predicament was made worse by seeing Didi in a chocolate-brown dress, looking like she was going for a Governor's

Ball or some such. Then again, there may have been all kinds of cool men at the Hyatt. Prince Charming, the shining knight etc. So it made sense.

Finally Ma made me wear my school shirt, and insisted I looked very handsome. It went with the jeans, but I didn't really want to wear my uniform for a social do. With all the fussing—Ma and Didi took their time with their makeup—we only bundled out of the flat by about nine. Baba kept complaining that we were never anywhere on time, that we should know better, that this was a five-star so we should have been more punctual. I guess we were in some sort of subservient awe of the five-star universe. Well, Baba was on time this time, but let's not get ahead.

We all got out of the Ambassador—painted a lemon yellow, about twenty years old, but still faithful. I remember the ambivalence with which Baba gave it for valet parking, which was sort of new then. We waited in the lobby for a while, taking in the sights and sounds while Baba dialled Neeraj Uncle's room from the house phone. Ma and I sat on the plush sofas in the lobby. Didi walked up and down thrilled at the entire experience. I was still sulking about the shirt, so I couldn't match Didi's enthusiasm, but it was exciting to be in the presence of polished marble, chandeliers, suited English-speaking staff, and so many different nationalities. Pink-faced Britons, ebony black Ethiopian women, large white Russians, flight crews, diplomats and other rich people. It was all so new, like a peep into the big world that lay outside Green Park. We weren't out of it, just not in it.

Finally, I can't remember why, but it was decided that

we weren't going to one of the restaurants, but instead going to get room service in Neeraj Uncle's room. We weren't particularly unhappy at that, anything five-star was cool. A room perhaps was cooler, since Ma, Didi and I had certainly never stayed in one. I don't know about Baba.

We took the elevator, which had no attendant, glided upwards smooth as silk and pinged a very classy ping. I wanted to spend more time in the elevator, but my parents asked me to not behave like a ghotka. It's a word we Sens used a lot in those days. It means awkward, uncoordinated, buffoonish in an adolescent sort of way. I wonder who came up with it? It has the sound of my mother's side of the family. So I controlled my desire to go elevator riding and accompanied my family out to the corridor of the fifth floor, when Baba started huffing and puffing and quite nearly bringing the house down. The rest of the evening is a blur. I don't remember eating or drinking or anything—just Baba telling, pleading, with Neeraj Uncle not to travel, to get a medical test done, to stay with us, to feed black dogs and whatnot. Baba was assuming of course, that none of us were going to cop it there in the Hyatt. I was embarrassed and so was Neeraj Uncle but Ma and Didi took it in their stride.

The next day Neeraj Uncle checked out and came home. Baba had organised a purohit at short notice and we did a small havan for the good health of Neeraj Uncle. I think the purohit's sons were employed to repeat the *Mahamritunjaya* mantra, because they were sitting in the corner, repeating something, looking mighty bored. I don't think Baba was terribly satisfied by the proceedings because

I found him sitting up in the drawing room at night, talking, apparently to himself. You can't tell with our family.

I was up studying for the mid-term exams so I checked on him when I surfaced from my room for a drink of water.

He was sitting on the sofa that he usually reserved for praying and sulking, mumbling something. It felt like he was complaining to someone superior, say a boss, about the unfairness of life. The sofas were striped a sulphurous orange and black by the streetlight coming through the grilles in the drawing room window and Baba sat there looking imprisoned in a tiger's skin, arguing with the powers that be. He started when he noticed me. 'What're you doing here?' he snapped.

'Water,' I said, holding up the reused Black and White whiskey bottle.

He stared at me, not registering what I had said. After a second or two of silence he asked, 'You know what this is like?'

'Yup,' I said knowing very well what he was talking about and what it was like.

'Well, what should I do?' I think he was asking the gods or some higher power, not me. 'It's terrible to live like this, knowing someone is going to die.'

Since none of the gods came to his aid, I told him, 'You can choose to give it away. To someone. Will it away.'

He looked at me long and hard, as though wondering where I was getting these answers from. Well yes, they weren't my thoughts, I'd heard at a religious satsang that you could give siddhis or powers away to people who were willing to accept them. It would take some work, some willing, some kriya, but it could be done.

My father waved me away gruffly. Not satisfied. Needing to stew in his abilities, his duties as a friend, his plight as a much mixed-up man. He doesn't know these things, he's not me, I could see him thinking. He just wanted that smell to leave him. He didn't ask why he smelt it in the first place, it would have been easier if he had. He just wanted to part with it.

I, however, am not like my father, at least in the matter of not valuing gifts. I am glad I've got his piece out of the way. If I had spent any more time on him and his problems, there would be no telling my bit. If you're interested, Neeraj Uncle didn't die. He's alive, well and still takes my father's trip about that night. I think after that time, because of the doubt or whatever, my father didn't speak about the smell of death anymore. People however, haven't stopped dying. I can't comment on whether he's stopped sniffing.

So what is my gift really? You could say it's a gift, but it's more an ability. More than mere palm-reading. For now, for the purpose of moving forward, just think of me as a very gifted fortune-teller. A very empathetic psychic, something like that X-Men girl who could absorb other people's powers, except that I'm no leech. I guess I started displaying signs that I could do more than just palm-reading early.

I remember I was very young when I first read a book

on numerology. Older when I first came across Arthur Avalon's *Principles of Tantra*. Between the two I'd read a bunch of books on runes, astrology, I Ching, teacup readings, all the fortune-telling books I could find. I moved on to more spiritual fare after the book on tantra. Kundalini yoga, aghora rituals, but I did read the fluff as well—the claims of Uri Geller, Nostradamus and Jeane Dixon. The tales of Atlantis, Nazca Lines, Ripley's, Guinness. Anything and everything on the supernatural or paranormal.

At any point of the day, I know when which constellation is rising, when Saturn goes retrograde, or Mars changes houses, what a broken girdle of Venus means, what happens when you get Mist over Earth in a hexagram, what number 9 means or the number 33, what you should do if your third card is the Blasted Tower, or sometimes depending on the way you use your fork, whether one of your parents is suffering from cancer or not.

It was a monsoon evening in Bombay—Mumbai, if one had to be politically correct, but I can't really bother with all that, it would always be Bombay for me—at my boss's house. It must have been because I was wearing a full-sleeved shirt. One of the less loud Fabindia ones, so it must have been cool. By this time, which was between my fourth and fifth year at work and an equal number of rum-and-cokes, I was speaking about my psychic abilities.

It was a silly party for our all-male marketing team. Because the rest of us were unmarried and our boss was not, I think he felt guilty or proud and called us home for dinner. Given how dull we all were at work, it got no better at his place. We were forced to watch our manners carefully, lest we lost such future honours. Or perhaps because his wife was just so damned attractive and flirty, it felt like a test. She displayed a whole lot of cleavage to a room full of men. Wore a bright blue dress not a starched cotton sari and emphasised a point by placing her hand on your arm. Modern chick.

We didn't want him to catch us eyeing her or saying something foolish. Increments were due soon or appraisals or KRAs. We drank till late and then Kartik started singing because he was the accepted singer among us and we all joined in. Trying our best to drown him out at the chorus, but letting him handle the tricky wordy bits in the middle, it was just like work. Kishore Kumar, Hemanta Kumar, RD, all the songs you can really belt out because they are just so singable.

Meanwhile my boss's wife flirted, offered refills, made eye contact, arm contact, laughed excessively at stupid jokes, etc. Dinner, like at most of these dos, was ordered-in and served when people were no longer in any condition to tell what they ate. So when I got around to serving myself in the kitchen I found my boss's wife eating by herself. I'm tiring of calling her boss's wife, but at the moment I've forgotten her name.

So there she was eating, sexily may I add. Leaning on the marble top or was it a black granite kitchen counter. One arm supporting herself, the other wielding a fork. I watched the passage of the morsel from the melamine plate to her shiny fork, the snaky fluid movement of her arm as the morsel made its way to her mouth and the tongue jutting out just a little in anticipation, while serving myself portions of chicken curry, a seekh kabab, some daal makhni and two greasy tandoori rotis.

'So,' she pronounced, pointing the fork at my chest, 'tell me something.'

'Something,' I said, not trying to be funny at all, just the rum and lust speaking.

'You said you were a psychic, what can you tell?'

Her eyes narrowed, her arm nestled against her breast, enhancing her cleavage.

It may have been because she was so sexy and my boss was not, the injustice of it, the alcohol, the cramped kitchen, the takeaway, the blue dress, the cleavage, but I really wanted to prove a point. Now when I think about it, a simple 'You are very passionate and are stuck at what you do' or 'You were once very close to becoming an actress' would have suited all my purposes, but no, I had to say something that would show her I wasn't to be trifled with, the psychic thing wasn't just a party boast, an alpha dog pee, I wasn't going to let her snicker condescendingly while slowly sliding the fork into her mouth with little bits of gravy-smeared rice.

In what seemed then to be the only psychic thing I could say, I said, 'One of your parents is suffering from cancer, it's serious,' while following the fork go into her mouth and then staying there, her high slowly vanishing.

'My father,' she said finally, putting the fork down.

'I thought so, but didn't want to say it,' I said nodding.

'How did you know?' she asked.

'I told you I'm psychic, I just feel these things.'

'What else can you see...feel?' If it was a come-on, I didn't respond to it. It would have been a fatal mistake, anyway. I think I muttered something about her childhood, growing up in colonial houses or something—trees, animals, servants. It must have been something like that, after all, I was feeling a dozen things but she was my boss' wife. It was way too risky to try a daring compliment even for a drunk member of an all-male marketing team. I had to answer honestly as a psychic, not some love god.

No we didn't become lovers, nor did I get a promotion. My boss just looked at me funnily when he came to work the next day. But then we were all hung-over.

I hope that works as an example. I read things off palms or charts or the way one eats food. Anything one does is full of portents and it can be read. That's what comes of being a Sen, honest truth. I tell you, it must be because we discuss God at the breakfast table.

⁓

It's time you knew my name: Anando Sen. It used to be Anand Sen. My grandmother was a great fan (if you could be a fan in those days and not an admirer, as she maintained) of Uday Shankar. She considered him to be a modern man. He was, I suppose, in the 30s and 40s. She would have named me after him, if she'd had her way. But since everyone in my family is named with an A, it couldn't be Uday. So instead they chose the name of his son, Ananda. My father, needing to have his say in the process and in a fit of modernity, decided that since his boy would be growing up in Delhi he would make the spelling a little less obviously Bengali. So he dropped the 'a' at the end, and I was christened Anand Sen.

Numerologically 'Anand' equals 15, which as any Chaldean numerologist will tell you, isn't a great number. In fact, it's the number symbolised in tarot by the Shattered Citadel. Not auspicious to grow up with that kind of name. With the 'a' added back to the end, it becomes 17. A very good number—the Star of the Magi. A number that I could have been satisfied with, but when you are changing your name why just go with the first choice. If you add an 'o' to the end of Anand, you get Anando— which is phonetically closer to Bengali, but that's not it. Anando totals to 23, which is the number of the Royal Star of the Lion. A number that indicates expanding greatness. Success in personal and career matters. Good in many ways. A number you can grow up to.

As for my surname, there wasn't much I could do about it. 'Sen' adds up to 13. Not an unlucky number as many believe—just a number of change. I was content being the Star Lion who brought about change. I've ignored the recently in vogue, Pythagorean numerological analysis of my name. It's a dumbed down version which assigns the numbers one to 9 to the letters in order. So 'A' is one and 'I' is 9 and 'J' is one again. A sad travesty.

I mean, what's the sanctity in the order of letters, the Greeks had them one way, the Romans gave Latin a different order. What's worse is that it doesn't take into account the difference in use of the vowels and the consonants. No, no it's cheap divination. Next you'll be suggesting doing numerology by the order of the Qwerty keyboard, or the scores on Scrabble tiles. Let's just give the so-called Pythagorean numerologists a wide berth, okay?

I changed my name, I must've been what, twelve then. Yeah, class seven, I was twelve. My palms didn't always have these lines either. I had a pretty straight line of head, if I remember correctly, and knots in the joints of my fingers. The knots are gone now. Only one knot on my left hand ring finger remains. It's not sideways anymore, it pops out to the front—palm side. A finger that will never admit a ring easily, and if it does, won't give it up.

The only thing I couldn't change is my birth chart. But then the rules of astrology are so complex and contrary you can choose your own set of interpretations when making a reading. In fact all readings are about choosing to see things a certain way.

Two intersecting lines on the palm isn't an impediment but can be seen to be the Mysterious Cross.

A domed forehead isn't alopecia but the mark of wisdom.

A malefic planet in a bad house can be a damn good thing.

The last-born of the Sens of Green Park could be the real deal.

Let's not get ahead though. It's time you were introduced to more members of the Sen family, and their little gifts.

Three

My uncle, Abhijeet Kumar Sen aka Bubai, was the apple of my grandma's eye. Yeah, he's the one who married a Muslim woman, who broke my grandma's heart and with it his ties to our household. When Thamma fell ill, Abhijeet Kaka let bygones be and came visiting. Somewhere between running to the blood banks and waiting in a swish South Delhi private hospital for lab reports, I pried his story out. Not about the woman he married, no, his gift. See, I was damn curious to know the stories of our gifts, so that I could work out how my gift stacked up against the rest.

He was a skinny man, balder than Baba, with this air of academic gravitas. Very prototypical Bengali nerd.

'Gifts, did you say? Haha, are you sure they're gifts?'

'Everyone seems to possess some ability.'

'So what's yours?'

'I asked first.' I wasn't going to let him wriggle out. 'I've been hearing about your episode since childhood.'

'Then you know…'

'I want to hear it from you,' I insisted.

'You sure?' He was being unnecessarily difficult.

'Thamma used to…Thamma goes on about our family being touched by something special. So I just…'

'That we are. If you just meditate I'm sure the answers will come,' he said, in a calming voice. A voice a hypnotist would have been happy to have.

'Come on, Kaku,' I continued labouring against the calm he radiated.

'Well, I'm not sure this is the right environment for a ghost story,' he said half laughing. Then sighing, 'You must remember I was just a child when these things happened, so a lot of it may be things that were told to me later, memory enhancement, but if you want to know the story of the woman in white, then here it is.'

He paused. I waited.

'It was a long time ago.' He stretched the 'long'. Then after some internal dialogue he looked up from his hands and then straight at and through me.

'Still hear it, you may get your answers.'

Abhijeet Kumar Sen's story:

It must have been early in 1956, because that's when Baba was promoted and we shifted from our quarters in Havelock Square, I don't know what it is called now, to the bungalow on Rakabganj Road. It was before my eighth birthday. I was a sickly child, you've probably heard that, I was sick almost every year with something. Unlike Dadabhai and Chhordabhai who were always playing, I was almost always indoors down with some illness or the other. Whooping cough, dysentry, influenza, rubella, I had them all.

That year I can't remember what it was, chicken pox perhaps or measles. I was alone in the room I shared with your pishis. They were staying with us those years. Anyway, that day I was alone, I can't remember why. Oh yes, of course, Daku Mama, that's Ma's elder brother was visiting Delhi and I think Mami was scared of catching measles or they were worried about their grandson catching it, so I was alone at home with Baba, and our maid Jhornadi.

I was scared with all of them gone, because it was a large house and my head was full of Chhordabhai's scary stories about all that happens with children in empty houses. Perhaps a little upset as well, that they would all be having fun, while I was stuck in bed, but I didn't have much of a choice.

It was around six-thirty or seven in the evening, I was lying in bed, maybe reading, there wasn't much else to do those days, we didn't even have a radio, when I heard some strange noises from the far side of the house. Like someone in pain. I got up to go check. It was still winter, so it was dark already.

I walked up and down the corridor, switching on lights, looking around. Nothing strange or odd caught my eye. I put it down to a stray cat and turned to go back to my room. Just then I heard what sounded like footsteps, walking away from me. I turned, alarmed, but there was no one. I didn't know what else to do, so I walked up to Baba's door. You must remember we were all very scared of Baba and you never interrupted him, if he was working or reading and especially not if he was sitting in meditation.

But I was too scared to go back to my room. So I knocked quietly on his door.

'Ke?' he asked loudly.

I replied, 'Aami Bubai.'

'What happened?' he bellowed.

'I heard some noises.'

He opened the door after a few seconds. 'What kind of noises?'

'Like someone in pain.'

He looked down at me sternly.

'Did you find anything?'

'No.'

'Well, you must have been dreaming.'

I was sure I had heard something, but there was no arguing with Baba. So I had him walk me to my room and then went back to bed. For a while there was nothing then just as I was falling asleep I saw a white shape flit across the doorway. I couldn't be sure who it was, it could have been Jhornadi, so I let it pass and drifted off to sleep.

Later, when Jhornadi came to give me dinner, I asked her. 'Jhornadi, what were you doing in the house in the evening?' She would usually spend time in the servants' quarters when there was no work in the house.

'I was not in the house, babu, now eat,' she said.

'But I saw you, you were walking in the corridor.'

'I wasn't here, Bubai, now eat, you need to get strong.'

'I'm sure I saw you or someone,' I insisted.

'You must have been dreaming, now eat. Do you like it that you're alone at home, while your dadas are out and playing and eating sweetmeats? You need to eat well and get tougher.'

I insisted I wasn't dreaming but Jhornadi was little help.

Around dinner or slightly before, I can't quite remember when exactly, we got word that Ma, your Thamma, my dadas and my cousins would stay the night at Daku Mama's. It must have been judged too dark to come back safely, also because Ma was meeting her brother after a while. So they must have wanted to spend more time.

Naturally I was really angry. Not only could I not play with my cousins and eat all the good food that they were surely going to eat, but I would have to sleep alone in a new house.

I threw a tantrum and finally Baba, in a rare moment of kindness, allowed Jhornadi to sleep on the floor next to me.

It must have been late, because I could hear Jhornadi snoring, when I heard the funny noise again. This time I paid attention. It was late and I was scared. I shut my eyes and willed myself to go to sleep, too scared to see whatever it was. I didn't want to go investigating at night. So I stayed there in my room, squeezed my eyelids shut and prayed. It didn't help as all Chhordabhai's ghost stories started playing in my head. How this one ghost sat on trees and waited for kids to walk by alone at night. Then he would jump on them and eat them. How this witch, whose feet pointed backward, would walk alone in a house with a candle and would tempt people to follow her, as she led them to a well or a cliff. It varied with the telling and the location of the house.

There was no more crying, or pained sounds, instead I could hear a woman's voice, whispering. Laughing.

Inviting. Coaxing me to come, investigate. I couldn't sleep and praying wasn't helping so I called out to Jhornadi.

'Jhornadi, help. There's a ghost in the house.'

Jhornadi continued to snore. I stayed in bed, hugged my pillows close and not knowing what else to do, tried to sleep. Hoping, praying that the ghost wasn't interested in me.

A little later the voices stopped.

I opened my eyes a crack just to check if there was anything that had caused this. Jhornadi was still on the floor, oblivious, then I saw a movement from the corner of my eye. There was a lady in white standing at the door looking in. I immediately shut my eyes, reasoning that if I pretended to sleep she may leave me alone. I kept my eyes squeezed shut and prayed.

After about five minutes, or one minute, it felt really long, and I could imagine her coming slowly for me, I half opened one eye to check. She wasn't there.

I told Baba the next morning at breakfast that the house was haunted and I had seen the ghost of a white woman, but he wouldn't have any of it, saying that neither he nor Jhornadi had seen or heard anything out of the ordinary. He blamed the fever and asked Jhornadi whether I had been having my medicines and what my temperature was at night.

When Ma and the rest came back around midday I told them the story but Ma pretty much said the same things as Baba and Jhornadi. Only Chhordabhai seemed interested but that wasn't necessarily a good thing. When we were alone later, he told me, in his most creepy voice, 'See I told you, funny things happen to children when they're alone at home. You be careful, next time she might not let you off so easily. She may put a curse, or worse, a charm on you. She might sing you a magic song that will drive you insane, tempt you to follow her, then you never know, she might want to eat you, or worse, keep you with her. As her plaything. Then you too will be a ghost walking around this house. Forever.'

I hit him but he was so much bigger that he just laughed and brushed me aside.

I didn't see the woman in white for a while but Chhordabhai continued to keep me in fear of her imminent appearance. He was very loving but I guess teasing comes with the territory of being a much older brother. So there were stories of the petni or shankhchunni who lived in the house, who he had seen walking around too, who was especially powerful on new moon nights. He had spotted her near the outhouse, near the hedge that separated our house from the neighbours, but the locus of most of her hauntings seemed to be in or around the little garden shed. That was where according to Chhordabhai the shankhchunni performed all her scary rituals. Eating children or swallowing their souls and leaving just empty shells, casting spells to make people forget their way home, doing black magic on the house, so that our family had no choice but to sacrifice their youngest child to appease her.

The shed itself wasn't that scary, I had peeped in once. It was a small brick room with an asbestos roof. Inside was a small open water tank—a choubacchha—some gardening tools, a hosepipe, nothing to fear really, but Chhorda's stories being what they were, it became a place to avoid.

Chhorda himself had no fear of the place, but as far as I was concerned, he informed me that I was risking my life or worse.

When summer came, your pishis went to stay with their parents. Once again I was the youngest in the house and as was with me in those years, housebound with a fever. It was a rainy evening, a pre-monsoon storm and I was sitting looking out at the garden. Irritated that I couldn't play in the rain, while my dadas were out no doubt playing football or something equally muddy.

It was around sunset, because I remember being angry that my dadas hadn't come home yet, it was raining hard, so visibility was low, but I was sure I saw a figure in white stepping, almost gliding out of the shed. She stood there under the roof, her back to me, for a second or two. Then as if sensing my gaze, she turned. When I saw her face I froze in fear. She was pale and where she should have had eyes, there were two large black holes. Those black holes seemed to focus on me, she held her finger to her lips, signalling me to keep quiet, and then she smiled diabolically. For a few seconds I was so scared I couldn't move, I thought she would trap me with her magic, swallow my soul, but then I managed to find my voice and my limbs and ran in shouting, 'Petni, petni.'

Ma and Jhornadi came running out of the kitchen.

'Ki holo?' they asked, worried.

'Ma, I just saw the petni standing outside the shed.'

'Oof, Bubai, there's no such thing, don't believe your dada, don't you have a good book to read,' Ma said.

'I'm telling you there is a petni in the shed, I saw her,' I said starting to cry, angry that no one would believe me.

'Aachha, theek aache, we'll go and check, just as soon as the rain stops, theek?' Ma reasoned.

I told them that she might be gone by then, that they needed to do something right away, call an ojha or any other exorcist.

So poor Jhornadi was made to go out in the rain and check, she came back shaking her head. Furious at me. I wanted Ma to go, I didn't trust Jhornadi's abilities, but there was nothing I could tell Ma, that would make her believe otherwise. That night Ma scolded Chhordabhai for all his make-believe stories, telling him to be more sensitive about his delicate and believing younger brother.

Chhordabhai, if anything, teased me more.

'See, only you've seen her, so she must be out to get you. One day soon she'll tempt you with sweets and toys, then she'll grab you by your legs, dangle you upside down and be off with you to the netherworld.'

Chhorda must have had a black tongue, God knows he had gifts of his own, because something quite like he described happened.

There was this one day, during the monsoons that year, that I was complaining that Dadabhai's and Chhordabhai's paper boats were far better than mine and that no one was helping me. For their part they had made me a boat or two but I must have sunk them, or taken them apart, so I had little reason to complain, but I was feeling grouchy. I sat and watched as they sailed their boats in the puddles and along the little rivulets that ran along the front drive, darting to try and hijack the boats, but elder brothers have longer legs and arms.

Later that day, when I was done crying and it was done

raining, I saw this perfectly made paper boat lying in the front porch. I knew it wasn't made by either of my brothers, since it was folded differently from the way theirs were, there were no sails in it, also it wasn't wet. I grabbed the paper boat and took it back to my room, keen to be the first to sail it when it rained next. When Dadabhai saw it, he asked me who had made the boat for me. I didn't tell him who I suspected.

Then Chhordabhai saw it, held it in his hands and shook his head slowly. 'Bubai, you shouldn't have brought it in. You've let the petni's creation into the house, now who knows what she might use it for. If you're smart you'll destroy it.'

I half believed him, and I half thought he was jealous because it was a really well-made boat. Crisp white paper, with no excessive folds. I kept it hoping it would rain soon. It didn't. So I took to playing with the boat, on imaginary rivers, in buckets, in the high seas of the living room sofa.

She didn't use the boat to gain access to my room or my soul. I didn't know then how those things worked. Later, in one of my imaginary adventures, when I was fighting the British in the garden, I saw something bright lying close to the shed. Walking closer I discovered a little red top lying just outside the door of the shed. I picked it up, happy at a new acquisition, when I noticed that the door of the shed was ajar and there was something intricate folded in the doorway. On drawing closer I saw that it was a folded bird, a little paper swan.

Now I began to get scared. I remembered all Chhorda's scary stories. So I started backing away, keeping a keen eye on the insides of the shed, ready to run in case I saw anything suspicious or white. That's when I saw it. Floating on the water in the choubacchha—a gleaming toy ship. Complete with chimneys, portholes, three decks and other details. It looked like a toy made abroad or by someone with greater craft than regular toy-makers, in fact it looked like the miniature version of a real ship. It was too good to leave behind, I was sure one of my dadas would claim it, and then I would regret being such a coward.

So reasoning that it was still many hours to sunset, and that I was not a coward, I took a step closer to the shed, then examined the interiors as best as I could. I didn't enter for a long time, I wanted to be sure there was no whiff of anything other-worldly. Finally, seeing nothing funny, I picked up the swan. It was really beautifully folded, with two little dots painted for eyes. It was so beautiful, I don't think I had seen an origami swan before, and no petni had stepped forward. The sun was still up in the sky. All that was left to do was to pick up the ship and bolt back to the house.

I ran in, picked up the ship and turned to go, but my hands couldn't hold the top as well as the ship and the swan, so in picking up the ship, I dropped the swan into the water in the choubacchha. I was ready to let it go, but it really was a beautiful swan. I couldn't bear to see it get wet and lose shape.

So I reached out to get it, but I only knocked it out further. It tipped over in the water, drifting away with the ripples. I reached out some more, I could just about touch it and then it was like someone had tipped me over, I fell into the choubacchha.

The choubacchha wasn't that deep, but I couldn't seem to find my feet. I began to drown, I spluttered and tried to get out but I couldn't. Pretty soon I didn't know top from bottom and felt something weighing me down, I couldn't tell what. I regretted going after the swan. Then I saw her, the woman in white. I realised then that this was all a devious trap to take me with her to her world. She had lured me to the choubacchha and was now claiming me. As I thrashed around she reached a pale arm for me, I saw her nails caked in blood and tried to fight her as she pulled me in deeper, but I only ended up swallowing more water. She reached, I struggled, tried pushing her away, she grabbed me, I gulped, I knew it was all over, I blacked out.

When I awoke, I was in my room and Chhordabhai was at my side trying to wake me. Dadabhai and Ma were standing behind looking concerned. He had found me outside the shed and had carried me in. As soon as I got my bearings I began to howl, telling them as best as I could, how the petni had tempted me to the choubacchha and then tried to drown me. There were marks on my arm, so there was no disputing that. The only thing that was hard to explain was the absence of the toys. Neither Dadabhai nor Chhordabhai found the top, the swan or the ship. But I insisted I had picked them up. Chhordabhai put it down to more magic on the part of the petni, Ma to my imagination and spending too much time indoors. That night, either because of the shock or water in my lungs, or the touch of the petni, I fell sick. I was in bed for almost a fortnight with high fever.

When I got better, Baba came to my room and told me

that I had more delicate senses than others, which is why I was the only one who had seen the petni. He also added that that was why I fell sick so often. He told me to work on getting stronger, and forget about the petni.

Ma, on the other hand, believed I was blessed with higher faculties, crediting her prayers and assured me that while she was alive she wasn't going to lose me to any petni or shankhchunni. She insisted that I pray more for my protection and for the upkeep of my psychic abilities. Meanwhile somehow word spread in the family that I had survived an attack by an evil spirit.

Either as a result of the near death, or the attack of the petni, or just many years of carefully nurturing the psychic side, I have seen many strange things, but I never saw that woman in white again. But that's how it all started. Our gifts, haha, yes I think the petni attack was how it all started. At least, as far as I remember.

'What other things have you seen, Kaku?'

'Oh this and that.'

I wanted to know more, and Kaku I think was warming up to tell more, but just then the lab assistant walked up to us with the reports and there was no time for another story.

But this should be enough to give you some sense of the sort of gifts we're talking about. Unlike Baba, who was uncomfortable with his gift, Kaku didn't seem to fear it. He is a brave man to have survived a succubus as a child. How is it that he didn't have more powers? Enough about him though, he can write his own ghost stories if he wants, I'm sure he'll have his readers.

Four

I spent the years moving from class to class, divination to divination. A bit of palmistry here, a bit of numerology there. Astrology on the weekdays, tea leaves or something exotic on the weekends. Since our family was oriented in this direction anyway, there was plenty to learn from everyone or from what they read. I kept my eyes open for signs, omens, patterns. The connectedness between things, the clockwork that ticked under it all. I kept a check on my palms, my charts, my numbers, my trigrams. If I foresaw, say, an island forming on my palm or a planet transition to an inimical house, I prepared for it. Willed it to go away, willed it to split into smaller more manageable ills. Kept my thoughts and actions pure and spouted mantras. Boy, did I spout mantras. It started like this.

Prannoy Uncle came home. He was squat, dark, bulbous-eyed, muscular forearms with curly hairs, the looks of a rum-drinker. I never liked him. I couldn't stand his jokes, though some of them may have been funny. I could not abide his comments on life, though they were said half-seriously and I could not deal with his world view and his self-pronounced mastery of all things occult. He had disappeared for a few years in his mid-twenties. If the stories going around were to be believed, he had done penance in the mountains, been a sadhu in Benares, a yogi in South India. Personally, I think he spent them in a psychedelic haze somewhere less exotic.

My hatred for him wasn't due to his pretence that he was a powerful psychic like me, but because he was doing something wrong. Very wrong. His intent was wrong. Selfish, evil even, albeit in a petty way. Someone who does a lil' tantra for sex, a lil' hashish for a longer high, a spot of black magic to get ahead of the Jonejas. Still, in our part of the world he was the expert on all matters supernatural.

He came home one night, I was home, everyone was home, there were drinks and snacks for Baba and him. We would come in carrying refills, papad and peanuts and then stay on to chat. I must have been serving him his refill, when he asked me almost like a challenge. 'So I hear you've become a major palmist.'

'Numero-astrologer,' Didi corrected, teasing me by using the words I had used to describe myself to a previous guest.

He smiled, looking at Didi for just a little longer than he should have. And I read him. That grey lock in the front which he thought made him distinguished. His muscles which made him think he deserved better. The veins on his hand, not green, not purple, just throbbing under the skin, throbbing with evil. The way they twisted and branched, I could see his career moves, his petty politics, his hatred for his lot, his poor relationship with his wife. I could see the way he looked at women in his workplace, I could see the envy he felt for car owners, I could feel his life, and he was challenging me and lusting for Didi! He was taking a freaking risk.

'Yes, I have,' I said not hiding behind any false modesty. I mean I am usually humble but he was asking for a fight, I couldn't give in, not on my territory.

'Oh ho,' he said condescendingly, flashing Baba a look that was both amusement and disapproval. He hated me as well and couldn't really disguise it. 'So what can you tell? Can you tell me when I got married?' he asked, a gentle thrust.

'I know that. I don't have to read your palm,' I said bluntly, parrying.

'What else do you know? What else can you tell without reading my palm?' he laughed, a mocking slash.

'I know what you do,' I feinted.

'You mean where I work. Yes, that I'm sure you do, everyone does, but is there anything else or do you need to read my palm?' he thrust.

'I don't need to read your palm,' I defended and then I attacked, 'I know that you did some sadhana, but I don't believe you have any siddhis.'

Hahaha, he laughed the laugh of the older experienced predator, the posturing of the ageing alpha male. 'So you've heard about my trysts in Benares. Well, you're very well informed. Good. So can you actually read palms or do you just tell people, what you've heard about them?' he challenged.

I couldn't believe no one was cutting in to stop this. My family sat around like silent spectators. Spectators to our duel. For shit's sake, couldn't they see his game, picking on a child. I was getting angry, I had held my manners thus far out of deference for a guest, the family name, but could they not see how he was riling me, forcing me into a corner? There was only going to be one way, to come out blazing.

'You have no real experience with black magic or tantra, you can't really communicate with ghosts, much less command them, you've just made that up to appear mysterious and powerful.'

He laughed louder and longer, 'Haha, Anand, you have no idea. Would you like to see what my ghost can do?'

He leaned in, crouching over me without leaving his seat, his eyes bulging, his breath rank with my father's rum, his voice low, resonant in timbre, building in excitement.

'...He sits above my left shoulder...'

He looked left and right, his hands curling like talons, screwing up his nose and baring his fangs, imitating a devil or genie or jinn. '...He looks in all directions...' He swivelled, stuck out his tongue like a viper sniffing the air. Drawing us all in to the horrible world of his imaginary pet ghost. He continued, 'He has wings this large,' he moved his hands apart to indicate the wingspan, his hands on either side of my face, his voice rising, '...and when he finds something nasty or someone standing in my way...' his eyes were wide, everything was silent.

'He jumps up and...' THWACK and he slapped me hard on both cheeks.

He burst into laughter, thoroughly amused at how I

had been had. Everyone joined in, they all agreed I'd been had by a very good act. They didn't know to what degree.

The slap, it wasn't just noise. It stung. It wasn't a joke or avuncular affection, he was teaching me a lesson—not to challenge him. Like a good boy, I should have learnt it and moved on, burying the hurt under good humour. But I wasn't going to let him get away with it. He was going to have to pay for insulting me like this. I remained in the living room not knowing what to do. Whether I should reveal my embarrassment by leaving or whether to join the amused, a more measured stance but an admission of stupidity and being wrong. I was too insulted to make conversation and hurting too much to go back to whatever I had been doing before Prannoy Uncle arrived. I felt woolly-headed but angry. Oh, was I angry.

Fortunately we had to break for dinner. As he got up he looked at me, and I looked back. He smiled a victorious, knowing smile. I knew I was right, he meant it as a lesson but I was going to have my revenge.

He kept checking on me during dinner when I tried feebly to come back to good humour, but he kept poking away, reminding me of his pet ghost with the swivelling head, yellow fangs and wings that flapped ever so hard.

He was going to pay.

That night, I couldn't sleep I was hurting so bad, I was angry and teary so I got out of bed and went to sit in the living room in the dark. I couldn't turn down the rage that was building up, filling my insides like a demonic possession. All I wanted was revenge. I wanted him to hurt, like he had hurt me, and I started repeating it, 'May he be hurt, as he has hurt me.'

May he be HURT, as HE has hurt-me.

M a y h e b e h u r t a s h e h a s h u r t - m e .
Mayhebehurtashehashurt-me.

Through my teary eyes I saw the living room blur, the pictures on the walls became swimmy, swirling, time itself bent to the power of anger and insult.

'May he be hurt, as he has hurt me,' I said aloud.

It was a chant. It became a mantra.

Can you feel it? Mouth it, say it aloud, pause at the commas. Can you sense the balance of it? It has power. When you add intent and emotion, it becomes a potent spell. The repetition opens a channel, the mantra is the medium, the tears are the offering. The sacrifice is complete. A sacrifice the Destinies are bound to listen to.

When I had had enough of chanting, I guess I felt calmed, comforted, I had felt the world warp to my mantra, I had a sense of things fall into place.

The next day I got up on time, I didn't feel tired for being up so late the night before, I just upped and went to school and went on with class nine as normal. It was before the holidays so we must have been getting ready for the May tests. There must've been enough studying to do, as they were really laying on the pressure for the board exams next year.

I forgot about Prannoy Uncle.

The following weekend Baba got a call from the hospital. He got up, ready to rush off immediately, being that kind of guy. Just as he reached the door, the car keys dangling, he turned to me, to explain, but it felt more like he knew that he had to tell me.

'Your Prannoy Uncle had a crash on his motorbike, he's lost sensation in his hands.'

'What happened?' is all I could ask, not believing it, almost.

'He must've been drinking, I'll get to know when I get there.' And he left.

I was excited. His hands, his palms, his beastly wings. Hahaha. He had hurt me and now he was hurt. On the hands he'd hit me with, the palms he wanted me to read. This was just swell. Hahaha. Fuck with me and you'll get fucked Mr Mukherjee.

I had a great month. I topped the May tests. I used the same principle—mantra repetition. 'I'm going to come first in class. I'm going to come FIRST, in class'

I did. By half a mark out of five hundred. It was small but just to the right degree, to show me that it was no coincidence. Taking into account how much better Manish Gupta (who came second) was, I should have come second by ten marks or more, instead I'd pipped him. I could do spells. Life was going to be amazing.

～

You're still disbelieving? Clicking your tongue perhaps, or are you enjoying this family history of deranged stories? You probably have a family trait too, that mutates from person to person. Say the hatred of losing. It may make some aggressive winners and others passive and lazy but under both is the same thing. Hating the ache that comes with losing. It is usually something arising out of the home. An energy. In our home everyone, including Ma, who married into the house, displays variations of the gift. However, the gift is different in me. As if the rest were test cases. As though the family was preparing for me, like

I was the higher octave, the ustad, the maestro in a family of trained singers. And in a family that discussed God at the breakfast table? Well.

For the sake of autobiographical accuracy and because you need to know, the first time I was conscious of my gift was not when I read Bulu Pishi's palm; I probably had read Baba's, Ma's, Didi's or Thamma's before, but it was when Thamma recalled me making the prediction.

I had read Bulu Pishi's palm and forgotten about it but Thamma had remembered. Dear Thamma. I wonder what it was? Perhaps she was just ambitious for the family. Maybe she'd lost a lot too early. My father to his business, my second uncle to the Pakistan war, my youngest uncle to a Muslim woman, my grandfather to spirituality. She must have wanted someone in this house to count for something.

So she brought up my palm-reading when Bulu Pishi visited after her husband came back. It could just be her gloating over the failure of someone else, but it was also her attempt at stirring things inside me, playing catalyst to the eventual combustion.

It was just a casual visit. My parents weren't home. I opened the door. Bulu Pishi greeted me with an ebullient, 'Hi, little master, where's everyone?' A loud China silk sari to complement her voice.

'Thakuma is home, Baba and Ma are out. Didi's at her friend's place studying.' You could get all the information out of me in an instant. Fortunately she wasn't there to burgle.

The volume of her voice or the sound of the doorbell

must have woken Thamma from her afternoon nap and brought her out. 'Oh Bulu, ki khobor, how come suddenly?' said my ever-welcoming grandma in her equally complementing stern white sari.

'Nothing, Mashi. Was just visiting the doctor, so I thought I'd drop by.' She murmured now, volume down several notches. 'Routine checkup,' she added just in case Thamma started asking irritating questions. Or me for that matter.

They sat and chit-chatted in the living room, till they got around to discussing her husband's job and how she never quite went to Dubai. That's when my grandmother suddenly spoke up and announced, 'Ah, but hadn't Anand foretold this?'

It was a bolt from the blue for me who was just sitting there, running my fingers along the horizontal stripes of my T-shirt, racing imaginary planes. Brown white blue. Jet fighters in a clear sky and then this. I stopped swinging my legs, expecting Thamma to scold me, for invoking the inauspicious.

'Huh,' went Bulu Pishi.

'Hai,' went Thamma, wagging her forefinger. 'Yes, he told you, when was it…a few weeks back, that you wouldn't be going abroad.'

Bulu Pishi turned to look at me slowly, as if locating the locus of blame. Then she nodded slowly. Smiling for my grandma, but not really at me. 'So he did. So he did.' It was very quiet when she finished. Very, very quiet when you take into account Bulu Pishi's normal volume.

I resumed swinging my legs but I had stopped grinning mindlessly. The entertainment was gone. The good times

Shujoy Dutta

seemed over. Now that grandma Sen had picked it up, it was probably the time for a shouting or at least a severe scolding. No sooner had Bulu Pishi's Fiat left than Thamma called me to her room. This I remember vividly.

It was not nice to be called into Thamma's room. You had really buggered up if you were summoned. And even though some of my many summonings to the room were yet to come, there was already a history of it being unpleasant. So I stood there. Skinny legs, shivering slightly in my shorts, at the door to her room. She was at her cupboard with the mirror. I think taking hair pins out to do her bun right. The peach walls of her room seemed to turn redder, the distance from the door to where she stood yawned open.

'Tha…mmma,' I squeaked.

'Stop standing there like a coward and come in, what wrong have you done, that you look so guilty?' she barked.

'You…you called.'

'So?' she asked brusquely but then she eased up as she went on. 'Anand, to survive in this world you have to be hard. You can't be this scared and soft.'

I nodded, moving in slowly. I was a child, Thamma, I was scared and soft.

'Now tell me how is it that you knew that your Bulu Pishi wasn't going abroad?'

'I didn't know, I just read it in her palm.' Still very squeaky.

'That's knowing,' she thundered, 'and you read how to do this in a book, in Cheiro's?'

'No, not in Cheiro's, I couldn't see the right line, but I knew she wouldn't go,' I said.

At that she started beaming. She came over to me and hugged me. Put me on her lap. 'Anand,' she only called me that at that age when she was giving me a serious talk. Twice meant I had to remember it forever.

'Anand, you are special, you have a gift. Not everyone gets these gifts. Only special people do, because not everyone can handle them.'

I was listening but also since I was getting progressively happier, I might have only been listening to what was good to hear.

'…you're special to God. Because the sadhus get to be like this after years of sadhna. Your having these traits so young, means you're very very special.'

Thamma and I had tea together that evening, alone. She had made some nimkis—gojas, really, the sweet kind. As she chomped her way through them and sipped her tea while I glugged my tea-flavoured milk, she told me about spiritual powers, hinting at the potency of celibacy and moral uprightness. Mainly though about being special and the sort of life that one does not choose, but is chosen for one. Pronouncing me as the Sen with the Sense.

Five

It's high time the romantic angle was introduced, no? What's a rant after all without a little love-interest, huh? God is love, is he not? He'd like us to believe he is.

Mitali Chatterjee came into my life when I was fourteen years old. MC or Chatterjee, Mits or Chatters, if she allowed me some affection, 'de taali' if I was being sarcastic about her achievements or some such. Or Ma, if I was being old-world Bengali, or strange.

I met her at the Durga Pujo in the colony, which had started just the year before. As is common to most Durga Pujos, the organisers had broken off from the Hauz Khas faction and decided to start their own. There were many reasons for doing so. They didn't want to share the park with the Ram Lila that took over more space each year, they didn't get along with some of the people there. This side of the road had more affluent families and also because someone or the other was making or wanted to make more money.

I digress, but bear with me, pujos are important to me. As important as Mitali, maybe. Or maybe not.

Her family had moved to Delhi from Calcutta that very year and although she was only a year younger, she was two years junior academically. Blame it on Cal's schooling system or to her transfer to Shiksha, the high falutin' school she'd joined in Delhi.

She was your prototypical Bong chick. Even then. Maybe it was the Cal upbringing, they were more promiscuous or exposed or whatever, earlier.

I was the nerd, geeky fortune-teller. She was the confident going-to-be-head-girl kinda chick. I was the thin wiry, shy, yet to reach my full height Bengali boy. She was the almost at her full height, and consequently fractionally taller at the time, girl. She looked older than me too, but those differences waned with time.

I saw her on Ashtami (the main day of the pujos) when I rushed in at ten-thirty to give anjali.

(Pujo details: mashis, saris, dust, smoke, children, fluttering yellow and white pandal, sholar-kaaj, temperamental dhaakis, much communal love, set-ups, the oldies at the collection counter, the youngies at the snack counter. Camphor and ghee in the air.)

I knocked my slippers off somewhere, did a hasty dive for a pronam and then someone placed flowers in my cupped palms, small bits of bela-paata, and I mumbled after the purohit 'Esho, shochondono, billo potro...'

I heard a more than normally well-enunciated repetition close at hand. It wasn't an aunty-voice, it was younger, cooler. I opened my eyes, saw Durga Ma, turned a little to the left, to identify the possessor of the voice. And by some twist of mantras, it was a younger version of Durga. Wavy hair, cheekbones, that flawlessly translucent, just a tint of yellow Bengali skin and big almond eyes. She was wearing a really well-cut canary yellow and leaf green churidaar-kurta. To top it all I got no vibe from her. No sense of history or the future. A combination of qualities that you can tell, by the aforementioned description, has really stuck in my head.

She was just a kid then, but her face had what you would call character, for lack of a better word. Or perhaps presence. Whatever you call it, she had it. I saw it. Since class nine is the age you only really notice older women, it was odd for a girl in class seven to have that kind of effect. At the time, I was fantasising pretty regularly about my teachers. Pujos were a time to keep an eye open for some of the mashis in their silks, a girl in a churidar, well, that was new.

The anjali finished and I loped off to get the proshad. She was behind me in the line and it must've been her height or aforementioned overall impression, but she made me nervous. So I awkwardly but boy-school chivalrously, let her get ahead in the line and get the proshad. I think she smiled, I can't remember. I kept an eye on her through the remaining days of the pujo but never really got around to talking to her. I don't think we even exchanged a word when our families were introduced or even during the post-pujo colony bijoya get-together.

My first memory of speaking to her is at the bijoya do at home. All the families took turns hosting the colony families. My parents being senior members of the community, got one of the first shots, so it must have been soon after the pujos but before Kali Pujo or Diwali. I had run back home from my maths tuition class and pretty much continued running all the way into the TV room. Running the first part because I didn't want to miss the party and the second because one had to project scholarly energy when guests saw you with textbooks, I suppose. Well, there she was, sitting on the diwan with the other pujo kids. Heaped plates of food in their hands. I think I was still running when I stammered my introduction to her.

'Hello, my...a...a...aamar naam Anando.'

'Yeah hi, we met at the pujo. I'm Mitali.'

'Hi Aanu,' the others said.

I nodded at the others, who I knew from last year. The boys I knew from before, from the firecracker pistol chor-police games at Hauz Khas. Somehow the police team had made it to our pujo, the thief teams had stayed on with the Hauz Khas pujo. A symbolism that I see only now. I had run around the pujo pandal playing balloon volleyball, unch-neench, and catch and all kinds of games with most of them but I had no such shared stupidity with her. With nothing more to do nor any great reaction from the other kids, I announced that I would go get a plate myself.

'Anando?' she said, stopping me in my tracks, 'My father's name is also Anando, with an "o".'

She beamed a megawatt smile and then turned her attention back to her plate. It was time to heap some food for myself, give myself something to do since I had nothing clever to say.

The conversation that followed that evening was pretty routine. Which class are you in? Did you choose computers or commerce kind of thing. I think she felt a little embarrassed by the whole thing. For seeming backward in her class, for not being able to spout Sanskrit like the rest of us, and mainly just for being unfamiliar with Delhi and its types. If I had met her today, I would have spotted the chink, but I was too goody-goody then.

I'm sure I fantasised about her but it was one of the many things you do in class nine. So nothing out of the ordinary. Also I was preparing for the board exams the year after. Trying to figure out factorisation, dealing with being shorter than most girls and having a voice that wasn't dependable. So let her not seem less important or more so. She was on the radar but just about.

She kicked in big time somewhere during the end of my summer vacation at the start of class ten. She'd gone to Calcutta to meet her grandparents and had come over home one afternoon with her parents when they returned. It must've been the weekend, it was the last week of June, very muggy and warm and we were holed up in my room. She had come with her books. Both she and her parents assumed that she would get some studying done in my company. After all, I was older and a rattu-tota, topper type. So the elders had their adda in the living room. For the usual lazy overfed Bengali reasons, it had extended well past lunch.

I was at the desk in my room trying to finish whatever holiday homework we were still not old enough to avoid. I know I should call it assignments but it was homework then. She had brought her books but was happy skimming through her Mills and Boons on the bed. I don't know why her parents thought she was safe with me. Maybe because I was so small and thin. They should have known those types are the worst. Anyway. Sometime during the afternoon she started dozing.

It must've been the heat, teen hormones, whatever, I'm making excuses, but I felt that things wouldn't be complete unless I had touched her. After much counselling and arguing with myself, I gave up. I knelt by the side of the bed and watched her breathing, it was regular. Deep inhalation and rise of the chest. Deeper exhalation and fall.

I leaned on the bed to see if it affected her sleep, it did not. Time was running out and someone might just walk into the room. So in an almost scientific probe I stuck my forefinger out and poked it into her breast. It was a scientific prod, very gentle, as you would an animal that's lying down, to check if it is alive. There was no reaction. She may have twitched a wee bit but not enough to suggest waking. So I cupped my palm, and put it around her left breast. I made a mental note that this was the first breast I had ever touched, but more than the pleasure of a sexual first, it was surprise at the softness of the tissue. Completely unlike anything male and in a boy's school you have a pretty good idea of all things male. So there I was kneeling next to her, my right hand cupped on her breast, left hand deciding what to do, when her mother called out.

'Mitali cholo, let's go, it's getting late.'

Her eyes snapped open and she saw me kneeling next to her. I moved my hands but the speed of retraction, my entire posture, my eyes and perhaps my curled hand, frozen into her adolescent cup size, gave her a damned good idea of what I had been up to.

She said 'Coming' in a normal tone, but she had begun to hyperventilate. 'You filthy dog, how could you, you idiot?'

I remained on my knees, but I folded my hands.

'Please, please, please, I'm really very sorry, sorry sorry.'

'I'm going and telling everyone, what you've just done,' she said this angrily, but now in retrospect, I don't know if she was quite sure of what I had done. She didn't slap me or anything, she just got up to go.

'Please don't, I beg you,' I said, holding onto her feet.

She tried dragging me for a bit, but I was pleading hard. Holding on harder. She turned with a disdainful toss of her hair, and crossed her arms across her chest. Anger and breast protection in one pose. I got up and shut the door.

'Please don't, don't do it, I'll do anything I promise, just don't, I'm sorry.'

She stood there, arms folded, leaning a little more on the right foot, fuming. It was a classic Hindi film peeved heroine pose. Her father must have noticed she wasn't out yet, and called for her again.

'Mitali, cholo Ma.'

It was one of those extended Bengali byes. We had another five minutes.

'Aashi,' she said but now her anger was waning and I must've looked pitiable.

'Anything, huh?' she asked, a spark in her eyes.

'Anything,' I grovelled.

'Okay you have to do all my holiday homework,' she said triumphantly.

'All. Yes I will.' I thought I'd got off easily. I was sure

then that my suspicions had been correct, she had assumed I was being a perv, but wasn't quite sure what I had been up to. But all bunched up at her feet wasn't the best position for negotiation.

'Before you do your own.'

I think she figured that I was too willing, that she could get much more out of this negotiation.

'Yes.'

'And if there's any mistake I'll tell everyone just what a dirty boy you are.'

There it was, the loophole in the agreement, the one that she was going to keep for later as collateral.

'Okay, thanks, yeah.'

'But you are a really dirty boy.' That had to be said. It was a character statement, a statement that no atonement could really undo. Then she turned, picked up her books and harummphed out of the room.

I felt dirty, stupid, used, moronic, insulted, hurt, horny. They say that the wild storm gods, the rudras, rule over youth. I felt like the rudra dream-team was taking a very personal interest in me. Wild and mixed up and with much homework to complete.

The next day she arranged to meet at Green Park market two shops from Evergreen, near the magazine shop cum lending library and handed me her exercise books, and a list of her homework. It was a week to school reopening, and she hadn't even begun her homework. The indisciplined bitch had left it all to the last minute.

For the next three days I did her homework and mine. The maths and science being class seven level was a breeze, the real crapper was writing her essay and that too, in as close as I could manage to her handwriting. I wrote it in my hand the first time, and she tore out the pages. It drove me nuts and nearly to mutiny, but the memory of her standing with her arms crossed, threatening dire consequences, played up and I stuck to rewriting it. I thought I'd play with her essay on 'The Interesting Thing I Did This Summer' but I was too chicken. I dreamed up a day at the Delhi planetarium instead. Though I did insert the phrase 'heavenly orbs' in case some spirit guide was reading. Truth must be told.

When I returned the books to her, covertly, as arranged in the evening, near the tombs between Green Park and Aurobindo Place market, she took them with aloof anger.

Then noticing something, she pointed at her maths exercise book cover. 'This cover is torn.'

'What? Where?' I asked.

'Here,' she said pointing out a small tear in the corner. 'You tore my cover, now you have to change it.'

'What? It was like that when you gave it to me.'

'Change it.'

'It was torn…'

'Change it or I'll tell everyone.' The arms recrossed.

This bitch was going to blackmail me for life. You tore my cover!

I can't miss the Freudian symbolism now, it was one breast prod and she was treating me like I had taken her fucking virginity. I changed the cover, out of my measly pocket money. I also had to hide the brown paper and all when I got home, I mean who changed their book covers after two months. Who changes their exercise book covers, period?

Hazaar more homework followed over the course of the next few weeks, till she finally got bored with the game and the incident was so far gone that I too had become brazen enough to challenge her to tell people. I guess we were both guilty by then.

Considering her test scores and the many re-dos I had to do, it was clear that she was suffering the consequences of her manipulative laziness and had started flunking maths. I was doing not much better, my academic career suffering from being in two classes at the same time, but we met so many times over the next year, victim and assailant, that in a sense, we got to know each other better. Not pally at all—but she became the first girl outside the family that I was actually speaking to.

I remember a night when my mother came in and saw me sweating over her books, and smiled indulgently. She thought I was studying hard to make the family proud. I felt weak. I promised myself I would be wholly, completely moral. Never giving in to a moment of weakness ever again.

So it must have been soon after the proxy homework business that I turned very moral, almost entirely good. Never lying, never cheating, never pocketing undue change, always offering my seat, my help, my predictions.

After all I was born special, I couldn't let a few vices spoil that. It doesn't take too much to be truthful all the time, or to not smoke or drink. As for women, one just had to be careful, asexual if necessary. These are small things to give up to keep one's spirit pure, intact. So that one can keep doing what it is one came to do. Tell the future, tell the past, tell what's in someone's head, help people find themselves, help others find them, and in the process become what one is meant to be.

So I went on with class ten. Took the mid-term exams, kept off masturbation. Filled my head with only the syllabus, and yogic breathing. The pre-boards came, I did well enough. Things seemed fine, but then we were hit by pure middle class familial ambition.

The day my board exams got over my parents told me they wanted to shift me from St Sebastian Boys, where I had studied for the last eleven years, to Shiksha in Vasant Vihar. It was a school with a fabulous academic record, of placing forty students in the IITs and about fifteen in assorted medical colleges every year, of being the 'factory'. Of no failures in the last five years. Of more ninety per centers than millionaires in Surat, or wherever it is they polish diamonds. Of more (academic) records than Sergei Bubka. You may have forgotten him—he used to keep toppling his pole-vault world record, one inch at a time. It was also the school Mitali attended.

I begged them not to, not for any psychic reasons, though I did try that line, but because even a weirdo like me makes friends in his school. Because who wants to shift schools for only two years. I swore that if I studied I would make it to IIT, if I really wanted to. I reasoned that it would be better to wait till the results came out, as only if I did well would it make sense for me to go, since then I would get the subjects of my choice in the new school. I was buying time really, my papers had gone fine. I don't know what I expected of my parents. I guess I hoped that they would see the advantage of lasting friendships forged over thirteen years of school, over focused studying.

As it transpired, my results were excellent. I mean, come on. How difficult is it to get a sense of the questions to come? Worst case, if your abilities don't hold up, there's always the previous years' question papers to give you a pretty good idea. If there's one thing we do well in India across the board it is to spot a pattern and then milk it till it breaks.

I scored an eighty-nine point five overall, which was pretty big shit in those days. And a message. Seductively short of ninety. While my parents had second thoughts about the change of school, my grandmother put her foot down. So that was the end of that.

I went with my mark-sheets, letters of character etc. to Shiksha and applied for their science with computers section. Interviews with the parents and self followed. Actually a lot of unnecessary stuff followed.

Didi was the first person I met when I got home to tell them all that I had made it. She hugged me, thrilled like only a much older sister can be, 'Did you make Gifted?'

Gifted was Shiksha's controversial and very glamorised segregation system, of putting the brighter kids together in one section and then training them like Olympic athletes for the entrance exams.

'Of course I made Gifted, Didi'

I mean if I didn't make it to a section for the so-called Gifted, someone was really buggering up. A pity that it was a misnomer—it should have been called Focused or Blinkered Vision, but that may have put the students off. As things stood, it was called Gifted and the powers that be decided that I take it. Like all parental decisions made on one's behalf in those years, I hated it.

The first few weeks of Shiksha were my first as an outsider, learning their stupid ropes. Where which class was supposed to be held, where the labs were, and what a Shikshan or Shishya as they called it, meant. (Since 'shiksha' is education, when you're studying at Shiksha you're a student or Shishya, not a Shikshan or Shikshite.) How a Shishya was supposed to behave and act and shit. It was stupid and girlish even. Especially when I thought about the rough and tumble methods used in my former school. You had to study, play whatever you were asked to play and 'you better behave yourself when you're in uniform or get caned, boy'.

After a while, I learnt the ropes, met other newbies and things became almost passable. Aside of physics and maths; which were gobbledygook. In the Gifted section everyone was so freaking far ahead of where we were at St Sebastian Boys, that it was irritating just to be in class. I had done two months in SSB, before moving, but these guys had crammed almost twice as much and studied through the summer holidays.

From being the top three in everything in class, it was very disconcerting to be in the bottom three. I missed my former school, I missed my gang, football, dramatics and all the extra-curriculars that SSB forced me to do. But one had to survive. I did what came naturally—predictions, reading palms, charts anything to keep my mind off calculus and the distressingly bright guys in class.

The good thing about Shiksha was that they had plenty of students, so I had many palms to read and predictions to make. In fact I could be walking down the corridors and batchmates would ask me 'pass' or 'fail' while keeping their test scores hidden. I would get it right usually. Well, I guess a lot of people could do that by reading the smug expressions of the Shiksha Blazered Gifted Section Snobs (the toppers got a school blazer with an ugly hastily embroidered crest, the rest wore sweaters). As for the others, well, there were always some clues. The way they crunched their answer sheets or carried their school bags, or how they walked, or the tilt of their heads.

It wasn't a big deal till one day the chemistry teacher caught me reading palms. A boy's palm to be precise, so I guess she assumed there wasn't any hanky-panky going on. She called me out of the lab. I thought I was going to get it. Get suspended or miss class, do maths problems or detention or whatever feeble punishment they had at Shiksha for the Gifted section. Once outside the class she asked me what I thought I was doing.

'I was reading his palm, Ma'am,' I said head bowed, feigning an apology.

'So you can read palms?'

'Yes Ma'am.'

She held out her palm. 'What does it say?'

This was odd, very odd. It was like the breaking of a wall or the crumbling of a hitherto unquestioned social edifice. A teacher asking me to read her future. Teachers weren't supposed to have a life that students were aware of and to get a student to voluntarily peer into yours and your secrets. Whoa. She must have been brave or very keen to know something. I, however, was blank. So to compose myself and to sound somewhat professional, I said, 'Ma'am, could you tell me your date of birth please?'

She didn't answer immediately.

'Ummm…don't tell your classmates,' she said with a nervous giggle, 'it's September 20, 1961.'

Right. Brain calming, but the psychic eye was not open yet.

'And your full name please, Ma'am.'

'Vani, Vani Gupta.'

I looked at her palm and then suddenly I felt it. 'Ma'am, you've recently had an operation. And it was successful.'

She looked at me open-mouthed. Surprised. I could see that I was right. However, before I really got going, both of us saw the principal doing his rounds and she withdrew her hand.

'Okay, that's enough for today,' she said hurriedly, a trifle embarrassed. I was still a little thrown by the entire experience of reading a teacher's palm. This, man, was breaking new ground.

Of course, the rest of the class had stopped trying to work out the constituents of compound salt and were watching the entire exchange. This was not the usual thing to happen in Studious Shiksha. No, this was front page, advertising be dammed, 72 point headline gossip. So sure enough, after that I became Shiksha's resident psychic. No one was too big or too small for a reading. All my classmates and one or two of the cooler teachers offered their palms and birth charts to be read. It got to a point where I thought I'd be advising the principal soon.

'Sir, to get more students into IIT you need to appease Rahu, the foreigner, by sending one of your new male students on dates with the prettiest girls in school.'

I was doing at least fifty predictions of different sorts

every day. The sort of practice that any expert on geniuses will tell you is the difference between the merely Gifted and the Exceptionally Cool.

The routine persisted till they tore down Babri Masjid. Then we were all homebound and there were no palms to read. So I used the time we got off school brushing up on my palmistry and astrology, reading all the books lying around at home. The rest of my class I'm sure did IIT joint entrance exam questions.

Life returned to normal in January. By then I was a regular at Shiksha and felt much more at home. Aside of that there were two positives—Mitali in the school bus, who was getting disturbingly prettier every day, and the Shiksha swimming pool. St Sebastian was too poor for a pool—Shiksha, which had no pretence of running on Christian charity had enough money for a 25-metre glisteningly blue pool. After school hours, with the relevant permissions in place, you could swim for two or three hours, or whatever time it took for the sun to set. So I swam and swam and swam, and underwater for increasing lengths, as my lung capacity and shoulder muscles grew. There's little that compares to swimming underwater, save meditation and space travel. (Not that I've experienced space travel but I've seen the videos and can abstract what it must be like.)

My abiding memory of the Shiksha pool is swimming deep underwater and looking up. There was another guy swimming underwater above me, and then the splashers on the surface. I remember thinking to myself then, that this is what Duryodhana (before he got killed by the Pandavas) must've been doing. It was such a healing feeling. If I could hold my breath for longer than the twenty- thirty-odd seconds that I could manage then, I may have been cured of all the crap I had within.

About the other good thing: Mitali. When I saw her get up at the school bus stop after mine, on day one at Shiksha, at first, I was worried. I was dreading that moment. I mean what if she exposed me in a bus full of schoolchildren. So when she did glance at me, I gave her the respectful 'Hey' upward nod. She, on the other hand, gave a surprised tilt of her head and what could have been a smile. I wasn't able to decode what exactly, since soon after she proceeded to put her arm around a guy in my batch. Also in Gifted but a different combination of subjects. When I found out who he was, I remember thinking how ahead of her times she was. I mean no one in school had a boyfriend two years their senior, but she had broken through that barrier.

That upward nod and tilt of head was perhaps the real start to our bizarre friendship. An almost peace-making exchange of looks. It's a friendship that's lasted many years, and I don't know what else to call it except a friendship. One must not scoff at small starts because God does work in funny ways and throws dice where we can't see them.

That's Stephen Hawking, admittedly on black holes, but it's so pregnant with meaning it's got to apply to life in general. I could have been a guru, a really great guru. All understanding, with one foot in the ancient Oriental and one in the modern Western, one in science, the other in the paranormal, both rational and intuitive. You raise a threaded eyebrow? Well how's this then. What do you know about meditation, you do know about meditation, don't you? Finding yourself, focusing on a point, a mantra. Watching yourself breathe, shutting out thought. You know the shit, right? Sit with the palms out, thumb and forefinger forming an O, twisting your knees, straining the thighs and ankles to get into the padmasana or lotus position for you anglicised yogis. I doubt whether you've asked yourself why it's called the lotus position and not the dead duck position? It's a simple enough answer, it's a meditation trigger.

You don't get to be a lotus simply by being flexible. The asana just makes it easier for the body to accept the meditative state. The pain in your lower limbs is only half the story, what you have to do, is imagine you're a lotus, with your head as the bud. Breathing in light, love, compassion. Slowly opening up to become a well-formed lotus as the light fills you. A lotus at one with the universe.

So believe me when I say, I could have pulled off the guru thing. I had my chance really. Sadly I don't have the time anymore. But I must get back. I didn't want to jump about in the telling like I have, I would have liked to have kept it chronological, or in some logical order at least but memories and other thoughts jump back and forth uncontrolled. I never expected it to be like this. I will keep going, or you'll never know the full shebang. I am tiring though, I hope I can keep awake, keep this up. I think I'll have some more water, take a break. Just a little recess, I can't afford much more.

I'm back. The water tasted bittersweet. Now isn't that a charming comment on life. Okay, I promise, no more asides. Where was I? Right, swimming, Mitali, Shiksha. Yep, more of the same till the class twelve board exams. Mitali had broken up with her boyfriend. Everyone was single and studying. Especially the Swatters-Gifted. They had to worry about the boards and all the entrance tests. Living in Green Park, it was my job to submit all the IIT joint entrance exams forms at the Hauz Khas post office. They were all taking it. And they all wanted to be in the top 250 so they could get the subject of their choice. Not me. I submitted the forms for altruistic reasons. I had to do something of greater cosmic significance. Not engineering, perhaps astrophysics. It had to be pure and godly. Yep, my target was a BSc in physics, and then who knows, some university abroad that could deal with a psychic scientist. What discoveries could lie hidden for long?

I loved physics, I truly did. Not just the area covered in the course, but the stuff hinted at as well—relativity, superstrings, dark holes, dark matter, I didn't get it, but I was interested.

So it was no surprise that I was well prepared for the boards, well before the actual date of the exam. I had read my notes, and re-read them. I had read the textbooks cover to cover, done the previous years' questions, done all the IIT '89 and Roorkie '85 questions. All the questions that came with the little pointy hand in the margin. In short, I was on top of things. I studied well into the night and fell asleep with the books around me.

I must have woken around three a.m. Standing level with my shins and about a foot from the bed was a dark shadowy figure in a shroud. He, for that is what his build suggested, was standing almost respectfully, his palms clasped together in front of him as if ready to declaim. Or what must have been his palms. I describe this as though I had time to observe him, it must have been an instant.

I mouthed a scared 'Hello' and then 'What do you want?'

He seemed to look up, as in his shroud seemed to move. I don't remember a face, though he wasn't faceless like a ghoul. Just too shadowy to tell. He raised his hands to indicate the books around me. I said an expectant 'Yes' to encourage him to explain, but then my eyes opened and the image dissolved.

I was sure it wasn't a dream. For one, the scene around me was exactly as it was with my eyes closed, just that he wasn't there. Now some neuroscience experts feel that objects and sounds of dreams persist into waking such that we feel we've heard or seen something to which there is no ready explanation. But what then is a vision? I mean was Joan of Arc dreaming? Was Saul of Tarsus projecting on the road to Damascus? Was Nostradamus in some great schizophrenic seizure? That's a lot of scientific mumbo-jumbo that masquerades as an explanation, all it aims to do is to deny the possibility that one can have visions.

I slept poorly and woke late, rushed to the examination centre, hurried to my desk in the hall and had a good paper, or so I thought, believing that the vision I'd had the previous night was a good omen for my future in physics. Alas, as it transpired, it wasn't a good paper.

I got 50 per cent in physics. I suspect a bulk of that was the practical score, because the lab assistants and the examiner pretty much tell you how you've done. This was an aberration without precedence. I had never done so badly in an important examination. With a sense of what was to come and studying hard, how could I? With that my PCM with an 85 in chemistry and a 90 in maths was a 75. Let me put that in context. When I went to see the physics cut-off in St Stephen's, it was 92 PCM. When I ventured to the outer limits of North Campus and saw the Khalsa College first list for the physics class, the first fifteen had a PCM of 99 or more. I wasn't going to get physics anywhere on campus, I wasn't going to be any sort of physicist, far less an astrophysicist, and if there was something pure and godly for me to do in college, I would have to find it outside the curriculum. Meanwhile, I had to get enrolled in some course.

That dastardly Shroud Man. It was his doing. I still have this recurrent dream that I have to take my physics exam over again, except that I have two days to study. I wonder what the heck Shroudy was trying to tell me, and if he had nothing of importance to say, why did he not let me just sleep in peace and go on with my love affair with physics. He reappeared once again later. I'll come to that in good time.

Dropping physics in my best four subjects, improved my eligibility for the arts courses, and as things came to pass I enrolled in English at Hansraj. Not my first choice, Hansraj being on the fringes of the university and social acceptability among the upwardly mobile Bengalis, also my family thought English was a course for girls. Wouldn't I be better off taking the IIT exam and dropping a year? But I had a feeling Shroudy didn't think I ought to do science.

So I stuck to English. It wasn't bad. Two girls in class were pretty. The dramatic society was composed mainly of the students from English and they smoked pot, drank a fair bit and kissed around. Two years blitzed by doing collegiate things. Studying prior to the exams and doing whatever else you wished for the rest of the year. If you did fine in your exams, there was greater licence to do more collegiate things. Singing in the lawns, lusting after your teachers, trying insanely hard to get your first kiss, sex, if possible, just talking to everyone and doing nothing at all. For hours on end. In my case, also reading palms, reading charts, using the library to read up the history of divination, astronomy, religion, philosophy. I couldn't do astrophysics but I could still find things that were pure and godly. There was such joy in being young and free that you forgave the twists of fate.

Great things were happening around us. We were at first scared of what the new liberalised India promised. We were told the foreign companies were going to kill us. Sure enough, McDonald's opened in Vasant Vihar, and Pizza Hut came soon after. They were going to fatten us before they killed us. On the whole however, things seemed to be getting better. You could get a decent pair of branded jeans without depending on your relatives living abroad. For me, that meant fewer trips to Mohan Singh Place, where they stitched you a pair of jeans of any fit that you chose and any label that you desired. I would go to Mohan Singh Place today, anytime, over going to a store, but those were different days.

Then computers left the school labs and came home. When I first went to my classmate Rohit's house to check what the big deal was I couldn't get the computer to do anything. I was waiting for a command prompt. A:> or a C:> because that's what I remembered from school. At Rohit's, I was looking at a coloured screen with no blinking letters or symbols. Hitting random keys on the keyboard made no difference. I discovered that I couldn't get the computer to do much, till I used the mouse and clicked at different places. That computers weren't only for writing programs, you could also type letters and make cards and draw things.

Then there was this grand new thing called the Internet. The cool kids said it was Wow, spelt with three wwws.

Some of my friend's dads used to send emails at Rs 5 a pop, and post on something called bulletin boards. There was a lot more, better and freer, on offer. People were getting Hotmail addresses. Others were seeing pictures of Cindy Crawford. Some of my friends had alter egos called Slasher and Duke and could be found skulking around the Delhi or the India chat room.

We didn't have a computer at home, but there were enough people with one, with things like a partitioned hard disk and a dial-up connection. So I too got introduced to the grating buzz-chime of the dial-up, and the two-tone static that signalled that you were online. I learnt over time which of the three telephone numbers one should dial at which hour, to get logged on. There was a world full of connections to be made, connections that didn't require psychic gifts.

Then on the first day of the third year of college, I saw Mitali board the university special from my stop. I hadn't seen her in the pujos the previous year. I think she'd gone to Calcutta to be with her grandparents for pujo. So it was nearly two years since I had seen her. She looked ready for college. Radiant. Her aura was golden. If I didn't feel like such an old college hand and wise in the ways of the world, and knower of all-things-university-special, my heart may have skipped a beat.

Instead, I smiled and gave the knowing nod of a senior. Soon the freshers, with mixed feelings of apprehension and excitement, began to get ragged. After the usual running down Safdarjung flyover like aeroplanes and singing of the anthem near India Gate, the tried and tested routines began.

'Do you find this funny, fresher?'

'No.'

'No, Sir.'

'No, Sir.'

'Well then, why were you smiling?'

'I don't know.'

'Know what?'

'Know why I found it funny.'

'Know why I found it funny, what?'

'Know why I found it funny that I smiled.'

'Know why you found it funny that you smiled, Sir.'

'Know why I found it funny that I smiled, Sir.'

Ah, the infantile rites of passage, establishment of hierarchy. It's the same game, played out over and over again in life. Only the players change and in the university special it is pretty straightforward. Mitali, it being established by glances and Bengali names, as someone who knew me, was asked after equally silly standard ragging rituals, to come and propose marriage to me.

The twelve-year-old in me panicked, but then I eased up, reasoning that that was years ago, and she would only make herself the victim of more and perhaps vicious ragging if she tried something funny on a well-established senior.

She walked up confident, looking like she had this in the bag. The look of someone who would never be humble.

'Will you marry me, Sir?'

Gallantly, 'Why?'

'Because I've been asked to ask you.'

This candour would not do for everyone's entertainment, where was her sense of sport.

'Well then, there's no reason to marry you, is there?'

The guys who had put her up to it, piped up, 'Convince him you silly fucchha. Otherwise we'll keep ragging you till next month.' Which I suspected they wanted to, since Mitali was the prettiest of the fresh crop.

'Because I love you?' she laboured on.

'Is that reason enough to marry you?' I was trying to egg her on, get her to play to the galleries.

'Yes, I love you and you will be happy with me.'

'Ah, and how pray will you make me happy?'

'I didn't say I'd make you happy, I said you would be happy with me.' She raised an eyebrow in challenge, but the others who had put her up to it, thought that was meant for them and got aggressive.

They spotted the sexual and hence more promising line and goaded her on. 'Don't get cocky, fuccha, tell him how you will make him happy.'

'I will cook for you and clean for you.'

'I could get a maid to do that, marriage might be a little excessive.'

'A maid won't cook or clean as well.'

'I'll make do with her standards, a wife must offer more.'

So it went on with the same silly thrust, parry and innuendo. I don't know why she just didn't give in and state how sex would be better with her than a maid, which would have called an end to it. Perhaps the joy was in the deliberate postponement of what everyone expected.

Till she said, 'Please marry me, Sir' and in a lower voice, 'My college is here and I have to go.'

I looked out of the window, it was St Stephen's. So she was going to be a Stephanian. She must have had the marks. 'You are joining St Stephen's school?' (That was the running joke. Stephen's still maintained pretty strict rules for things like assembly and attendance, unlike other colleges which were more liberal and treated you like an adult.)

'Yes,' she said.

'Okay, go, we can marry some other time.'

She didn't seem at all pleased with the prospect. Though I don't know whether she was visualising more ragging or a real marriage. I, on the other hand, watched her go with a feeling of sadness. No, there was no vibe yet, just a sense that as far as she was concerned, I'd always have homework to complete.

A trimester passed. I visited Stephen's to grab a bite and catch glimpses of Mitali. She seemed popular, from what little I saw, and serious. I saw her once at a demonstration and once at a seminar on English in our college. At the time I didn't know what subject she was studying but I assumed from the seminar that it was English.

Late October, Durga Pujo came and that's when we got chatting. We had a fair bit in common. The same bus, North Campus, interest in the upcoming college festivals. Also interestingly, as I discovered, she had an interest in English literature and wanted to do it, but her score in English didn't allow her to make the cut-off, so she'd opted for history. So we both ended up doing a subject other than our first choice. She, however, seemed to enjoy history, I was just biding my time, getting a degree studying literature. We spoke at length through the pujos, interrupted only by her then current boyfriend's unwelcome visits. An unwashed second year musician, in totally inappropriate pujo clothes, I mean, torn jeans and T-shirts were fine for college, I wore them as well, but in the pujos, c'mon, you dressed in your Indian formals. Or you didn't land up. I guessed he wasn't a Bong. Or trying to be cool. As soon as he showed up, they left the pujo pandal— smoked, hung out, did what they had to—things that I wouldn't approve of. But no one asked my opinion on the matter.

The year drew to an end; it was time for exams, to decide one's future. After three years of not caring, it was time to take a peek at the real world. Except I hadn't a clue what I could do. While my family approved of all my divination stuff, an astrologer or equivalent wasn't an acceptable occupation. Surely that wasn't the point of sending me to Shiksha and then putting up with English literature for three years.

They wanted me to get into a programme that would get me a good job, law, the IAS, or the MBA. Though my mom, in a small voice, at the dining table, did sort of say that it was okay, if I wanted to study more English, that becoming a professor wasn't such a bad thing, my grandmother and father wouldn't have it.

When I looked at my ambitions all I discovered was a great desire to spend more time with Mitali. The only way to do that would be to join St Stephen's for the Masters. So even though I didn't quite disagree with my grandmother or my father—I spoke up for my mother and for all professors. That was exactly what I wanted to do, I said, and concedng some territory to the power figures at home, I added that it kept the door open for the civil services exam.

We fought, but finally they gave in. I took the relevant tests, the interviews, and my English score was decent. I got into Stephen's for the Masters. It was like getting into Shiksha all over again. Cliquey, exclusive, and if that wasn't bad enough the Masters students didn't even count as regulars. Also there were far fewer students in Stephen's than I thought, so everyone knew each other, but they didn't know you and it was made pretty clear to what degree they didn't want to know you. That didn't bother me, I hadn't joined Stephen's for its much vaunted parties.

My life was sorted. Mitali and I boarded the bus from the same stop, walked into college together, said our byes for the day, then bumped into each other once, maybe twice during the day, and typically took the university special back home together or to whatever extent I could live my life around her schedule. If she was doing any extra-curriculars, I would skip the 1.30 p.m. special, sometimes the 2.30 p.m. one as well, but even my love wasn't strong enough for me to miss the last special of the day. Because missing that meant the trudge to Mori Gate. Two buses, and then a crowded bus back to Green Park. I must have done it quite a few times, since the scars of those journeys linger on, but yes, it was to be avoided, unless you had bona fide plans of your own.

We got to bonding big time at the Durga Pujo in my MA first year. MA Previous as it's referred to. She told me about her ex-boyfriends, her growing love for history, and her plans for life—which involved going abroad to study more. I spoke to her about my apathy for English, my lack of clear plans about my future and my growing fear that I may be gay. She laughed at the last bit, then got serious saying it wasn't to be feared, and if I was, I was. She added that anyway she had always suspected that I was not quite the norm. To which I grilled her about the norm, and then revealed that I didn't think I was gay, but just had no evidence of being heterosexual since I'd had no real relationships. I wasn't fishing or anything, just in the spirit of opening one's heart out in front of the Goddess during those late pujo nights when everything is somewhat more charged and emotional.

I can see her still. She was by my side in a sari, I think it was pink and blue, a chiffony, georgetty or whatever material the slinky saris come in. We were sitting on the pavement just outside the gate of the pujo, sipping milky sweet tea that they served at the pandal. It was cool, and she had wrapped the aanchol of her sari around her shoulders, which made me want to put my arm around her. She, I think, was craving a smoke.

There was this lingering incense and camphor in the air from the evening arati, and also the smell of those wintry eucalyptus-like leaves so typical of Delhi. Amaltas, I think it was. There was a hawker with toy bows, arrows, maces, in the usual cardboard and silver foil. He wasn't bothered with us, we were pujo regulars, he was looking out for visitors. A policeman sat in his chair with his back to us. His walky-talky made static appeals from time to time.

When I told her I had never been in a relationship, she turned her head slowly, a grin forming.

'Really? Why?'

'I dunno.'

'I would set up some of my friends with you, but you're an odd one.' She chortled at that.

'I guess so,' I said, looking down at the dregs of tea and malai in the thumb-sized plastic cup.

'Isn't there anyone you like?'

'There have been.' I should have said 'there is', but I was shy. Or perhaps I didn't know what I felt for her back then. Or how to say it.

'And?'

'And nothing, what and?'

'Well, did you do anything about it?'

'What am I supposed to do?' I said, evasively.

'You show interest, you ask them out for coffee or tea or dinner or something. Spend time with them.'

'What? I'm not sure that's the way. I mean just because I like someone doesn't mean I have to do anything about it,' I argued.

'Oh ho, then how do you expect to get in a relationship?' she asked.

'I didn't say I wanted to be in one, just that I hadn't had one.'

'You said it with regret.'

'Look, liking isn't enough, I lust after my professors, you're saying I should ask them out?'

'Oof, you silly horny Bengali boys, can't you have a normal approach to life?'

'Like you and your five exes, that's normal?' I had been holding that in and it came out sharper and more explosively than I intended, it also betrayed the fact that I had been keeping count.

'If I like someone, I like to be with him. It's more normal than not doing anything about it and letting it sit inside you and make you crazy,' she responded with surprising equanimity.

'I'm not crazy, I just haven't liked anyone enough yet.' I mean I did. I liked her, I just couldn't say it. Not when she was being the counsellor.

'Well, you're probably gay then.' She said it like a challenge, but also ready to accept it, in case I agreed.

'It's not likely,' I said crossly, then playing on her indecision on how to treat my sexuality, I added, 'but since I haven't been with a girl yet, and some boys I do think I could kiss if I had to, it could just be possible.' I said that with what I hoped was an argument-ending smirk.

'So will you be here for the Shondhi Pujo?' I asked after she'd taken a longish drag on her cigarette. That's a pujo that's held typically very late at night, it's quite charged, and supposedly the hour when Durga vanquishes Mahisasur.

'Doubt it, but let's see,' she said, flicking the ash, then crossing herself, in case that was seen as an impious gesture.

I was there for the Shondhi Pujo. God and I go back a long way, so I had to be there out of loyalty and also because for the four days of Durga Pujo, one felt quite alive and all Bengali. There was little else to do, anyway.

It was about two a.m., so it was a ragtag group of the pujo regulars and the few strays like me who decided they wanted to be there for Shondhi Pujo, this year. As the hour approached, the housewives began lighting the lamps. One hundred and eight. There was one big lamp and the rest were diyas placed on the tenthouse table.

One of the colony uncles, sensing the aesthetics of the moment switched off all but one of the pandal lights. Then the dhakis started their drumming.

Dum dum dum dadumdum dum, thiki-thiki thiki thiki.

The priest began to ring the bell. Some of the women ululated. Camphor filled the air, my pulse must have quickened with the beat of the dhaks.

I looked hard at the Durga protima expecting her to come to life and speak to me, she gazed back at me, her clothes and perhaps even her eyes shimmering in the flickering light of the lamps. It was almost as if she was trying to say something with those bloodshot battle-crazed eyes.

'What is it, Ma?' I asked the Goddess, shutting my eyes. The image of Durga stayed for a second or two and then dissolved into someone familiar. I asked her not to kid me. I opened my eyes, saw Durga's eyes glitter with meaning, then I shut my eyes. I tried to keep the image of the protima there. She was reluctant to stay, only her eyes remained and then they too began to dissolve. I opened my eyes and I saw the same eyes, or perhaps my eyes hadn't opened. Perhaps as a psychoanalyst would have me believe, I was projecting an image from my subconscious.

She said a long 'Hi'.

She'd put a sweatshirt on over a salwar kameez that she must have slept in, it didn't matter, she was lovely.

'Gosh, Shondhi Pujo is so special. Just look at the setting, it's goosebumpy,' she said, and folded her hands into a devotional half pronam.

I couldn't speak. I could only hear the blood in my ears, drumming away, out of sync with the dhaks.

She was standing next to me, close enough for me to feel the heat of her arm on mine. The heat of sleep broken and then hurried dressing for the pandal. Durga was speaking to me quite plainly.

'You came.' I whispered, not out of piety, just because that was the only sound my vocal chords managed.

'Yeah, my parents wanted to come, and then you and I don't really hang out the rest of the year. When you're not talking about relationships, you're fun.'

'You know, about liking someone...' I began

'Yup.'

'There is someone, I really...'

'...You like me, Andy, don't you?'

'Yes,' it was a relief to say it. 'Yes I do.'

'I'm seeing Manu, Andy.'

'Manu?'

'Manu—musician Manu. With the li'l goatee.'

'Oh!' Damn him.

'Besides we'd be terrible together. I don't think I'm your type anyway.'

'You don't...'

'Yeah, you like boys or something, don't you,' she giggled. She'd offered me an honourable escape.

I smiled what I think must have been a very weak smile. 'Boys,' I parroted.

'You know I'm right, you just haven't met enough girls, which is why you like the only girl who's willing to speak to you. Haha.'

She was speaking a little too fast. Perhaps she felt something too when she saw those angry shimmering eyes.

Maybe the eyes weren't shimmering at all, maybe that's just the way things look when you try to see through tears.

'Yeah, I should meet some girls.' It was a croak. Pathetic. Even in retrospect.

'Yeah, you should, you can anyway get to hold their hands while you pretend to read their futures.'

Yeah that I could.

'See you tomorrow then?' she asked. It was a goodbye.

'Yup, for the anjali, if you're up by then.' A scolding, moralistic bye from me.

She drifted off to her parents, who were about fifteen feet away, and a few days later, to Manu.

I put up with one of her set-ups. I think her friend and I were both arm-twisted into meeting, but there wasn't a single vibe between us. Anyhow, seeing her with Manu and Manu's guitar put me off. So I stopped hanging out in Stephen's. My classes were at the arts faculty, so there was no real reason to go to the college anyway.

I let my father convince me to take the management school tests. I was late in starting, so it wasn't easy. Still, the need to keep Mitali out of my head made me study. I didn't make it into any of the Indian Institutes of Management but I got into the Faculty of Management Studies in North Campus. If Mitali got over Manu, I wasn't too far away, and if not, then I could always lose myself in the MBA and the corners of FMS and Delhi School of Economics.

She did break up with Manu, it must have been my first year at FMS, but that was because she had made it to Cambridge for the Affiliated BA and he hadn't. (With a name like Mitali Chatterjee, your application form had to look promising. While Manu Singh is a name destined to get into middling real estate management.) He wasn't really academic, he'd just applied because she had.

Three days before she left for King's College in Cambridge she called me.

'Congrats,' I said.

'You know the Stephen's machinery is well tuned to get you to Cambridge. You should have tried too.'

'I'm not cut out for more education.'

'You're doing the MBA.'

'Like I said, I'm not cut out for more education.'

She laughed a full, throaty laugh, 'Oh I'll miss your stupid jokes.'

I kept quiet.

'You'll stay in touch, right?' she asked.

'Yeah we have email now.'

'So you will mail, right?' there was almost a plea there or was it just a higher pitch. Maybe she was just excited to be leaving. Maybe I was hearing things. Telephone technology of the 90s.

'I guess, unless the Y2K bug kills my email software.'

We exchanged maybe five mails in total while she was at Cambridge.

One of which informed me she had a boyfriend named Jack. And another that she had broken up with him, as 'He was too much of a boy.'

I had little to report, other than the fact that I now had a job, at a multinational company. I was going to sell potato chips. She accused me of selling out, going against my Commie Bengali DNA and being another rat in the rat race. I mailed her just how much they were paying me to run the rat race and that ended that.

We stopped mailing after that, I started using the work mail ID more, and didn't really enjoy sending personal mails from office or my work ID. (There was always this nagging feeling of someone looking at my screen over my shoulder the second I started keying in her address.) She, I think, was studying more, or searching for a new boyfriend.

The years passed, we drifted apart. I sold chips and got fatter. She got some degrees, had more men and shifted continents. Then the planes crashed into the World Trade Centre.

She was in New York at the time. I tried very hard to get in touch with her. I tried calling her, I mailed, messaged. I was pretty panicky. It would be just like her to be around the WTC, or go there if she heard that something was wrong and then get crushed by the second tower coming down. I kept redialling her on a loop for a long time, but there was no getting through.

She called a week later, I was at work, hence couldn't talk as affectionately or for as long as I wanted to. That

Shujoy Dutta

tone just didn't get used in office. She said she was fine, upset but fine. Someone she knew very well was in the North Tower when it came down. I couldn't tell who, it was either Fred, or Al or Alfred, or Frey—the connection wasn't great. I was just grateful to know that she was all right. Just before she hung up, she mentioned she was coming back to India for work. I heard 'Bombay', before the line went quiet.

So she was coming back to India. Good, that could only mean a break-up with whomever she had been with. She would be in Bombay, and I in Delhi-NCR, but there was hope.

I drove home in a happy mood that night, belting out ten of Kishore Kumar's top fifty hits as loudly as I could. Complete with the sway of the head, the index finger pointing to the pals in the audience and the little dashboard drum roll at traffic lights. It had been a healthy summer, chips were down. Pun intended. Even when we bundled the packet of chips with fruit drinks, there were fewer takers than previous years. My boss avoided eye contact for two days. My increment wouldn't be great, the promotion may get stalled, but there was good news finally. Life was looking up.

Six

~~~~~

I knew something was wrong the moment I entered home. Not psychically, just. Didi was sitting on the sofa in the drawing room, hugging a cushion to herself and pointing the remote at the TV, I guess, flicking channels. I had seen the light flickering from the TV while climbing the stairs. I peeped into the drawing room, she didn't seem to register me. So I walked inside pulled out some orange juice from the fridge, put as much ice as I could fit in a glass and poured the OJ in. Then I went back to the drawing room and collapsed on the sofa next to her. She kept changing channels, holding the remote with her arm outstretched, as though she was just scanning channels, waiting to return to the programme she was watching, so I waited with her. She didn't say anything for about two minutes, neither did I, I was happy to look at the trash she was scanning through.

I heard a small sob and saw a single tear trickle down her cheek. Before I could ask what had happened, more followed. Lots more. I was still buzzed by the news of Mitali returning, so I couldn't even get in a question. She wiped her face with the arm that held the remote and said, 'I lost the baby, Aanu.'

I didn't react, I couldn't. I just sat there looking at the TV and her. The guys on 'Worst Case Scenario' describing how to deal with a shark attack and my sister on the sofa, in a Worst Case Scenario herself, with no white ex-Marine in cargo pants to help her out.

'I felt a little sick in the loo—nothing serious...but I knew something...not right...I ran to the hospital...I couldn't save it...I couldn't save my baby, Aanu,' and she broke down, tipping over until her head rested in my lap, crying uncontrollably.

I think I just turned to stone, we weren't that affectionate—Didi and I. I mean we hugged from time to time and knew what was going on in each other's lives, vaguely, but I didn't know the appropriate physical response. So all I could do was put my hand on her head and sit still, while she wept. My eyes moved from the TV to her, to the ice melting in the glass, to the damp patch on my trousers, which grew with every tear.

I felt for her, I think I did, but I don't think I quite felt her pain. Or I had just switched off. So I just sat there. This should have been one of the things I sensed, warned her about, but I hadn't seen it coming. I was angry at myself for not being able to warn her, to not be able to help protect her child. Heck, it wasn't me that I should have been thinking about. There should have been some way of consoling her, something I could have said or done to make it easier, to bear her grief better, but nothing came to mind.

If we had been closer, in years or emotionally I might

have known what to say or do. It was only about a fortnight ago that we heard that she was pregnant. She and my brother-in-law Ashok had been trying for years, but something just hadn't worked. Sperm motility and uterus environment or some such. And then finally she'd gotten pregnant. She called the morning after she'd been to the doc at the end of her second month. Ma had received the call, 'Oh Abira, that's so wonderful, I'm so happy. For you and Ashok. That's great news. I get to be a grandmother,' and she'd danced a little, the first time I'd seen my mother dancing, and then spent the day laughing at most things.

Ashok knew of course and he did what he did when there was any good news—took us all out to dinner that night. I guess my parents were the happiest, I don't think either Didi or Ashok had started planning yet or gotten into the parent act, I certainly hadn't registered any avuncular emotions, just a certain objective happiness for my sister and my parents.

That was gone now, and here was Didi crying in my lap. I sat there, a major cryer myself, without a tear in my eye, hardly feeling anything except a certain stoniness. Ashok came home soon after and I left them alone. They sat for a while in the living room, with the lights off. Ma was in her bedroom lying down in bed, she too looked miserable. Thamma was sitting very quietly in the puja room. Baba had gone out, I don't know where. I wandered around the flat, which though full of people, felt very empty. All feeling pain. I sat at the dining table not knowing what to do. What, how? Why didn't they call me at work to tell me? Why hadn't I felt anything? How had this happened to a family that prayed all the time? Had I lost my sense of things about to happen? I could usually turn it on but now it was off. Even if someone had walked up to me, dripping with omens, I wouldn't be able to tell a thing now.

There was some change lying on the table, the balance left over from buying the milk. I picked up a coin and gave it a spin. It spun. It fell. I spun it again. It spun in a small revolution.

Then I remembered.

It was a humid August day in Didi's second year in college. She, her friend Radhika, Urmila aka Urmi, and a fourth friend who was new to the group, who I couldn't place, all came home excited in a swish of dupattas. There was something they had learnt in college and couldn't wait to try at home.

My parents were out. Thamma must've been on some pilgrimage. So there was just me. Didi wanted to keep me out of it but I wouldn't have it. Also Radhika was a major hottie, and after Mitali the one I would think about most often. Whatever Radhika was going to be involved in, in my house, I wanted to be a part of, or at least witness to.

So they all trooped into the living room, cleared the central table of all the cutglass and ashtrays. They were jabbering in an adrenaline high and ignoring all my questions. 'Aanu, if you're going to be a pest then you can't be here,' Didi said.

'I'm not being a pest,' I replied, miffed. I was old enough then to want to be taken seriously by older women.

'You are, and if Ma and Baba get to hear of this, I won't speak to you again, ever.'

'You hardly speak to me even now,' I said cheekily, figuring there was going to be something surreptitious and grown-up cool.

'I'll show them that magazine that I found,' Didi continued.

'That's been disposed of.'

'Okay, get out then,' she said giving up.

'No, no I promise, I'll be quiet.'

They sat on the floor around the table. Radhika, with something of a magician's flair, whipped out a sheet of paper from her satchel. Those were the satchel years.

Didi took out a little triangular-shaped cardboard.

There were holes at the vertices. Through these holes she inserted three pencils and made sure they were level on the sheet of paper. Only one of the pencils had the lead bit touching the sheet, the others had the unsharpened end.

Once Didi was happy with the balance of this odd eight-inch tripod, she started.

'Okay, we're ready now. Remember, under no circumstance are we to let go, I will do the talking, the rest of you can ask questions.'

Radhika beamed (with a Madhuri Dixit-like radiance, making Mitali wobble at the top of my list) then she and Didi exchanged glances and everyone got serious.

If it wasn't all so interesting and covert I would have been sneaking glances at Radhika throughout. Her bare shoulders, tanned and magnetic, her face glowing with the youthful radiance I knew only came with admission to college. Lust would have been the dominant state. Instead, witnessing this strange ritual there was another feeling, anxiety or something like it. Something heavy.

They sat cross-legged on the floor, around the central table. I sat a little distance behind them on the sofa. I had no idea what the heck was going on and it was best to observe at a safe distance.

Didi nodded, and as if it was an instruction, Urmi pulled out a newspaper cutting from her purse. I peered at it, it was a picture of Rock Hudson. He had died of AIDS a few years ago, but we had only recently seen *Giant* on the video, so he was fresh in our minds.

Didi started. 'We are all to concentrate on the picture, asking the spirit to join us. I will do the talking. Concentrate hard and don't let your thoughts drift.'

They shut their eyes and concentrated, I assumed. I certainly did.

'Rock Hudson, if you are here we ask you to join us,' Didi summoned.

Nothing happened for a bit, it was just the sound of the ceiling fan creaking with every revolution and the sound of breathing. Four of them almost in sync and me a little faster.

Didi asked, 'Rock Hudson, are you with us?'

Nothing happened.

She asked again, nothing.

Then she waited. The third time, she said 'Rock Huds…'

Before she could complete the question, the tripod shuddered a little. I nearly jumped.

'If you are here, write something to show us you are here.' Didi's voice was more oratorical, older even. Like she was playing some ageless Delphic priestess.

The tripod moved, the pencil traced a curve.

'Are you happy to be here?'

The pencil circled.

'Okay, then.' Didi seemed relieved.

Then the pencil circled a lot faster, it started drawing a violent spiral.

'Please write something if you are unhappy to be here.'

In very poor handwriting indeed, I saw the pencil trace an H, followed by what I thought was a C, but it could have been an E as well. The third letter looked like an L, but before the word was complete, Didi finished it.

'Hell. He's in hell. Oh my God!'

Then the pencil went wild, it scribbled all across the sheet, random and uncontrolled. Like a spirit burning. The scribbling got scratchy and the pencil moved faster and faster till the paper began to tear.

'Please leave if you're unhappy,' said Radhika.

The pencil stopped moving.

'We have no more empty sheets,' Urmi said.

I piped up, 'I'll go and get some.'

Didi spoke in a voice almost not her own. 'No one is to move. Radhika.'

Radhika nodded. She reached with her free hand into her bag and pulled out a folded sheet. With their free hands the girls unfolded it and spread it out. Urmi reached into her purse and rummaged for a long time. No one spoke. Everything was quiet. I could feel the sweat trickle down my back and into the crack of my ass, but I didn't move. I didn't want to upset Rock Hudson.

Finally Urmi pulled out a one-rupee coin. They were quite large in those days. With enough space for four manicured forefingers.

They must have adjusted how they sat, because I saw the sheet clearly only then. The alphabet along nearly three sides and numbers—the digits on the fourth. There were three circles in the middle of the sheet, more or less aligned. I had never seen an ouija board till then, and while it was a makeshift, student's version, it seemed loaded with mystic significance.

The coin was placed in the central circle.

'Rock Hudson, if you are here, please leave this tripod and come into this coin.' Saying that, Didi put the forefinger of her left hand on the coin. Seeing her do it, Radhika joined in. The fourth girl, I still can't recollect her name, was looking quite nervous, but she reluctantly joined in.

'Are you in the coin?'

Nothing.

'Are you in the coin?'

Nothing.

At this point, the fourth girl spoke. 'Look we've done enough for one afternoon, let's do this some other time.'

Urmi was also ready to be done with it, I think.

Didi, looking very stressed spoke, 'Damn you, it feels like there's someone pressing down on my finger, why have you two left the coin?'

Urmi and the fourth girl looked panicked.

'C'mon he's pressing down,' Didi insisted, anxiously.

'Is there anything you want to say?' Didi said, trying to keep control.

The coin darted to the circle marked 'No'.

'May we ask questions?' Radhika asked, also sounding very anxious.

There was a little tremor, and reluctantly the coin moved to the 'Yes' circle.

'Will we get married?'

Yes.

'Who will be first?'

Urmi.

'Will we all pass our exams?'

No.

'Who will not pass?'

One of you.

There was a flurry of questions. I can't remember all of them clearly but they asked about their studies, about their careers, about going abroad, about whom they would love and who they would marry. The coin swishing across the sheet like some possessed figure skater, and Didi or Radhika calling out the letters that it paused so very briefly at. It was moving so quickly I was amazed that they could keep up with it.

At one point, Radhika asked, 'Who will be the most famous among us?'

The coin seemed to be in two minds. Finally, it spelt out—HEWILBE.

Till then I had been just an observer, an outsider, with that answer I was a part of the drama.

I could feel the room get darker, colder, dryer.

Then Didi asked, 'How many children will we have?'

The coin seemed undecided, moving this way and that. Would he just add up all the possible future kids, or what?

'Does anyone love us right now?'

The coin stayed passive.

Then the fourth girl spoke, 'Okay, what about Abira?'

The coin went on a dance.

Finally it spelt NEMO. Then it paused, as if struggling with the future, and then TISCA. An odd name. Probably a future love.

'Is there anything else you want to tell us?' Didi asked.

The coin spelt WONTON, and the fourth girl spoke out the word.

Odd, Rock Hudson was craving Chinese, I assumed therefore that there weren't any Chinese cooks in hell.

Radhika spoke, 'No, idiot, it's not wonton. He's spelling backwards.'

Didi spoke, 'Spelling backwards, that's not a good sign is it?'

As if on cue, the coin once more began to move, slowly at first, then faster.

EVILOTNAWI

I had lost it on Evil, wondering what dangers Rock Hudson was warning us of.

Radhika spoke slowly, seriously. He's saying, 'I want to live.'

Didi, her voice quivering, 'Are you really Rock Hudson?'

The coin danced between H and A, it took me a couple of seconds to figure that it was laughing. My throat was dry, there was no saliva to swallow, I felt like I was going to choke and I was too nervous to cough.

Then the coin spelt, what looked like 'ZDOBADEENI'.

'He needs a body,' my sister spoke.

By this time, I was bursting with nervousness, the fourth girl was also panicking—she said, 'Rock Hudson please leave.'

I meanwhile had started mentally reciting the Hanuman chalisa, making sure I was enunciating the doha 'Bhoot pisaach nikat nahin aave, Mahavir jab naam sunaave' clearly.

Radhika noted, surprisingly calmly, 'I don't think he's Rock Hudson at all, he must be some passing spirit.'

'Who are you?' my sister asked.

The coin spelled 'OL' then slowly, very slowly, it went to B,A,I, D

DIABLO.

I had had enough. I asked them to please ask it to go. The fourth girl was crying with big heaving sobs.

Urmi, weeping herself, said, 'Please leave, whoever you are, go. Please leave us.'

Didi and Radhika joined in asking the spirit to leave, Urmi was begging and so was the other girl. I, of course, was repeating the Gayatri mantra at full speed. Hoping that nothing crazy would happen. That there wouldn't be a possession or some such. Possession films were bad enough, having one of them here in X-35, or worse still getting possessed myself would be unthinkably bad.

Finally the coin stopped.

The fourth one wiped her tears. I think Didi, Urmi and Radhika also wiped tears or perspiration. It had been an intense afternoon. I can't remember anything bad happening after. Perhaps the doors in the house slammed of their own accord a couple of times. Rock Hudson or whoever it was, had a temper. That was the last time my sister's gang did planchet at home.

When I look back now, all the other answers seemed okay, even guessable or open enough to be true, just one of them stood out for its oddness.

NEMO TISCA.

What a strange answer to who loved Didi. I could only think of Captain Nemo, but what did Tisca mean. Tisca was not really a surname, if anything it was a girl's name. That couldn't be it, there had to be something else in it. Prior to this answer the coin was almost well-mannered, it was at this point that it had turned strange. Perhaps, Nemo Tisca was not Nemo Tisca at all. The not Rock Hudson was possibly already spelling backward at this point.

It could have been 'OMENACSIT'. That still made no sense to me. So I went online and keyed in the letters, I googled. Went on random sites. Then I started splitting the letters into different combinations of words. One of the windows opened on a page with Latin phrases. I scanned the page wondering what piece of relevant information had caught the attention of Google's software spiders. Then it practically jumped out from the blur of text.

In Times New Roman Bold the phrase: Absit Omen. Translation: Let this not be a bad omen.

The coin meant to spell TISBA, but instead, due to the panicked pulling of four college girls had spelled TISCA.

Rock Hudson or whoever he was, was warning Didi. Diablo, he'd said he was Diablo, the devil. I should have worked it out. He had switched to spelling backwards. That was the signal, that he was shifting to more serious business, or that the spirit, the energy had changed. He was warning all of us, but most of all Didi about today, about the miscarriage.

He hadn't been evil, or if he had been, he had still managed to slip in a warning along with a curse, had we been willing to pay heed. Damn it, I should have known better. I had had over a decade to figure it out. With all my abilities, everything I'd read, I couldn't see a little backward-spelt warning for what it was. Heck, I could have helped Didi, I could have made sure she took precautions. I had failed her. I didn't tell Didi about it. What would have been the point? It was too late for warnings now. Too late to tell her to be careful. I didn't have the empathy to console her, and sadly, I had no words either.

I shut down the computer and came out of my room. It was dinner-time, but no one was hungry, Ma didn't even ask me whether I wanted to eat. That was a first in twenty-five odd years.

Ashok and Didi left soon after, they went home and dealt with their loss as best they could. I should have offered to be with them for a few days, or to stay with Didi, till she felt better. Instead, I began to stay longer at work, there being no point coming home, the house was in mourning. Baba shopped more or went for longer and longer walks, Ma slept more. Thamma, I assume, prayed more. I wasn't home to know better.

Seven

Didi went very quiet for a few months after that. Very unlike herself. She began praying, sitting in the dark. When she wasn't at our place she was out cult-hopping. One day at a Tibetan chanting group, the next day at a godman/godwoman's ashram, the third day at a centre that helped street kids, the fourth offering a chaadar at a dargah. It was unnerving, but good, we thought. As long as she didn't stay at home and mope. For about three months all she could speak about was spirituality. I mean more than what was the average at home. I never knew there were so many people in Delhi interested in God. Suddenly my family didn't feel that abnormal anymore.

About six months after her accident, Didi's conversations stopped being vague, quasi-philosophical principles on living life, and I started hearing the word 'channelling' tossed around in her conversations. Despite my copious readings on all things spiritual I hadn't come across the word. So it sort of stuck in my head.

A school pal of hers had introduced her to this group that held—well, for lack of a better word, seances. Among the various activities that they claimed to do, they seemed to be able to chat with higher energies. Most of the people in the group went to ask for life advice and speak to the recently departed, but there seemed to be some talk about God and the universe. Didi just went to talk to her unborn child and ask 'why'.

After a couple of sessions, Didi seemed to be much better. She came home and told us how much better she was and that she had accepted her loss. She felt responsible for her life and her decisions. It was funny language, but as long as she felt better, it was fine with us.

One night after dinner, she took me to my room and asked me how I was doing, whether I still hated my job or not? It was vaguely unnerving, but I replied.

'It's the same, Didi, the promotions don't matter. We marketing types are treated quite poorly by the product and sales guys. The boss, the sales head, the R&D guys, they act like they're doing the real work and we're the necessary evil. So I'm more senior than I was a year ago, but it's the same shit every day.'

She looked like she wanted to talk, so I made space on my bed, picking up the clothes that I had tossed on coming home.

'It's recurrent dramas, Aanu,' she said, plainly, professorially, sitting down after making space for herself.

'What is what?' I asked, sort of half in the room and half in the loo, where I was chucking the clothes into the bucket that held the dirty laundry.

'The Pups told me that.'

'Pups?' I asked, in a squeaky, getting-worried-for-the-sanity-of-my-sister voice. She was speaking to animals, acceptable, but little dogs?

'Pals upstairs,' she laughed.

'Ah, pals upstairs.' I had heard her speaking about these exalted energies at the sessions, though I hadn't ever paid any real attention earlier.

'When you seem to be going through the same situation over and over again, then that's a recurrent drama.' She sat back on my bed, wringing her hands. She obviously had come to explain the entire channelling phenomenon to me. 'It means you are supposed to learn something from it but you're not. So you keep repeating the lesson till you learn what you have to.'

There was a long 'hmmmm' from my side. 'What else did they tell you, your pups?'

'If you promise not to tell Ma and Baba about this, there is something I want you to hear.'

I nodded.

She walked to the dining room and brought her purse, from which she extracted a cassette. There was no cover, it looked like one of those T-Series cassettes. I wondered what the late Gulshan Kumar or his singers could have said or sung that was so pertinent. Maybe the tapes played backward or something like Led Zeppelin. She inserted the tape into my music system, rewound it and then pressed play.

There was the customary silence and then Talat Aziz began to hum.

I shrugged my shoulders, asking—what?

'Wait,' she said sternly.

There was silence, or periodic swishes as the tape spools spun. Then it began.

'Beloved Abiiiira, (swish swish) greetings.' It was whispery, croony, yet somewhat official. Like a nineteenth century letter-reading. Didi's voice but unlike anything I've heard her vocal chords produce. It was so creepy it gave me the shivers. She rested her hand on my arm, perhaps to calm me but also as an instruction to sit and listen. So I sat and listened.

'You are loved and treasured, by all of us…so you must stop living in regret.

'Regret and other negative emotions create a vortex…a vortex through which positive energy escapes (swish swish swish).

'Whatever happened was in your karma…You must learn to let go…to forgive.

'You had to work out your karmic baggage and move on. Those were debts you had to repay.

'If you can't learn the lesson from this and move on…you will have to keep repeating the lesson till you learn.

'It's not in your best interest…to keep reliving the same recurrent drama.

'Your child is safe…he was an exalted soul who only had a little karma to live off.

'He has, and has since moved on to the Causal Plane.

'Where he waits for you as your guide…

'Don't mourn his loss. Live your life to the fullest.

'Let go, allow yourself to heal, spread the message of love and remember above all you need to forgive to heal.'

Swish swish swish.

She pressed stop, before Talat Aziz came on again and changed the vibe. If she hadn't stared at me, wide-eyed through the whole thing, I would have thought she was playing a prank.

'What?' is all I could manage.

'I have no memory of making this,' she said, ejecting the tape and putting it back into her purse.

'You're kidding me.'

'No, I'm telling you,' she insisted. 'All I remember is going into my meditation before sleeping. I found the tape by the side-table in the morning.'

'And these are your Pups?'

'Yes, it certainly sounds like them.'

'It must be very important for them to use technology,' I said.

'I guess so.'

'I wonder what the long-distance rates are? Astronomical I assume,' I joked.

'You idiot, it's serious.'

'It sounded like the usual Didi, except for the insistence on forgiveness. I mean I get it, everyone needs to move on. And they're asking you to. It's decent advice.' I was sort of spooked by it, one way or another, either my sister was losing it or she'd become some sort of medium. Given her history with spirits I didn't think it was a good thing.

'Yes, it is,' she said, looking at her palms.

'Why did you want me to hear it? I mean other than showing me your spooky side.'

'You too need to forgive, Aanu, to move on.'

It did seem like it was about her more than me, so I

asked, 'Didi, who do you have to forgive? You lost the baby? Who is there to forgive except God?'

'There is someone, Aanu.' She stopped playing with the pillow, held it and sat still. 'I've never spoken about this to anyone, but now it makes no sense to keep it within me. You remember Prannoy Mukherjee Uncle?'

'Of course I do, he and his talk of Benares and ghosts and what-not. He had a crash and lost sensation in his hands. He recovered I think.' I was getting slightly worried here. Did Didi know that I had willed his crash? What or who would be there to forgive? I mean I was the one to blame.

'He did, but not completely.' She sat looking down at her hands. The room went quiet. The tubelight stopped humming, the cicadas stopped chirping, the traffic outside must have stopped too.

'What about Prannoy Uncle?' I asked.

Eight

Abira Sen Mitra's story:

(With my interjections or questions almost entirely edited out.)

I must have been around fourteen that night when Prannoy Uncle came home. Ma and Baba weren't there, they were probably out for dinner, Thamma was on one of her pilgrimages with her pilgrimage pals and I can't remember whether we had any domestic help then. It was just you and me at home. You were eight, so it was okay to leave us at home. You were reading one of your stupid fortune-telling books or playing. I can't remember what I was doing. Homework, most likely.

The bell rang, I got up to answer, 'Who is it?'

'It's Prannoy Uncle, sweetheart.'

He was always going 'sweetheart' or 'dear' or 'baby', you remember that, right? All of us thought it was very English and Western then. Except I don't remember him using 'sweetheart' for you.

I opened the door and there he was. Standing, reeking

of cologne at the head of the stairs, whistling an English tune, spinning his keys with one hand and a plastic packet dangling from his other hand. He always came bearing gifts for us—the kids—so it seemed like a regular visit. People dropped in unannounced all the time then, so nothing seemed odd or wrong then.

I told him Ma and Baba weren't home.

He said, 'Oh well, anyway this is for you.'

It was chocolates, and I was happy to get an unexpected gift. I asked him if he'd like water, since he'd come from so far away and, well, that's what we all did. He agreed to water and stood around in the living room.

I went to get water from the kitchen, took out a bottle from the fridge and a glass, shut the fridge and turned to pour it.

'Let me help you with that,' he said giving me quite a start, he was right behind me. Unnecessarily close.

I hadn't heard him follow me to the kitchen. He reached for the glass but instead put his hand on my breast. I didn't know what to do. No one had really felt my breast before, I don't remember if they were even developed.

Before I could react I could feel him pushing against me. I didn't know it at the time, but he had an erection, because I could feel something very odd in his pants rub against me.

I dropped the glass and shouted for you, asking you to come meet Prannoy Uncle.

You didn't answer, you must have been really involved with whatever it was that you were doing but it did seem to break his mood. He backed off.

He said he'd have the water some other time and left.

I didn't know what to make of it, I didn't even know if anything had happened so I didn't tell anyone, but I felt guilty for the whole thing in some way. I forgot about it, went on with life. Then many years later, in college, we were trying to get a lift to come home. It was Radhika, Urmi, the usual gang, you know, there must have been four or five of us. We were standing a little distance from Jesus and Mary College, so that the professors wouldn't catch us. A car stopped, I think there were two boys sitting in the front, dhikchik music—the typical loafers outside girls' colleges. There were enough of us for safety, so we we started piling into the back.

Just then I heard a 'peep-peep', and I saw a man on a bike taking off his helmet.

It was Prannoy Uncle. 'Arre, Abira, what are you doing,' he said.

You remember his office was somewhere near Chanakyapuri, so he must have been on his way home.

He saw the situation and how packed the car was, and shook his head disapprovingly. 'There's no need to travel like this, and that too with strangers. These young boys are never up to any good.'

It had been years since the incident in the kitchen, so I thought nothing of it, besides I was in college. You feel so much braver and crazier than you really are, in college. So I got on behind him. Nothing really happened right away, he cautioned me about young boys and what they were like, that I should be prepared, that I was to be more self-reliant than asking boys for a lift. We were somewhere on the empty roads of Chanakyapuri, when he asked me if I knew how to ride a bike.

I remember I laughed and asked him how he expected me to learn with Baba and Ma and that anyway no one around us had a bike. He suddenly braked and I fell against him. He got off the bike and said, well, it's time for you to learn.

He explained how the bike worked, the accelerator, the clutch, the tap down or pull up to change the gears. Then before I knew it, he asked me to sit in front and operate the bike.

It took a while to figure how the clutch worked and how to change gears. He helped of course, he was quite patient. Soon we were moving and it was so liberating. To have something that powerful move at your command, it was fab. We weren't going fast or anything, I was too scared to speed, but the wind was on my face and I could feel the bike jump ahead with the slightest turn of my hand, it was a great feeling. So great that I hadn't noticed when Prannoy Uncle put his arms tight against my side. He was feeling me up and rubbing himself against me.

I couldn't stop, we would have crashed, so I tried pushing his arms away. I hadn't quite mastered the brakes. I tried pushing out with my arms, but that only got him more excited.

'C'mon, you're not a little girl anymore, you find this exciting too, I'm sure.'

Before I could do anything, he reached over and grasped the handle and took over the bike. We went faster and faster and all the while he was pushing against me. I was crying, asking him to stop, pleading with him that I was his daughter's age. It had no effect—if anything, it seemed to get him more excited. Then finally when we were around Safdarjung Enclave, he shuddered and moaned. I guess he came.

His grip on the handle bar relaxed, I squeezed the brakes and the bike skidded to a stop. We nearly fell down. I pushed him away and began to run. I must have run nearly all the way home. I had never felt so humiliated, so weak. I was crying and running and cursing myself for getting on his bike and agreeing to let him teach me to ride it.

I was feeling so great commanding the bike, I'd forgotten who he was and what he'd done to me before, I should have realised there was something wrong from the start. The worst thing was that he was practically Baba's age. I couldn't believe that someone that old could think of me sexually. Could be sexually crazed by me.

I felt utterly helpless that night. Helpless and soiled. I hated myself, my breasts, being a woman. I cursed him and I cursed myself for being foolish. I hated my body. I hated all the organs, the body parts that had made me so vulnerable. That hate didn't go away for a long time. All that hate, all those curses. It slowly turned my uterus to poison and killed my little baby.

Didi wiped her tears.

'He paid his price, and anyway I forgive him now.'

'There's no reason to forgive him, Didi. What he did was unpardonable. Why didn't you tell anyone?'

'I didn't know what to say, Ma-Baba were against asking for lifts. There was no evidence either, I felt stupidly that they would turn it against me or worse say that it was my teenage hormones, that I had imagined it. The Prannoy

Mukherjee they knew was very different. Anyway we sort of lost touch with him after his crash. If he had come home, maybe I would have made a scene.'

'I don't know what to say Didi…'

'There's nothing to say, Aanu, you have to forgive, if you want to move on.'

'This is what your Pups advise you? This is what you get? Forgive the guilty?'

She shrugged her shoulders. She had stopped crying. She put my pillow back in its place at the head of the bed and smoothened the creases on the bedsheet.

'I don't know why I told you this after all these years, I think I had to get it off me, the secret itself had started feeling heavy.'

I'm not sure how I felt. Angry at Prannoy Uncle. Awful for my sister, surprised that she thought the hate turned to poison within her. Helpless at not being able to do anything. I had always hated Prannoy Uncle. I wish I had asked for worse. All I could manage, squatting at her feet was, 'I hope you feel better now, Didi.'

She smiled a tear-streaked smile, and patted my cheek. Then she got up to go. As she was walking out of my room, she stopped and said, 'Maybe you should go to the Pups too, you know,' with her eyebrow raised, suggesting that this may be just what I required.

Confronting and forgiving all those I considered guilty. That was my Superboss and the GM Sales.

'They can answer a lot of your questions you know.'

'Like what?' I said, sitting down on the chair at my desk.

'Lots of stuff, Aanu, like why you're here, your life aim,

life after death, whatever you need to know. I could help get you started. We could even meditate together.'

I looked at her not knowing how to react, while she said her stuff. She'd just dropped a bombshell and now she was almost cool. It was like she was advising me to go see a shrink she had used for mild anxiety, and now recommended to her baby brother for his on-off work related stress. I couldn't imagine meditating with her, I mean I can't remember Didi and me doing anything together, aside of eating perhaps. We hadn't even played house-house together.

I did believe that they could answer questions. I had been absorbing the trivia that Didi dropped since she started with the whole channelling business. If Didi said they could help, what was there to be antsy about. I would follow Didi into most causes in the state that I was in then, after she'd opened up to me. There was nothing to be gained by holding on to my scepticism.

However, I fished, 'What do I need to know? I'm okay.'

'For example, why you're so miserable in your job and then you're interested in all this afterlife business anyway,' pat came her reply. She did really know me. An elder sister may not really understand seedy men, but she knows what her little brother's buttons are.

Nine

⌒

It was on a Wednesday that Didi had stopped by for dinner and dropped the bombshell about Prannoy Uncle, and by the following Saturday evening I had decided to go for a session. I started making the relevant noises early on Sunday morning about going to attend a session set up by Didi, so that if there were any objections Ma and Baba could voice them well in advance. You see everyone at home had pretty strong opinions on what paths were and weren't allowed for spiritual or intellectual progress. Speaking to spooks wasn't a path you took. So no surprise that Ma was not at all happy. I caught her several times in the day, shaking her head, and clicking her tongue in disapproval. Rehearsing the argument with me in her head. Finally it was time for lunch and near about the hour for me to go and discuss the topic openly.

'Why are you getting mixed up in this bhoot business?' she told me while serving me the chhanar jhaal cooked in red chillies and mustard (just like you would do with fish) but vegetarian, since non-vegetarian fare may have stirred up my baser emotions and reduced the workings of the intellect.

'Didi goes.'

She shook her head. 'Didi is married, she can do what she wants. She's been through a lot,' she said, putting the chholar dal in a steel bowl as old as me. I could see what this was about. Ma had cooked up my favourite meal. This was her way of arguing. Food conquers all logic.

'Ma,' I said using my calming voice, 'I don't think it's about ghosts. It's not like the planchet. Going by what Didi says, they seem very wise.'

She clicked her tongue. From the timing I could tell that this was obviously going according to the argument in her head. 'I don't know baba, why can't you just meditate or read something, we have so many books.'

Baba and Thamma had eaten earlier or weren't eating. I can't remember why they weren't there to lend their considerable philosophical weight to the subject. So Ma sat down after she'd served me. We both ate together, silently. She knew I would go despite how excellent the lunch was. Anyway, she didn't really have a strong reason against me going, just distrust of these new-age cults and fiddling with things one didn't completely understand.

'I'll be careful Ma, and anyway I want to ask somewhat deeper things than ghosts would know. Physics and metaphysics.'

She wasn't even hearing me, she just shook her head, I think she'd played out the rest of the argument in her head and seen that there was no dissuading me. 'I don't know, take God's name,' was all she said.

Didi had informed the centre which she attended that I would be coming and I had opted for the three o'clock slot. Half an hour before the Sunday afternoon group session. That would give me enough time, and also would draw things to a close quickly, if things were not going okay. With Ma's reluctant permission and muttering all the protection mantras I knew, I went to the house in Defence Colony.

I stood outside and tried to take it in, get a vibe. It was one of those multiple storey, kota-stoned houses. Six apartments on three floors and a basement. The centre was in the servant's quarter part of the plan. You know the sort of place SOHOs and things work out of. Two-room set. I would have rung all the wrong bells had Didi not given me instructions. I don't know, considering all the ashrams I had been to in life, maybe I expected this to be grander.

I knocked on the door. It was opened by a very well-moustached yet solemn-looking man, gaunt, with sunken cheeks, he looked worldly-wise yet friendly. The sort of look my mother and her siblings would have described as 'shukno' or dry. Don't ask why. The etymology is long and bizarre. He was standing barefooted and wore a simple white safari suit top and white trousers, tinged blue with Robin or Ujjala or some equivalent bleach. He saw me standing there looking suitably humble with palms folded in a traditional namaste and broke into a toothy grin. Some of his abundant whiskers going up his nose and merging with the hair there, and the ones nearer his ears merging with the hair that grew there.

He asked me, in a very low, gentle voice to wait as Shivanginidi was meditating. He was 'shukno' all right. I wonder why that word was swimming around in my head.

I must have been nervous. It's what's supposed to happen when you see a dead body or something, right. You keep repeating the words you speak when you see a corpse. That's why you chant God's name in a funeral procession and not anything else. I forget the exact workings of the superstition, but it's something like that.

I tried putting the word out of my head, and looked around. There weren't too many choices for seating. You had the pick of the bare floor and a small Rajasthani jhoola-type sofa that was right next to the entrance. So I plonked myself on it, half expecting it to swing. The man meanwhile, still solemn, went in and checked on Shivanginidi. He nodded and then stood by the door. I looked at him, but he hinted at no communication. His whiskers were stationary. I looked around. The walls were bare, off white, aside of a Krishna calendar which seemed to have been donated by the colony printer. After about five minutes, on cue from some telepathic messaging or from the sounds in the room, Mr Shukno informed me that it was all right for me to enter now.

I left my slippers in the rack outside the room and entered. There was no indication from Mr Shukno that I ought to do so, the rack seemed to demand the removal of footwear. In a way that was good, it indicated a temple-like piety. Ma would have approved. This was not regular bhoot business.

The room was empty. I mean of people. I guess that was what a private session amounted to. It felt emptier than it was because it was a largish room almost the size of a hall—the two rooms of the set had been combined. The walls were white—a distemper finish. It was carpeted wall-to-wall with a beige-brownish office-like carpet and there were a couple of worn durries on the floor, a low table with an empty book-stand, a white sideboard that reached about two feet high and ran all along the wall across the breadth of the room. There was nothing on top of the sideboard, whatever the room needed to have, or the sessions required, must have been inside. So full marks to them on organisation. The curtains were drawn shut and the sole illumination was a less than standard brightness tubelight. Other than emptiness the other feeling was that the place was cold. Wasn't that what they said about being in the presence of ghosts? There was no Shivanginidi, I could however, hear some sounds from one of the doors adjoining the room. It might have been my mother's words or the entire otherworldliness of what they were supposed to do, I was quite spooked. I made a mental note to keep this part out of the telling, when I spoke to Mitali about the session. She would consider it greater proof of my wussiness. Yes, she was back in India. In Bombay. More on that later. Meanwhile, I was breaking into a bit of a cold sweat and full speed repetitions of the Gayatri. The bathroom door opened and Shivanginidi stepped into the room. She was a forty-something salwaar kameez-clad, fattish, typical Punjabi aunty. Ergo, nothing like I had imagined. She had no makeup and behind her spectacles she had two small fiery, piercing eyes. Or some curious form of astigmatism.

'So you're Abira's baby brother, the one who hates his job.'

She spoke perfect English, I had half expected that.

I smiled, nodding, still trying to reconcile the image of

the tall reserved saintly seer in my head, with the aunty I saw struggling to sit in front of me.

'Sit, sit,' she said pointing to the durrie on one side of the low table, she was trying, with what appeared to be some pain in her joints, to get into a cross-legged position. Shivanginidi, was clearly no yogin. What kind of higher energies was she in conversation with?

I hitched my jeans, crossed my legs and squatted, a little quickly, sort of making a point. She spun to her side, reaching across to the sideboard and pulled out a white board, a small face towel and a small stainless steel glass. Also through some sleight of hand, she pulled out a Bhagavad Gita and placed it on the stand. After a quick pranam to the Gita and some incantations I couldn't quite catch, she opened her eyes. She then laid the board on the table. It was an ouija board with ballpoint pen scribblings. Oh Ma, this is bhoot business. Amateur bhoot business.

I mouthed my own mantras. She pulled out a coin from the pocket of her kameez and placed it in the centre of the ouija board. It was a one-rupee coin. Some awful memories came back. The stainless steel glass was, curiously, placed on the towel at the edge of the white table. I couldn't tell what its purpose was.

She smiled at me, sensing my nervousness.

'I believe you have lots of questions, you want to ask them now or should I get started?'

I shrugged, still too spooked to speak.

'Why don't you ask me the questions, I might know some of the answers and then we can get started.'

'Okay,' I said completely blank. 'What's the glass for?'

She laughed. 'That's for later, for me to have water when it's done. For some reason I get very thirsty.'

I smiled a stupid nervous smile. I was ready for a drink already.

'Anything else you'd like to know?'

I took recourse to the standard question all spiritual types ask, 'What is the purpose of our being born?'

'Everyone has a different purpose. We all have an aim and we come to settle our karmic dues,' she said.

It was precise, not overstated. I was quite impressed. But if she was this good, how would I know she was a genuine medium, sorry channel.

'Why do we need to come down at all?'

'To learn, this world is a school of duality. We need to experience what our higher self only knows conceptually.'

'Who or what is God?' I asked.

'We should begin,' she said. 'You're ready to ask them now.'

'Kaka,' she called, and Mr Shukno appeared almost instantly and then squatted down without a sound. He obviously was a yogi. They sat next to each other, their fingers on the coin. They both looked at me and Shivanginidi said, 'We shall begin now,' then they shut their eyes and went into some sort of meditation or trance. I sat and watched. I felt reassured almost, good too, also on the edge of some boundary. Like I was really going to learn something important if I was ready to look forward and step out. I was ready to get to know God.

Ten

It was a wonderful new world. After that initial session with Shivanginidi, where I learnt a little about all the lives I had led and some bits and pieces on metaphysics and karma, I went online and started reading. I read almost every night after dinner. It came to a point where I couldn't go to sleep without reading some channelling session transcript or the message from an archangel or some higher entity with electromagnetic properties, involved in loving or saving the planet.

Consider for example:

'Be greeted, and know that you are not here by accident, friend. You are special. You have always been special which is why we are speaking to you dearest friend on Earth—the wonderful school of duality! Many blessings to you! It is with great joy that I speak to you this way, just in time for the great transition occurring for Earth and Humankind.

'Many of you can feel that these are special times; some can even feel the energy coming towards Earth from the central sun of the galaxy in a constant beam. As we shift vibrations, transitioning from the third dimension to the fifth, some of you can feel your powers grow. There will come a time when you will need to use them. For now be content and know that irrespective of the changes, you are loved and treasured by us all.'

Hocus pocus to you? Well, it had me grabbed. I don't know if it was just clever guys writing pseudo-spiritual or indeed pseudo-scientific copy or real messages from spiritually exalted beings but you had to give it to them. It was the best-decanted, hopeful, spirituality from all the religions. Besides, what absolutely enticing entities! Archangels. Magnetic Vibrations. Energy forms. Healers, Creators, Causers, Designers, Guardians. Erstwhile denizens of Atlantis and Lemuria, Alexander, Ashoka, Gandhi, or their higher vibrations. With names like Rametheses, Antarnuman, Barathenom. What's not to like?

For a few months my parents must have thought I was working on some mega project or doing a PhD on the sly. And when I needed more there was always Didi. With wisdom from the Pups, or from her own experiences or readings. I was like Columbus and the New World, Galileo and the telescope, Michael Jackson and childhood. Boundless excitement with much to discover. Other twenty-somethings were flocking to the pubs and nightclubs that opened and shut every three months in Delhi, but I couldn't get enough of anything new-age spiritual. It was almost enough to make me forget that Mitali was tooling around Bombay. No doubt looking for another man to fill the vacuum of moving back from the First World. That wasn't entirely fair. In adulthood, she had become involved with development and the rights of the downtrodden, the minorities, the fringe dwellers of India's great GDP-demographic dividend story. She'd got a job with a magazine that dealt with the arts and culture—a snooty affair that stank with the pressures of saving the environment, the world, and all of middle-brow culture.

Yes, so despite my new interest, I was also festering with the knowledge that Mitali was a domestic flight away and that I was not doing anything about it. Ever since she had moved back to India, communication had been low. I put that down to moving pangs, but I think it had a lot to do with me being distracted. I used to initiate the emails and messages to her but with Antarnuman holding forth on karmic theory and the need to fill ourselves with lights of different colours, it was a little difficult to compose a suitably cool, yet reply-generating mail.

One evening, I was reading up on Indigo Children. Who, for the uninitiated, are the next wave of spiritual evolution—children born after 1978 with greater powers. Even though I was born in '76 I was slowly getting convinced that I was one of the first, say a prototype. Given that my ancestors died farming indigo for the British, I thought it was vaguely appropriate. So I was reading, when surprise-surprise, I got an SMS from Mitali.

'Sup,' it said.

This would have been sometime mid-2002 and I'm not sure I was conversant with gangsta. I thought it was an extremely pithy invitation for dinner, and naturally I got excited that she was in town. So I called her. She first had a fit of giggles that I thought 'sup' meant 'to sup'.

Then true to her style, she broke a little piece off my heart by saying that not only was she not in town and therefore unavailable for dinner, she at that moment was headed for dinner with someone called Danny Rodricks.

I asked if he was a Bandra boy and she said no, he was an East Indian from Kurla. A community I had never heard of before. Why were the East Indians settled in the west of India? Were they descended from the East India Company? Was this a new Westernised nomenclature for an existing community like the Anglo-Indians, on the lines of East Asian for Indians?

She laughed out loud. I had never felt this ignorant in a conversation with Mitali before. I had to remind her that for all her fraternising with the lesser known communities of India and her undoubted mastery of US slang, she still couldn't tell me the formula for the area of a triangle.

My bantering skidded to an abrupt halt when she told me 'Andy, he's my first serious involvement since Alfie.'

Was I supposed to cheer aloud for that? Of all the people in the world, she had to pick a Danny. I'm not against the Dannys of the world, I'm sure they're good. I mean look at Danny Denzongpa. He's been an arch villain in Hindi films for about four decades and he still looks like he could step out of a helicopter in an Armani suit, brandishing a million-dollar arms deal with the muscles and wiles to put a hero a couple of decades younger through a lot of shit, before the final showdown. But Mitali weds Danny, just didn't sound right. It's like Hermione weds Noddy. A mix of genres. I told her as much, without quite the turn of phrase I can manage now. Hurt impairs wit.

I had been fooling with new age spirituality for too long. It had addled my brain and made me forget the more immediate reasons for living. To wit, love. I had to get to Bombay. Quickly, before she got any more serious with Mr Rodricks. I had to take a shot at a life with her.

I spoke to the headhunters, I circulated my CV, I waited. Nothing happened. I expected the worst in the form of a wedding invitation from Mitali. The weeks passed. Then completely against expectation, my boss, the apple of the eye of the potato chips industry (I'm sure there's a turn of phrase I've missed) decided to up and leave and join the serious business of selling detergent and mineral water.

'Yes, they're counterproductive, that's why I guess it's a win-win for the company.' His words, no kidding.

For this he had to move to Bombay. In an even more unexpected move he asked me to move with him as his deputy. His actual words at his farewell were I think inspired by Steve Jobs's wooing of John Sculley, 'So how long are you going to keep selling junk food, pretending it's okay.'

I had no idea he loved me that much. My increments hadn't reflected it but I said yes. A little too eagerly I think, taking into account that I didn't know enough details of the job, the pay, the rank or title. Perhaps he too saw a loyalty he hadn't noticed earlier.

He moved, no communication for a few months, then true to his words, the HR of a Big Bad Fast Moving Consumer Goods major in India called. I hadn't really checked with him, where he was moving to, or perhaps he hadn't really said, but the call was a shocker. I thought he'd have joined a local player as the boss or number two. So I was suitably surprised when it was ULCI. There were a couple of rounds of telephonic interviews, and then I had to fly down to Bombay for the closing interviews. It was quite exciting. I had never been sent tickets for an interview before. This was the sort of stuff you only read about or saw in films starring Tom Hanks or someone equally earnest. It was twice as exciting since it was a chance to drop in on Mitali. Not surprise her. I would have to ask where she stayed, if she was free and what-not. Didn't want to feel crushed, walking in on her wrapped around Danny's East Indian torso.

I messaged the details of my trip to her and asked if it was possible to shack up with her for one night. The interview was at nine-thirty in the morning and I reasoned that it was December, so Delhi could be foggy and the flight delayed and I didn't want to risk all that. A good case, but I'm sure she guessed that I wanted to spend the evening with her.

She messaged back saying 'Cool', and then that 'u'll hv to crash on the futon in d hall. ok?'

That was more than okay with me. Being within twenty feet of her at night was a situation charged with possibility. I had to think of some intense, moving and delirium-shattering-conversation-openings on the flight. She would have to recognise that while Jacks, Johns, Alfies and Dannys were okay as playmates, for real joy she would have to pick an Anando. Or The Anando.

I got myself an open ticket from the Indian Airlines office near work. Oh the joys of the days of the open ticket. You could just land up at the airport, get it endorsed for the next flight out and off you were. There was always place. I had once even wrangled my way to a seat in Business Class. That's unlikely to happen anymore. They'd rather run loss-making budget airlines.

I booked myself onto an evening flight so that I could leave straight from work. Since so many of us were always flying for work, the suitcase under your desk wouldn't even get a raised eyebrow from my new boss. He'd just assume I was dousing some fire in some corner of the potato-growing heartland. More to the point, it gave me more or less the entire evening in Bombay. An evening with Mitali. There was time for a few drinks and dinner. Time enough to show her that we had only been kept apart by not cohabiting in the same city together.

I was so excited I was almost tipsy. The cab to the airport wasn't fast enough, the check-in line was dawdling, the security check was glacial, the bus ride to the aircraft was at a snail's pace, the aircraft took its time to admit passengers, get its logs cleared and whatever else they needed to do before take-off. I'm running out of synonymous phrases for slow, but you get the drift, right? Once the flight took off, I felt better. I took a long relaxing breath. The arrow had been fired. Now it was only air-resistance in the way.

We circled around Bombay at least five times, which put me off. That was one drink less for Mitali. I had no check-in baggage—just a change of clothes, a toothbrush, a roll-on deo and less than 150 ml of cologne. One of those tiny bottles, the label of which said Gucci, but it smelt so cheap I was sure it was a rip-off. I can't remember how I had gotten it, it had sat in a groove in my toilet bag since I had started travelling.

So no sooner had the bus deposited me at Arrivals, that I started running. I sprinted all the way to the taxi stand determined to beat the queue and any others who may be travelling light. I jumped into a cab bag first, before I got too sweaty running, which may put Mitali off, and gave him the address in Bandra. There was music in my voice. He bickered, since he wanted a longer route but I told him I'd tip him, so he should get a move on. He did, except entering Bandra was painful and sweaty. The loop that the Western Expressway took to get to S.V. Road was clogged. Bumper to bumper. It was enough to get me mighty pissed off. I drummed the back of the front seat, threw my little backpack on the floor and then threw it on the seat, flapped my shirt for the perspiration to evaporate and gave the driver all kinds of instructions. It was already nine-thirty p.m., this was going to be my only evening with Mitali in the foreseeable future, unless I landed the job, and all of Bandra and suburban Bombay traffic was determined to minimise the time I had with her.

Eventually I walked up the three floors of Nazneen Apartments. It was never this humid in Delhi at night, and it was supposed to be winter, did I really want to move to this city? I rang the bell outside a door with a hand-scripted Kaizad on the nameplate, wondering why she hadn't changed it.

The door was opened almost immediately and there she stood. Mitali. A little heavier than I remembered, but not in an unattractive way at all. Her hair was a little longer, falling to just below her shoulders. She was all dressed up. Lipsticked, eye-lined, a partyish top, tight jeans, God she was a revelation. I couldn't believe she'd dressed up for me, she was planning dinner out too. Woohoo.

I dropped the backpack and we hugged. A more intimate hug than I expected, and for longer. I could feel her breasts press against me, I think I could feel her heartbeat. I could have held her there for very long.

She disengaged and said almost crossly, 'Thank God, you've finally made it. Another five minutes and I would have asked you to join us, bag, baggage and all in Gazebo.'

'What's Gazebo?'

'Where we're going to party. It's a club.'

'Oh great, what a surprise!'

'Yeah, you're lucky, Danny just signed on to do music for a Hindi film today. Big banner, big budget. So we're celebrating. Oooh, I'm so excited for him.'

My throat suddenly felt very parched but I managed to gulp down what must have been the salivary manifestation of deep disappointment. I put my bag down next to the futon.

'Great for Danny,' I said. It sounded fake even to me. 'Are you sure I should come, I could just stay here and rehearse for the interview.' I had to sulk for a bit. It gave me time to console myself and prepare for a night that Mitali would spend with her successful boyfriend.

'Don't be stupid Aanu, who rehearses for an interview? We want you to be with us tonight. It's one of the biggest days for us and you're one of my closest friends. Also there's someone I'd like you to meet.'

She used 'we' and 'us'. This trip felt shitty already, I wanted to take the morning flight back without taking the interview. But then I would have to pay for this bullshit trip.

'Gazebo, can I shower?' And then added with the wiliness of the sweaty, 'For this someone.'

She sniffed from about two feet away, 'You smell fine, and we'll be late. If we make Ruma wait any longer, she's likely to find someone else interesting and that would be a waste of all my talking and effort.' Saying that she started shutting doors and switching off lights and fans.

'She's that kind of girl is she?' I asked.

'Don't talk shit, Aanu,' she said pushing me out of the apartment.

'So what's the film? Is Shahrukh Khan in it?' I tried to feel upbeat about the night.

'You can ask him when you meet him.'

'SRK will be there?'

'No idiot, Danny. Ask Danny.'

As we were walking down the stairs, me a few steps ahead of her, she suddenly placed her hands on my shoulders and leaned with nearly her full body weight on my shoulders, like a gymnastic piggy-back. 'So you're moving to Bombay, oh how exciting. There's so much to show you.'

It was high-pitched and squeaky enough to be genuine affection and excitement only she'd lost me at 'there's someone I'd like you to meet'. I didn't want to meet anyone else, I wanted this evening to be private. Just the two of us. A couple of drinks, nothing excessive, she could drink more if she wanted, I'm sure she'd developed Anglo-American appetites. Just some small eats, dessert, then back to her place, conversation, a post-dinner liqueur and who knows. But no, my simple desires were not to be, instead I had to sit in the penumbra of Danny's musical brilliance and feign interest in some Ruma. I wanted to stab myself in the neck with an ice pick, be both Sharon Stone and her victim.

She managed to flag down an auto almost immediately and off we were, with the inevitability of matter moving towards a dark hole. She pointed out spots in Bandra, her favourite this and her favourite that. I didn't bother paying attention. I was just looking at her. The way her hair fell, or blew in the breeze, the curve of her neck, the way her eyes danced when she spoke, the feeling of her touch when she slapped me for playing silly. The roads wound, the cars honked, the pedestrians hopped and skipped but all I cared about was absorbing as much of her as I could. So that I could recall all the details of being with her later, when I was alone in Delhi, and heartbroken. Then we stopped outside some ground floor unit dressed up to look like a shack.

Gazebo was as stereotypical as it got. Brick walls, low lighting, classic rock, lots of filmi and media people in sandals, ugly ill-fitting T-shirts and green pyjama-pants.

There was a booth in the corner where there was a group of people who got excited at seeing Mitali. So we walked that way. Danny came across first. He was densely bearded, my height but big, muscle and fat in equal measure. He grabbed my hand in a firm, almost too firm, handshake.

'Anando! Maacha, glad you could make it, Mitali's told me a lot about you.'

'Not all of it is true,' I said.

He grinned with his shoulders. I thought oh no, he's one of those maacha types. Fake Bombay fondness, he could've said man, or hero, or dude even, but no, he had to be East Indian West Coast Suburban familiar. I was forced to feel bonded, familial. I should have replied with something smarter, snappier, something to keep a distance without being rude, but I was upset with Mitali's plans for the night, and it served as a greeting.

A round of introductions happened where I remembered no one's names except Ruma's. I did check her out to see if she made the cut. I sat across the table from her, even though Mitali asked someone sitting next to Ruma to shift, but she was making it too obvious. I made some polite conversation with those around me. I wore an air of aloofness. Danny tried to involve me in all the conversations. He seemed easy, friendly, elder brotherly, bearish. The sort I would have ordinarily liked, if he wasn't seeing Mitali. As such, I nodded interestedly at all the details he gave me about the movie business, I just didn't get too pally.

Drinks came, appetisers appeared, the night wound on. Witticisms led to laughter, the laughter got louder, the music got louder, people began to sing the songs they knew. Ruma moved around till she was sitting next to me. She was fair, small, short like her name with large kohl rimmed eyes, would have been petite had she not been on the slightly fatter side. Nearly cute, just something was missing. I don't know if it was her face, figure or what. Just short of my type.

'So Mitali tells me you're her genius friend.'

'Did she? I didn't think she had a nice word to say about me.' I said, still bitter.

She giggled a nightclub conversation giggle. 'Why is that?'

'Well, she's always treated me like the idiot cousin.'

'Are you related?' She looked genuinely puzzled.

'No, no,' I denied, a little too quickly. Almost betrayed emotions there. 'No, we're friends…you know we've known each other a long time, so…'

I let it trail off, leaving it ambiguous on how cousin-like we had become with the passage of time.

'And you're moving here?'

'I'd like to, I have a job interview tomorrow,' I said, needing to sound more important and real-world than the filmi crowd.

'Who with?'

'I'd rather not say, if that's okay with you?'

'Cool, cool.' She shrugged her shoulders and took a long drag of her cigarette.

'I mean, it's no big deal, just, you know word, gets around,' I continued, since she obviously thought I was anal.

'You think I'm going to tell someone?' she asked.

'It's not that, I'm just uncomfortable talking about things before they happen.' Which as you know, is not true at all. If there was one thing I specialised in, it was speaking about things before they happened.

'It's okay, chill man.' That was patronising. Or had I been rude and she was just reacting?

I didn't want to come across as being an anal bore. Not to Ruma. I didn't want her to dismiss me before I made it clear that I had dismissed her. 'You know when you're interviewing with another company you just sort of stupidly worry that your bosses will get to know before anything has happened.'

'It's cool, Anando, I really don't want to know.' She gave me the eye.

Mitali looked up from what she was doing, which was playing the hostess with the filmi hangabouts. She gave me the eye, too. Not the same as Ruma, though. A more matriarchal one, which said, 'Don't bugger this up. This is as good a setup as you're likely to get.'

I tried to patch it up with Ruma. 'Let me get you a drink, what are you having?'

She seemed to thaw a little with that.

I located the waiter for our table, which took a while since Gazebo had in the meantime gotten quite packed. I placed the order for Ruma and myself and then turned to walk back to Ruma, making a mental note of smiling more. Hoping that it would make amends for being terse earlier.

Before I could make eye contact with Ruma, I saw Mitali snogging Danny. I had known about her relationships, but I had never seen her in one. So this is what it was like. It hurt. Hurt deep. Like a hammer on the inside—a sledgehammer swathed in cloth. It knocked my wind out, and damaged some internal organs only it didn't break the ribs. An internal bashing.

I met Ruma's eyes with a grimace. She must have seen that I was not happy being the Idiot Cousin at all. I don't know, I stopped caring after that. I began downing the drinks as soon as the waiter brought them. It didn't matter who the drinks were for, if they were in front of me I downed them. I chatted with everyone, and in faux friendliness took sips from all their glasses. I sang with the Rockers, I gossipped with the more gossipy and I did the eye-dance with Ruma. That's when it happened. An epiphany or lucidity or alcohol-induced clarity. Everything went quiet. I mean I could hear the music, but it didn't matter. I saw the people around me but they felt less like people. I turned my head left and right and things seemed slower and a bit out of focus. So far this is sounding like just being very drunk, there was a critical difference.

I could sense what I wanted to sense. If I wanted to hear the tinkling of the glass at the bar, I could hear just that, louder than the other noises. I could tune in to someone's conversation at the far side of the bar. I could see the earrings on a girl's ear, notice even the little stones set in an octagon, in the earring. Hell, if I tried I could see the cut of stone too. I could see the fine hair growing out of the bartender's ear. I could smell the ingredients in the kitchen, the various spirits at the bar, the different perfumes mixing with smoke, fried onions and potatoes, and breath and body odour and the chemicals of attraction, age, decay, illness and health. My senses were awakened, actually even more, I could sense the essence of each individual present.

I turned my new hyper-vision eyes to look at Danny. Oh, he'd never break into Bollywood, even this movie would get into trouble, with star-dates and releases. I looked at Danny's friends from the movie business. I saw their small petty lives. Their homes in modern chawls and shared one-bedroom houses. They lived on the money they earned at photo-shoots and edit rooms. I felt their futures too, nothing exceptional. I was nudged by the waiter, and I felt his family back in the boondocks of Jaunpur. An ageing mom, a young bride, younger brothers, one of who wanted to sleep with or had slept with his wife. I looked at the bartender. I sensed his family living not far away from this place. A daughter he wanted to educate, a son he hadn't wanted in the first place. I sensed his wife doing two jobs a day, trying so hard to move up the class structure. I looked at Ruma, of the doe eyes and nearly cute petite frame, and I felt a boyfriend in the near future, someone she didn't care for much, but needed for social credibility. I sensed a promotion at work and her vying for a job with someone else.

The world was calm, quiet, what peaked were people's individual energies. The one or two things that were unique to them. While I had probably sensed the effects of this very phenomenon, all these years, this was the first time it was so manifestly clear. Everyone was energy. Since you can't help but receive energy, you feel their energy. If your mind and your internal sensing organ are up to it, that energy can be read, felt, transformed through cards and charts and other devices. It's essentially energy resonating with energy. All the so-called psychic gifts are just variations of the same resonance. Mutations that the resonance undergoes when being interpreted. Like a ripple and water, like time and a clock, like a piece of iron that slowly gets magnetised, like light and silver nitride, like hydrogen and helium. Like all of these and yet with meaning, with life, with a plan, a path.

I started seeing with more than just my eyes. I saw how the energy shaped their beings, their bodies. I saw how a girl in the filmi group who'd started working very early in life, had turned more masculine, in the placement of her eyes. They were closer-set than most women, smaller and predatorial. I saw how insecurity spoke in just the tiniest misalignment of the shoulders. So that's why they called it a chip on the shoulder. I saw how differences with the parents over the choice of one's girlfriend showed in a stiffness that ran from the chest through to the arms. I saw how ambition made the brow curl, I saw how horniness dilated the eyes, how envy was a vacuum that sucked from the heart, how happiness lifted the spine, how love clothed one in an aura. I could see the swirling balls of energy that we call humans. This emotional, flickering wave-form that each person was. Some blueish, some orange, some shone with a white radiance—an intellectual brilliance, some with healing greenish light, Mitali of course was golden. Radiant with an inner light. The only one in this gang with something of a future. The rest, despite their celluloid dreams, were just going to have to go through the motions of living.

I smiled my biggest smile at Mitali. She smiled back. It nearly blinded me, the light of her iridescent aura. I swayed up to her, 'Listen Mitali, the most amazing thing is happening to me, and you know I've never really told you about your future, so if there's anything you want to ask, ask now.' That's what I thought I said, I might have slurred it a bit or not said these exact words

She said, 'Listen, I promised Ruma that you were a great guy, so if you don't start giving her some attention soon, you're not crashing at my place.'

I couldn't believe it. She had a chance to know what lay in store for her, her future, who she would finally hook up with, what life held for her, and she wanted me to flirt with someone who just really wanted her boss's attention and the next promotion. Fine.

I turned to Ruma and flirted. I can't really remember details, but I remember holding her hands, and telling her how good she smelt, the obvious stuff I'd seen the rake or the charmer pull off in films. She played along, I think. No one else was vying for her attention, either through Mitali's expressed wishes, or from lack of interest. The music had gotten loud enough for people not to care what anyone two feet away was saying anyway. I had Ruma's ears to myself. I had to lean right into them for her to hear me, that was all right, since I was slouching and feeling loose-limbed thanks to the alcohol.

I didn't usually drink that much, I believed it came in the way of the powers and keeping the body clean as a temple. Considering the revelation that night, alcohol was a newfound elixir. A cleansing solvent if you like, for all the grime that my temple had collected over the years.

I can't remember what happened next, but I was not on Mitali's futon, it was seven-thirty in the morning and I had a pretty massive headache. I made a mental note that this must be what a hangover felt like. It wasn't fun. Hangovers were romanced in films, quite a bit. Dark glasses were always within arm's reach, everyone gave you sympathy and alka seltzers. This was the nasty bastard brother of clairvoyance. Things were loud and bright. Just normal things, not hidden essences and stuff.

Loudest and brightest among those was the naked

form of someone lying next to me. Size indicated that it could only be Ruma.

This was crap. Crap, crap, crap. I was naked too and I found a used condom on the floor. Oh heavens, so we'd done it. What an unmemorable first time. I absolutely couldn't remember anything. Had Ruma slipped in a date rape drug? I'd come for Mitali and ended up with the Beta version. Things couldn't be worse, and how was I ever going to make it to the interview? My bag was at Mitali's and I was at Godknowswhere.

I tried to get up, found I couldn't and sat back down with a thud. We were on a mattress on the floor and the hangover wasn't helping standing up. I looked around for my clothes. They were in a heap in a corner. Then I noticed my backpack under them. A memory flashed from the night before, of Mitali laughing at an open door and handing me my bag, as I tried to embrace her.

So we'd been smart enough to get my bag, but obviously not smart enough to avoid a hangover before a really important interview. I got up, picked up my underwear, got my toothbrush out of my bag and opened a white plasticky door which seemed to be the most likely candidate to lead to a loo.

I sat on the pot with my head in my hands and despised myself some more. Once I had sufficiently regretted the night, and hated myself enough, I tried my hardest to crap. The whole bathroom smelt of partially digested alcohol, it was making me sicker. I washed up and flushed. I had about half an hour to get myself fixed. Bad night or not, I had to make the move to Bombay.

I stood at the sink and looked at the mirror. My face—

puffy, red-eyed, bloated with immorality and Gazebo's vilest mixes. The unmistakable smell of booze, reeking out of every pore. I wouldn't hire me. Besides I'd done the dirty dance with Ruma, my first dirty dance. Why oh why? I threw up. Then I retched till there was little left to vomit aside of my intestines. I brushed, went out to get the towel from my backpack and get showered.

Ruma had woken with the sound of retching and didn't look too happy.

'Everything okay?'

'Getting better.'

Both of us looked at the condom lying on the floor.

'Listen about last night…' I started.

'Don't worry about it, we were both drunk,' she said rather professionally.

'Right,' I hung my head. 'If you don't mind, can I shower? I have an interview to get to.'

'Sure,' she said. 'The geyser is an instant one if you need hot water…you'll find shampoo on the rack.'

She was much cooler by day.

'Listen…' I said, not quite at peace, 'I don't remember much after telling you your future. We did it, huh?'

She looked at me, now in my VIP Frenchies, at the crumpled bedsheet, and said, 'We'll talk after your interview.'

There was no getting an answer, so I showered, got dressed, gave Ruma, who had something of a top and pyjamas on, but no bra, a tentative hug and dashed out of her place. She did make some sounds about breakfast, but I was too embarrassed to stay on any longer. Besides I was late.

I hailed down a cab and asked him to get me to Lower Parel in double quick time.

In the cab, I checked for drunken messages. There were none, who would I message? Mitali was with me the whole time, well nearly the whole time. Then I remembered I didn't ask for Ruma's number. It wasn't very civil to not take her number after leaving a condom on her bedroom floor, but heck, I didn't feel gallant. I felt sick. I needed something to kill the bitter-sour taste. I needed something to kill the drunken Anando. I needed someone to kill the last twelve hours. How, how, how could I have done it with Ruma?

The interview was actually interviews. The first was a non-event. The HR lady made some remark about my red eyes. I told her it was from the early morning flight. The words popped out before I could consider whether she would look at my ticket, when I submitted it. I met the Vice-President of Laundry, a skinny, balding man, who I took an immediate distaste to and couldn't see myself working with.

I answered the silly questions, spoke of all the marketing promotions I'd run to sell more potato chips. The crap I'd learnt from Testizos, the nacho brand in the US, and Eqi, the wheat crackers in Australia. I went through the motions. I didn't offer them any sparkling personality or wit or anything other than prosaic answers to their dull questions.

My thoughts drifted towards Mitali and the night before. I remembered her kissing Danny. Was it actually just proximity for her? Would there ever be anything between us, if I did get this job? I mean Danny was a nice guy, but not remarkable. I was a corporate man not a filmmaker or from that ilk, but surely she'd come around. I didn't need to depend on the scraps thrown by the producer-director machinery to make my living. I had a regular salary. With any luck Indians would eat more unhealthily and I would do better.

VP Laundry made some dry concluding remarks and we shook hands. I wasn't going to get it. Waves of hangover nausea notwithstanding, the higher senses were still alive. Though a third party observer wouldn't need higher senses to see that I wasn't going to get the job. My ex-boss would be disappointed that I'd botched it up. Before turning to go, I enquired after him, to no real excitement from VP Laundry. So a recommendation from my ex-boss wouldn't help either.

I walked out of UCLI desperate for some fresh air. I took a deep breath in of oxygen, hydrogen sulphide and sulphur dioxide. It cleared my head, so I called Mitali. She sounded groggy, it wasn't even eleven yet, and it had been a long night.

'Andy,' she slurred, 'did you have fun?'

'At the interview….'

'…No.'

'…No I don't think I'll get it.'

'…I meant with…oh shoot, I forgot about the interview, how did it go?' Sounds of waking from her end.

'Not great!' I said.

'Not, huh?' There was a pause as I imagined her extricating her limbs from Danny's. 'Let me call you, in a bit. When you flying out?' she asked, concerned. I hoped.

'Well, the flight's in the evening, I took the day off from work,' I said, implying she ought to make some time.

'Okay, why don't you come this way and we can do lunch together.'

'Don't you have work?' Diffident ole me.

'I called in sick,' she said.

'Fine, I'll come Bandra side then.' There was going to be some upside to this trip after all.

'Right,' she said, now sounding more awake.

I was about to click off when I heard her say, 'By the way, what were you on about last night?'

Oh-oh, her senses were coming alive.

'I can't remember,' I lied. I remembered enough to know that I had said a lot of shit.

'That's convenient. Do you remember that you had a long chat with Danny?' she asked.

'No.' I didn't.

'You went on and on about how filthy the film industry was.'

'It is.'

'And that he should keep me away from it.'

A memory flash: Me leaning on Danny.

'He should.'

So far nothing to regret. Mits on the other hand was getting worked up. I wasn't the only one with memory flashes. 'You also asked me why I had a new boyfriend every six months,' she said, pitch rising.

'It's not every six months, is it?'

'You asked me if I needed a man that bad.' Now there was some other emotion in her voice. Is venomous an emotion?

'Did I?'

'Yes.'

'Right.'

'Frankly, it's none of your business, but I don't need a man. I love Danny.'

I could sense that she was moving around, probably out of Danny's earshot.

'Right. Of course,' I said.

'And no, I don't date the first available guy.'

'Did I say that?'

'Something like that.'

'I can't see myself saying that, I don't think that,' I countered.

'You mean, the rest of what you said, you think.'

'Er…what did I say?'

It's so irritating to have a drunken whitewash. People can misquote you and make things up, and character assassinate and you have no choice but to agree.

'You told me it wasn't going to work out with me and Danny.'

'Was I telling futures or just offering my opinion?'

'How the heck am I supposed to know?' she screamed.

'Well, it makes a difference. One is…'

'You know what, I'm suddenly not feeling like lunch. Bye.' Click.

She hung up. I thought of calling back and apologising, but I didn't remember the details. All the silly things I could have, must have said. It could get worse.

I had five hours to kill, and not one person to kill them with in Bombay. I had also begun to remember bigger chunks of the night. One particular bit about leaning in to kiss Mitali and ending up in her hair, as she turned to kiss Danny. What a loser! It was after that I think, that I began showering all my attention on lil' Ruma.

What exactly I did with Ruma, I couldn't quite remember. There were no edifying memory flashes. It struck me that I should try to contact her. She hadn't been entirely unfriendly or unhappy. Maybe I should land up at her place and see if she'd called in sick as well. No, that would be way too shady. I looked at my phone and the ninth number dialled, read Ruma. So I had saved her number. This then was a sign. I called her, she was at work, but was up for lunch. We met. She told me some more embarrassing bits from the night before and asked me how the interview went. She was cordial, friendly even. I liked her better in the daytime. Much more. After Mitali's flare-out she seemed so much saner.

'People get drunk, and do silly things, it's okay,' she pronounced and then proceeded to take a long hangover-thirst driven sip of her iced tea.

Truer words weren't spoken. Nor more embarrassed sips taken. Though I couldn't tell what she meant by silly things—the stupid things I'd said, or the sex we had had.

'If you get the job, where will you stay?' she asked to break the embarrassing silence.

'I don't think I'm getting the job,' I said, no point getting anyone's hopes up.

'Ahh, don't be so negative, you were so fun and positive last night,' she smiled as she said that. I couldn't tell if she was kidding.

'Was I? That's not like me at all.'

A giggle, 'Well you told me that you loved me.'

Oh well done.

She continued, when I didn't say anything, 'I think you said that only to do it with me, I thought it was cute.'

She laughed, I blushed or whatever it is that brown-skinned men do with their cheeks when they're really embarrassed.

'Drunken cunning,' I offered.

She giggled some more. The rest of lunch was peaceful. I couldn't remember telling her I loved her. Maybe I thought she was Mitali. How drunk was I?

When we were leaving Ruma said, 'So you'll call me, when you're in Bombay next?'

'Yeah, sure,' I said. I mean you have to have some sense of loyalty with your first girl, right? She gave me a peck on the cheek, perilously close to the lips and bounced away. She seemed happy. Who was I to break her bubble? Confucius I'm sure would agree with me today. 'Want the girl you have, if not have the girl you want' or words to that effect.

The HR lady called just as I had finished paying the bill.

'Hi Anando, we really liked you but at the moment we can't see you fit in this team with your experience. If there's an opening in another team I'll let you know.' Was it the act of giving bad news, or did her voice sound more electronic on the phone?

Playing the role of the rejected applicant, I gave her my stiff thanks and enquired about the submission of the ticket, reimbursement etc. She gave me the details and that was that. So no Mitali and Bombay in the near future. Or Ruma, for that matter. It was going to be more sexless selling of chips. The only positive from this trip was the feeling of omniscience before the drunkenness took over. I made a mental note to tap into that. There was something waking inside me, and it needed help waking right, alcohol couldn't be the only way. Oh yes, I'd lost my virginity as well.

Why this long recollection of a sad evening and a failed interview? Well, sex, your first time is important, even for people like me but more importantly, you needed to know about the feeling. That calm, that all-knowingness or all-feelingness. The feeling of tapping into the universal code. That deemed remembering. So it came with Mitali cravings and other things, so what? It's important for you to know that I had it. That it was very real and that it felt like the unlocking of something that had long lain dormant.

I did travel to Bombay in the following months, and though Mitali and I had gotten over our little hangover tiff, we seldom met. There were enough sales conferences, shoots for advertising films or products to bring me to the city every odd month, except Mitali was always busy with something.

Her job at the magazine had gotten more demanding. There were more environmental issues to chase. She was getting more involved in the life of Danny and his filmy friends. She once told me she had this script idea, that she had bounced off the first assistant director of Kunal Hassan. The AD was impressed even though it wasn't mainstream. Maybe she would get around to writing it, when she was done researching ground water depletion.

I was of course, cautious discussing work with Mitali. I didn't want her magazine to examine our company too closely. Not that we were doing something wrong. Just that in India, everyone is doing something somewhat irregular somewhere. The MNCs get screwed by the local government and press for something tiny, of which local players are guilty tenfold. So I never revealed to her about the farmer's strike, or the various lengths we had to go to, to get water for the few potato fields we owned. Even though I was stressed as hell about all these things.

It helped that Mitali wasn't concerned about my work anyway. She dismissed it as something unimportant and menial. Ruma on the other hand, belonging to much the same world, she did PR and dealt quite often with the ugly side of things, sympathised a lot with all my stresses. She was also available to meet a lot more often when I visited Bombay. Things moved in ways I hadn't quite foreseen. Which was odd for me. I found that I was in a relationship with Ruma, by virtue of sleeping with her and her being willing to meet every time I visited Bombay. Or was it the other way around? Sometime into this new equation, Ruma told me that she was applying for a job at the agency that handled my company's business and asked whether I would recommend her to the boss there.

I said, 'Sure, that means you want to relocate to Delhi.'

She said 'Yeaah, duh,' as though it was the most obvious thing in the world. It wasn't to me.

'You're doing this…to be…with me?'

'Andy, for a smart guy you're mighty stupid sometimes.' She started tidying her room. While admittedly her room needed tidying, I thought she was doing it to avoid eye contact.

'But I'm thinking of moving here.'

'Are you applying to anyone currently…'

'No…'

'…then someone's got to make a decision right?' she said.

'What's the problem with how things are?' I asked. She was an independent girl in Bombay. What shared complexities did she want in Delhi?

'What's the problem? Are you trying to be difficult?' Her voice began to rise. She was also no longer shy of making eye contact.

I could tell futures by looking at tea leaves, runes, I-Ching, tarot, astrology and god knows how many other methods, sometimes by no methods at all, but I could not have predicted the scale of her tantrum.

'I have a boyfriend I see once in two months at best.'

That was the first time she'd referred to me as her boyfriend.

She continued, 'I have sex once in four months if he has been considerate enough to spend the night and not fly back the same day.' Her voice dropped when she said 'sex' then it got loud again. She threw T-shirts, pyjamas, soiled cushion covers and other things in one corner, while I shifted my weight from one foot to the other.

'I have to continuously explain to people why my boyfriend is not with me and how I'm making it work long-distance. I have to go to bed alone and be lonely and miserable…and you ask me what's the problem?'

'I thought you were fine with this?' I asked calmly. It worked for me. I actually enjoyed the sailor coming in to port thing.

'I'm not.'

'You want to come to Delhi, fine. What's to get angry? We've just never spoken about these things,' I said, pacifyingly. It didn't work.

'What's to get angry?' she started screaming. 'You treat me like some booty call, who has to be there for you and God forbid if I'm busy, then you'll sulk like a schoolboy and act all hurt. I have to hear how shitty your job is every time, but you can't be there for me, even once. You never even once offered to help me with job openings, even though you well knew that I was applying. I had to come out and ask you.'

'Ruma, listen. Don't get upset. I really didn't think...'

'...Yes you didn't. You never think,' she said crying. Instead of throwing the next pile of dirty clothes into the corner, she crumpled them and held them to her chest. Rocking with hurt and sobbing loudly every few seconds, falling onto her side and curling up. I stood around not knowing what to do. I was reluctant to put my arm around her. I was uncomfortable being her 'boyfriend'. Heck I'd only met her all those times, because Mitali had no time for me. Sex was a plus, though on many, many of those occasions, I had to think of Mitali and sundry other women, to get myself going.

I observed her, hurting as I knew I had myself, but without any real empathy. Eventually acting out of civility and a sense of duty, I put my arm around her, but I knew I would have to break this off soon. I couldn't get into an official thing with Ruma. Mitali out of loyalty towards Ruma, wouldn't hug me tight, ever again.

I decided. I had to get Ruma the job in Delhi, and

make the shift to Bombay. There was simply no other way. I couldn't introduce Ruma to the Delhi gang as my girlfriend. That was just not on. She would have cornered me into accepting this relationship. I was no expert on women, but this much I knew of their wiles. I was a good catch. Earning well, in a good job, would only get better. Good family, decent school-college credentials. Ruma was getting older every day. If she was good to wait for me for two months between meetings, she was obviously not getting much attention. I was a boyfriend that she needed for her self-respect.

Then I had a flash from the night of Danny's film-music party. What was it that I had seen in Ruma's near future? A boyfriend she didn't care for much but needed for society. That would be me. I didn't want to be this trapped boyfriend. It was tough enough to hold one end of a conversation with her for more than an hour, without suggesting sex, how was I going to deal with her fulltime? No, no, no. I was in love with Mitali. This had just happened. My psychic abilities be damned, I hadn't been able to see where this was heading. Now I had to get out of it. I consoled Ruma as best I could. Which is not to say we had sex. I wanted to, she looked quite attractive with her mascara streaky, but it would have been improper.

When I got back to work, one of the first things I did was to call the head of our business at the PR company and gushed very eloquently about this friend of mine who was very capable, sassy and full of Bombay pizzazz, who would be just right as Group Account Director at Huntington & Associates. The next thing I did was to call the headhunter who had been badgering me four months back, about openings in Bombay.

Come February 2004, Ruma was in Delhi, well NCR to be precise. She got a flat in Gurgaon, a red Hyundai Santro to get to work in and winter clothing. Like any Bombayite moving to Delhi, she wore more woollens than an Antarctic expedition team, and boy, was she thrilled about it! I did my duty, accompanying her to the malls that had sprung up in Gurgaon, but I was getting desperate to end whatever it was that we had.

The sex, even in her more modern apartment in Gurgaon and with the Delhi end-of-winter chill had gotten monotonous. Monopositionus, monoprocessonous. We would meet post-work, grab a drink, a bite, head to her place. I'd remove her top in her living room, drop my pants near her bedroom door and we'd get rid of the remaining clothes in a heap by the chair in her bedroom. Then I would start with my mouth at her breasts, kiss my way to her navel, come back up again, penetrate, thrust, come, wash up, dress, head home. She must have had a similar version in her head. I don't want you to think I was cold-blooded about it. I'm sure she wanted 'our thing' over as much as I.

I was so bored and so trapped I started mumbling a mantra to myself on the drive to work. I had learnt from my mantra with Prannoy Uncle, that it's important to construct it right. You must feel for the balance of words. It should have a meter. The rest is a matter of repetition, intent, the clicking of gears in the cosmic clocks and whether your incantation syncs with one of the clicks.

'Letitbe overwith Rumaanme.'

You see how it works, if I pronounced the 'd' in the 'and', the mantra would lose its meter and balance and so cease to be effective. Also you must ask, not command. It's more humble. Now worrywarts will tell you that it's too open-ended, that this sort of mantra could cause any kind of ending between Ruma and me. Or what's worse that it could cause all kinds of endings, that Ruma and I would share nothing in common. If one or both of us were to disintegrate, that would be tough luck. So unintended results do often accompany mantras and you have to be careful.

Intent however, plays a big role. You have to intend it to happen without any ill-will. That way the destinies can't twist ill-will your way. I bore Ruma no malice, I simply didn't want to be in a relationship with her anymore, I would be happy for her to find someone else. Very happy and relieved.

So every day that I remembered, I would repeat this on the drive to work, that is if there were no crisis calls from work. Or back from her place, unless she wanted to talk.

The first syncing click came when our company sacked Huntington & Associates from our business. They had done a terrible job of handling the press reports that we had bullied the farmers into planting genetically modified potatoes and were now controlling the prices, keeping them away from more profitable crops and/or free market pricing. All in the course of what happens in India, except that farmers in various parts of the country were dying. This got us into a terrible spot and we had to spend crores of rupees on a 'Farmer ka bhai' campaign. Ruma was upset that I hadn't given her a heads-up, since she had agreed to take on the account just two weeks before the sacking, and this would now reflect on her record even though she had nothing to do with the management of the so called 'aloogiri' incident.

The second click happened on her birthday.

I had a red-eye flight to catch early the next day, so I dropped in early to her place, gave her the customary bottle of perfume, and left as soon as I was sure she had enough friends for company. The PR crowd loved their alcohol and their antakshari, and had I stayed on, I'd have been singing myself drunk to catch the flight, and would have botched up a major presentation. After Danny's do, I wasn't up for a repeat.

She called me just as I was leaving for the airport. She was very high and somewhat weepy. I feigned sympathy, as I was feeling a little guilty about not staying on for her party. Then she let out the magic words. 'There's something I have to say.'

Now any man in a relationship knows that's a relationship thing that you will have to react to. Either she's going to let you know that she loves you and that it's your responsibility to take it to the next level or that something or someone else more important has come up.

'I was low after you left.'

'I'm sorry, I had to go. I'd told you before.'

'I know, but I was feeling bad that you weren't there when the cake was cut...I'm sorry...'

'No, I'm sorry,' I said, my voice unnaturally stoic.

'What you saying?' she said.

'Nothing, you tell me,' I said, she after all had the 'something' to say.

'I had so much to drink and Keshav was flirting with me all night.' Keshav was a colleague of hers. 'He stayed on when the others left and we kissed,' she finished.

I remained quiet. I was weighing possibilities. After a few seconds of silence she spoke.

'Say something…I feel terrible,' her voice was cracked, oddly cute.

I was ready to forgive her, I really was. I mean I was actually feeling bad for her, for the routine pleasureless sex that I offered her, for being absent for the best part of her birthday party, for not informing her of the sacking of her agency in advance.

'What?' she asked, the static adding to the dangling question.

'Ruma…' I said, enunciating more than necessary perhaps because she was being so inarticulate and raspy, '…you can kiss whoever you want, it's your birthday, it's up to you.'

'Don't say that,' she said sobbing, 'I was missing you.'

'It's all right, you kissed him, no big deal.' I was cold.

'So is it okay, withyouanme?'

If she hadn't said those words, I would have most likely let it pass. But then the mantra clicked in my head. The missed 'd' and the meter were eerily the same. I saw the chance that the destinies were giving me and took it. 'No Ruma, I think it's over. You're attracted to other men, despite what you say about missing me.' I laid down the cards. I'd called her hand.

'No, I really was missing you, it shouldn't have happened, it wouldn't have if you'd been here.'

'I think not. You keep talking about Keshav. You obviously meant this to happen, how could you not?' I said, cold-blooded.

'I was stupid, I was sulky.'

'You knew very well what you were getting into when you let him stay on after the others left.'

It went on like this, her apologising and taking the blame, and me pressing my case, cold-bloodedly, getting more convinced with my argument. The argument went back and forth like two tongues in a drunken kiss. Then I was at Palam at 1B, and had to go check in, security etc. I told her I would call her later and I didn't. She called me later, timing her call to coincide with my taxi ride from Bombay airport. I continued with my line of argument. Finally she accused me of being cold and calculating and wanting this to end. I accepted that, using the gruff voice of the righteously indignant. By the end of that night, we were over.

Itwasover, between Rumaanme. Magic!

I gave thanks to the gods of the mantras, they obviously outranked the Destinies.

Before any reconciliation with Ruma was possible, through a revolt of the Destinies, weakness on her part or mine, I got a call for a job interview, for a job in Bombay. This time, I was spurred by twin desires, to be near Mitali, and to put a safe enough distance between Ruma and me.

I hope you're not feeling sorry for Ruma. She kissed Keshav, not me. Besides, it was for the best. The Destinies don't take it out on the recipient of a mantra. The recipient only gets what is intended; it's the chanter-invoker who has to pay the price. She's happily married, though not to Keshav, and is pregnant. I think she already takes a lot of pride in wanting to be the working mother and soon-to-be soccer mom. Or theatre mom, I dunno what propensity her child will have. I could try and figure, only now is not the time.

Me on the other hand…Well we'll get there won't we? It'll be soon, don't despair. I don't have any other relationships to look back at fondly. Mitali not included. And Mitali is more a leitmotif than a relationship.

June 30th was my last day as Brand Manager Glow Crisps. From July 15th I was Brand Director of Fulscreme Body. I moved from selling potato chips in five flavours, to selling body care in soaps, moisturisers, and gels. While it was still a single brand, because of the variety of formats, it felt more like a portfolio. I'm just throwing this in, in case you're evaluating my decision with a marketing director's eye. I just took the job to be in Bombay, within shoulder-offering distance of Mitali when her break-up happened.

Eleven

Two days before I left Delhi, Thamma summoned me to her room. This was a lot like the summoning that happened many years ago. While my perspective of her room had changed with age and height, in her presence, I still felt like a little boy. It was Saturday evening and I remember that it was raining, but she hadn't switched the light on. The windows were open, letting in a grey-green refracted light. A cool breeze probably from the deer park next door, brought in the smell of wet mud, and what I imagine must be chlorophyll. A green and leafy smell, to go with the green leafy light. It was the light and smell of a lecture. A forest-tale full of caution and wrong turns and mishaps with a strong moral kicker. I was worried she would ask me to do something I wouldn't be able to without arguing, or worse still an admonition to get married. Or a contract to do or not do something yet undone by the Sens. None of which I could honour. A summoning with grandma Sen meant a life-decision, yours. Which Thamma had already made and you were going to be informed about.

She was sitting at the edge of her bed, her back to me,

looking wistfully out of the window. No doubt smelling the leafy greens of Sylhet or wherever the Baidyas harked from, before they travelled west and eventually became the Sens of Green Park. She heard me drag my feet and turned, her face changed quickly into the stern authoritarian that she was.

'Anando, sit.' She had used my name and not the more familiar Aanu. This was definitely a serious one.

I sat dutifully across her on the bed, glad to note that my legs no longer dangled. If Thamma said something strange, or foundation changing, I had firm ground to plant my feet on.

She crossed her legs, sat more upright and raised her right hand with the index finger up, adopting no doubt the pose of the preacher. 'You're leaving the house for the first time,' she started.

Yes, my friends had made fun about this. 'Yes,' I said dutifully.

'You must return the way you're going,' she continued.

It was one of those ambiguous sentences full of import, meant to invoke a sense of duty, but it was near impossible, and I told her so.

'You know what I mean,' she said, the sternness unabated, although the index finger did retract.

I was trying to guess. Did she mean not become an addict, or not marry a Muslim, like Kaku had? Well there was little chance of that unless Mitali converted to Islam. I promised her, 'I won't turn to intoxicants, Thamma, and I won't keep bad company.' I had trouble enough finding any company. She was not convinced.

'Whoever has left my home, has seldom come back,' she said gravely.

'Those were different times, Thamma, this is just a job, Bodo Kaku went to fight a war and Chhoto Kaku came back, you just didn't want to accept his wife.' I didn't speak about Dadu. That was a bit tricky to bring up with Thamma in a sermonising mood.

'Let's not talk about your uncles, shall we? It makes me upset and angry.'

I couldn't see a way out. Weren't we discussing family history? 'Okay, I will come back the way I'm going,' I gave in.

'You must promise me not to get involved with any girl who your parents don't approve of.'

I was surprised she was ready to trust the judgement of my parents. Would my parents approve of Mitali, would they have approved of Ruma? Mitali would make the cut. She was known to the family and aced all parameters. She was Bengali, Brahmin and beautiful. Of course if Ma and Baba got to know about her rather long list of boyfriends they may not approve. What about Thamma's approval? Why had she so humbly kept herself out of it?

'Okay,' I said. More to get out of this silly conversation than with any sense of grandchildly devotion or loyalty to the family name.

Then she handed me a pair of cuff-links. 'This is for you, you're going to a big job. You need to dress with a sense of status,' she said, holding them against my wrists. They were silver. One of them had an ornamental A inset in some blue semi-precious stone, the other an equally curly S. They must have been my grandfather's. We never really spoke much about him at home, especially not around Thamma, but I had seen his pictures and he was quite a dandy.

I was quite moved by this unexpected gift and a little guilty for having misjudged Thamma's intentions. I had come in expecting a sermon and little else, this on the other hand was a huge sentimental gift and clearly the reason for calling me in. All that 'come back as you're going' business was just her way of breaking the ice, or perhaps she was creating a sense of occasion.

The cuff-links looked, well, semi-aristocratic. She must have had them polished or something since they were at least fifty years old. So she had been planning for this day. I felt bad that I hadn't planned for a proper goodbye with her, that I hadn't even thought of getting her anything. That since starting work I had hardly given her enough attention, while she had gone to such lengths to give me something meaningful before I left.

I thanked her, and did a pronam. The Sens don't really hug. No tears in front of her, I said to myself, she found them weak. There were no tears in her eyes when I got up, a slightly softer matriarchal set of face, perhaps. The cuff-links however, were proof that this was a mask.

'I'll take care of them, Thamma,' I promised, ready to hug her, if she had given any hint that she would be fine with such a show of affection.

'They're yours to do as you please. Remember to use them.'

I would if I could get a shirt that had no buttons on the sleeve. How convenient the naming system of the Sens had turned out to be. It made heirlooms inheritable and yet personalised.

I couldn't think of any parting words, that would capture how moved I was. I left her room with the determination that I would sell more Fulscreme lotion than any brand director previously and woo Mitali at the same time. The first part, technically, I didn't see posing much of a challenge since the brand was growing, it was the second part that would be tricky. Still I had Ardhendu Sen's cuff-links, Dannys of the world beware.

I left on Monday, my parents came downstairs to the gate and looked sad, Didi called to say bye and cried, Thamma didn't leave her room. She had said her goodbye. Teary farewells weren't her thing.

I don't feel like going on. Pain, anger, disappointment and acidity are mixing and swirling, decomposing my innards. I need to cool down. I'll just surf the net, check my mail, whatever. Drink some water. Eat a biscuit perhaps, nothing too heavy. Breathe. Count to three. Hold to a count of twelve. Exhale. Consider something randomly conceptual.

Let's start with God. That's good.

Let's save you that soul-searching backpacking trip across India. The slumming around in Rishikesh and Benaras. The search for a guru. The ganja drags, the chanting, the kirtans, the satsangs. The visits to the bookstores in Auroville, the Ramakrishna Mission, the Sivananda Foundation. Let me save you the trouble of clearing Spirituality 101.

God all-powerful, the one and only, that guy: At the ultimate level he's the only thing there is. I use 'he' only for convenience. You have to be really small-minded to get gender questions into this.

Then there's God at a slightly lower level. Who is both the collective consciousness as well as the quality that pervades through all of us. This God still doesn't care much. At still lower levels God manifests himself as the higher powers, the arch angels, the Holy Trinity or the devtas and their consorts. Different names for different faiths. These guys may care for you, who knows—heck, they keep coming down as avatars or prophets so they must have some insidious interest. But they are also simultaneously Gods in their own right, burdened by the demands of continued creation. So you and your small prayers are an insignificant part of their daily worries. Or whatever unit of time they use.

Think of them as the chief officers of a really large company and yourself as the trainee mail-room clerk or an envelope in the mail or the stamp on the envelope, or the dust mote, the smallest thing you can imagine. God almighty is the entire Company.

All the work you do, living your life, loving, hurting, dying or just spinning in Brownian motion, the CEOs doing their own shit, it all goes into helping God experience Godness. So whether the CEOs tank the company or you spin to a higher state of entropy, the Company, i.e. God, experiences himself. It doesn't really matter who does what, all experience is godly, for God. By virtue of the most cosmic circular argument ever. God is ultimately selfish.

Don't bother with spirituality, do what God would do. Go to the Bahamas.

Okay, I'm calmer now.

It was raining when I landed in Bombay. Chhatrapati Shivaji airport. As if anything in this city was not CS. Well actually the Bombayites could say the same about Delhi, what was not IG or RG? How fabulous that our parochial biases and petty regional politics made it difficult to pick other historical figures, despite five thousand years of unbroken civilization. I had to hop, skip and jump from the stairs to the bus that refused to park closer to the aircraft, to avoid getting totally soaked, before I made it to the CS airport arrival lounge. The suitcases took their time coming and were wet too. This wasn't the auspicious welcome I had been hoping for. This was not the mental image one has of new beginnings, unless one sees the rains as some sort of cleansing agent, a bath provided by the gods. However, it was a little difficult to conjure a feeling of that kind of significance seeing one's shirt run colour.

I had a room booked in the corporate guesthouse so I wouldn't have to depend on Mitali's whims. I gave the cabbie the address in Andheri and we were off. Mitali knew I was coming, so I would wait for her to call. Now that I was in this city, it wouldn't do to appear desperate.

She didn't call that night or the next day.

I began work, searching for a pad, living off the comforts of the RG Group guesthouse, which admittedly had a great cook and caretaker, and managing Fulscreme.

The last part was painful. From day one. Not just because it was a new job, a new employer and body lotions not potato chips, the scale of difference was irritating in many different ways. For starters, you had to learn a new set of three-letter acronyms for everything: GDP, no, not

Gross Domestic Product, but Global Development Partners, BIM, Brand in Motion, which was the cool name for the brands which were being Indianised. And the best of all, FVI, pronounced 'Effvie' by old hands. Which stood for Flaunt Value Index. Or how much a customer wants to be seen with your product. You couldn't speak a sentence without using a three-letter acronym, hitherto, if required again, referred to as a TLA. Like mantras but corporatised.

Try it. Don't say 'You're looking good today, wanna do dinner.' Instead say, 'Your Effvie's dialed up today, CDM (Closed Door Meeting) EOD?' See what I mean? The meter's right, it just feels like an evil mutant clone—the shlokas of the modern world. The Vedic Brahmins who composed the sutras, the mahavakyas, would have rather lost a son than add a letter. Their modern-day counterparts, would rather lose a friend, colleague, why, a whole audience, than utter the full forms of TLAs.

Then there were a slew of new processes to learn. GATES, ISIS, RECORD and others. I won't bore you with what they were. Suffice it to say that they knocked the joy out of any marketing promotion or activity. Actually, it was just how dry the job felt in comparison to the more intuitive job of selling food products, that made it suck. The joke about the guys in my vertical (skincare) was that they were all double MBAs, because you couldn't get so screwed in your head with just one. They all simply loved their processes and their little corporate language. In India's new class system, skincare marketers were the new Brahmins, TLAs their most refined Sanskrit.

If only processes weren't such an enemy of intuition.

My essence alas, was defined by intuition. One didn't have to be a psychic to see that I wouldn't last very long with the RG Group. But here I was in Bombay, near Mitali and earning nearly twice as much. I would have to make it work. I would have to bring the rain clouds of Intuition into the Anal Thinking Desert of Body Lotion Marketing.

As far as the search for the *GQ* bachelor pad of the year went—after much searching in Bandra and Khar (single men were an issue, as was religion and eating preferences) I found a flat that I liked in Vakola. Yes, it was the eastern side and hence uncool for hip Bandra yuppies, but it was a decent flat. It was close enough to Mitali's, yet not so close as to appear desperate. It was also a short hike to work and yet not so close that you could be commanded to come in for any crisis, real or imagined.

Life began in Bombay. I bought things for the flat. It was liberating to have your own things instead of things bought or chosen by your parents, or in my case grandparents. If it wasn't for the sobering thought of 793 square feet of carpet area, I would have bought out whole shops. Mitali came once to help me, Danny was the more cooperative one. Telling me about places to get things, even loaning me his car to cart things around. Finally, tiring of his generosity and how difficult that made it for me to steal his girlfriend, I bought a Maruti Zen. I blended in with the double MBAs of RG. I tried my best to make Fulscreme the number one moisturiser in India.

My desk at work was on the way to the little niche that housed the water-cooler and coffee machine on our floor. As a result people would find it necessary to say something silly to me every time they needed a drink. It was short and inane to begin with, but as word got around that I read fortunes and other things, the hangers about and the time they spent with me increased. From saying 'I'm feeling thirsty but Fulscreme's making you dehydrated,' to 'Dude, I had no idea, tell me about my marriage. Wait, let me get you a coffee.'

So naturally Fulscreme didn't get all the attention it deserved. Oh, I did the due diligence—the research, the travelling to middle India, the rounds with the sales team, the store visits, but who cares for planning a brand's future when you can read people's.

Also I had discovered quite early that we were the losers in the marketing game. The competition was tough and savvy. Their advertising and promotions were so much fresher than ours. We just had beautiful women look fresh and vouch for the efficacy of Fulscreme in delivering softer suppler skin in seven, fourteen, thirty, sixty or 180 days or some such arithmetico-geometric progression depending on the size of the tube and the will of the legal team. The competitive brands, on the other hand, did all kinds of money-shots like splashes of water on the skin of a beautiful Brazilian model. A model whose skin was so hydrated it had condensation like a chilled glass of beer. I tried to get Fulscreme to get a little hip but was shot down by my boss, the legal team and the advertising agency. That sort of gimmickry, they said, was just not for Fulscreme. It was a salt of the earth or oil on the skin of India kind of brand and not a brand for Malabar Hill or Golf Links. Growth would be slow they said, but solid. I had always found the terminally dull patronising, but never this united, so it was lonely trying to get boring Fulscreme to challenge the market leader.

I took to trawling the RG intranet to pass the hours at work instead. Everyone who was employed by RG had a little page. With a link to their work, and a paragraph or two about themselves. It was shocking the sort of things people were willing to share with their employer and colleagues. I mean, why would anyone care that you think you're a typical Scorpio, that your mother bakes the best banana bread, or that your idea of adventure is brand building. Still, it was good entertainment. The more enthusiastic ones had family pictures up and updated their pages regularly. Lots of personal and professional achievements were bandied about. Clearly there wasn't enough to do.

The days passed slowly, the months blurred away. RG had managed to suck up all intelligent thought so completely that I forgot the main reason for my moving to Bombay. I had met Mitali thrice and one of them included my birthday. I wasn't sure if she was upset with my breaking up with Ruma, or unable to deal with me now that we were in the same city.

I was bothered by it too. She was my only friend in this place. I had pretty much nothing to do. I mean how many drinks could you have with the double MBAs. Their conversations were only about work and the sexual favours granted by the women who had overtaken them professionally.

It got so boring that I started going to channelling sites every night. If the times were changing, I had to be sure I stayed tuned, it wouldn't do to get left behind in the third dimension. It was like my bedtime story or counting sheep and a way of keeping my psychic side hydrated. Bombay, Fulscreme and Mitali were doing a great job of drying me up otherwise. If I returned to Delhi, Thamma would see that despite staying away from intoxication and women of disrepute, I had changed. Dried up. So I browsed Spiritweb, Antarrspake, Lovenlight, Greenhealing, and whichever site had the more stars, runes, hieroglyphics, angels or use of purple type. It did seem, even with a casual reading, like they knew they were speaking to me or at the very least to an intelligent psychically charged, spiritually potent human.

The months passed. The inter-dimensional transitions continued. The weather in Bombay stayed the same. It was winter but felt like summer. People began to ask me my plans for New Year's Eve. 2004 had been a bit of a let-down, I had expected so much and gotten so little. I guess things are cyclical, 2003 was quite eventful. 2005 had better be better, even if that required much meditation, some serious mantra-making, so be it.

Most important on my agenda though was to swing an invitation to a decent New Year's Eve do. I didn't bother asking Mitali, she would think I had no social life without her. I would have liked to spend New Year's with her, heck, I would like to spend the whole year with her, but that would mean tolerating Danny and his wannabe Spielberg friends. I couldn't understand what she was doing with her time. Why weren't we meeting more? Was her job that demanding? Was I acting obtuse, or any more obtuse with her, than I always had?

No, no, it wasn't going to serve me to think about Mitali. I had to get to a good party on the 31st. Wash away this write-off of a year and then start the New Year on a positive note. With all the right vibes, energies and chakras aligned, frequencies matched to the third, fifth, or whatever transitional dimension we were in, so that life in 2005 would turn out as planned or willed. Fulscreme would be number one, or I wouldn't give a shit, and Mitali and I would wind up together.

However, first for December 31.

Thanks to my popularity with the coffee drinkers at RG, I did get invited to a party on the 31st. It was a terrace do at a bungalow in Juhu. Obviously someone loaded was throwing the party. I was going as a friend of a friend. I knew Manav, who seemed to know the host vaguely. Manav was the media head for Fulscreme. That meant he decided how much money to spend, where and how, in which channel and which newspaper, during which show and in which corner of a newspaper. In RG, I had most of my arguments with him on budgets and duration of TV commercials, so you could say we were close. Enough at least for a New Year's Eve party.

Anyway there were so many people, no one really cared how well I knew Manav or how well he knew the host. The guests looked mainly like TV hopefuls or TV stars. Considering that I was heading the marketing function of a big brand I could wield some serious clout by pretending to be looking for the next face of Fulscreme. Going by the faces we'd used recently I'm not sure it would have been a compliment, but TV chaps can get quite desperate. It's a way of breaking into the big league.

Actually some of the film stars had, in the recent past, done their best work in ads. So it was no scoffing matter.

Imagine then, a pleasant night on a second floor terrace. Slums to one side, inversely affluent bungalows to the other. TV stars, hangers-on, marketers, socialites and waiters jostling each other. A counter for the bar, some tent-house chairs with white covers, kebabs and pakodas and some pretentious hors d'oeuvres, and me milling around minding my second drink, looking for some pretty face to seduce with the prospect of appearing on billboards all across the city. I drank slowly, I didn't want to wind up on another Ruma's couch or worse.

Then I saw her. Not Ruma, nor Mitali, no, another psychic, who had seen me too. We spent a few seconds sizing each other up, like two predators in a forest, wondering if this party was big enough for both of us. I'm not sure if you know how to spot a psychic. It's easy. There's something misplaced about their face. There will be some asymmetry when you look at it. The eyes or ears will be off axis. The nose may be pronounced, leaning to a side. The forehead domed. It's the eyes however, that will give it away. No one, not even someone placed within fifteen feet of a coffee dispensing machine, or standing by a bar forking down mouthfuls of kebabs can hide x-ray eyes. They're invariably small, piercing and sunken in. When they turn on you, you may feel somewhat smaller, dissected or unclothed.

We stared, then went back to what we were doing. I tried to find Manav or someone to talk to. Or just to hang with the hangers-about. If I didn't find someone soon, I might have had to tell a future or two. Seeing the overwhelming percentage of Bollywood hopefuls, and the spate of flops they were determined to produce, that might not go very well. So I pretended to be comfortable, leaning against the railing, but we were still sizing each other up. It stayed that way for five or seven minutes, then since I couldn't find Manav or any other loser in the party to chit-chat with, I decided to break the ice with her. She was at the bar, so I walked up, if things went off-kilter, I could always get a refill.

'Hi,' I said, almost suavely, 'I'm Anando.'

'Hello,' she said in response, neutrally.

She looked back, not like the TV guys, who broke eye contact after the 'hello' and ignored you. Usually a 'hello' for a 'hi' isn't a good sign. There's a suggested formality in the 'hello' which the 'hi' is trying to break, but since the 'hi' has already been uttered, it's a rebuff. That could be because the attention is undue, the person wants to warn a possible suitor about the presence of a mate, or because there is something unsettling or challenging about the person. I assumed it was because she'd met more than her match.

'Hi,' I repeated. 'And you are?'

'Prajna.'

No surname offered. Odd. Self-assured. 'That's the Sanskrit pronunciation, wow,' I said, making conversation.

'Yes,' she replied, monosyllabic.

'So do you get upset if people call you Pragya?' It's a good question, Pragya is the more natural form.

'I don't spell my name Pragya, so people don't really call me that.' Claws. Non-retractable it seemed.

'Right. I saw you...look, er...you looked familiar...I was wondering if we'd met before.'

She looked at me. I could feel her inner eye open and scan me. I maintained my neutral vibe, didn't want her reading too much off me.

'You're Manav's fr…colleague right, he mentioned that you'd be here.'

'Yes.'

'No, we haven't met.' Definitely not social.

'And you are…' I flailed my arms, implying how are you connected to this party.

'Hari is my partner.'

'Hari?' She obviously expected more from my psychic abilities.

'Hari Laroia, whose party and house this is. Whose booze you're drinking.'

'Oh, that Hari.' I tried to brush off the put-down. I was so excited to be invited to a filmi party, I hadn't bothered to enquire who the host was. Still I should have at least checked the nameplate at the gate. Hari Laroia didn't ring a bell. Was he famous? She said 'partner'. That was a weakness, an attempt to be modern. Why not boyfriend?

'Well, you must be busy, I won't keep you,' I said.

'No, it's okay,' she smiled. She was baiting me for another put-down. Someone called out to her, she raised her finger to say 'in a minute'. 'So you read fortunes at your company I've heard,' she said touching my hand lightly, almost flirtily.

'My reputation precedes me,' I offered as gallantly as I could manage. I was glad that after my faux-pas she wasn't ending the conversation.

'Are you any good?' she continued.

'That's for the others to say.' I shammed modesty.

'Don't you know?' she asked, the acid returning to her tone.

'I guess I'm okay,' I replied.

'Just okay, huh?' She had begun scanning the faces. I was boring her.

'Yeah.'

'Well, get another drink. And if you want to come for one of our sessions, it's every Wednesday at seven-thirty in the evening.'

'What session?'

'Why channelling of course. Aren't you interested?'

'You're a medi…a channel? I…'

'Some seer you are,' she said with half a smile that never reached her eyes.

I wasn't mollified, she could have at least shown some warmth. Her lack of sociability was off the scale.

'I wasn't really looking that hard.'

She held my hand, as she looked at some other guest, it was more of a bye.

'Well, enjoy and think about coming to a meeting. You could learn a thing or two. Now there are some people I need to catch up with.'

Yes, it seems abrupt even now. So much for a predatorial contest. I guess you can't compete with the host's partner. I nursed my drink, slowly circling around all the little huddles, till I found Manav regaling some TV types with what could only be his legendary tales of negotiating advertising rates.

'Ah there you are, my main man…' New Year's Eve had turned him into a black rap artist. '…Bros, this is Anand Sen. The Fulscreme Man.'

There were titters. Don't you just love being introduced as your work? Fulscreme isn't the sort of cream TV people use, so I was positioned as a clown, someone to be picked on.

'Anando,' I corrected.

'Yes, yes, the brilliant Bengali from Delhi.' Manav should have been a master of ceremonies, he was outdoing himself. Fortunately, no one picked at the usual Delhi rivalry bait. A buff dude with nerdy Clark Kent glasses spoke, 'Tell me, do you guys really use animal fat in your cream, I read it somewhere.' TV stars had started reading. We were doomed.

'Animal, mineral, vegetable,' I dodged. 'No fat is too good for us.' I didn't want to get into an animal fat discussion, there were bound to be some ingredients sourced from animals, this could get ugly.

'So we're rubbing pig fat on our faces.'

There it was. The trigger that was going to kill this party and start a communal riot. I could see the headlines tomorrow. 'Year starts with a bang: marketing executive provokes angry mob.' I looked at the trouble-maker. Early thirties, wanted to get into news reporting or the like but his pals convinced him he was too good-looking for that, that he could make more money in serials. Now he was playing a two-bit brother to the leading girl. Typical disgruntled Juhu Versova struggler.

'No, I was kidding, all our ingredients are sourced from vegetables and natural chemicals.' I looked at Manav for help.

'Fat is a natural chemical is it not?' This guy was so damn adamant and aggressive. What was it with people in this party, were they spiking the drinks with testosterone?

'Dude, all the ingredients are up on our website, why don't you look it up?' I said, as civilly as I could.

'Yeah,' Manav said. 'Let the guy drink man, its New Year's.'

'I was just yanking, Fulscreme Man. Let me get you a refill.'

'Sure,' I said, relieved. I wanted to ask him whether he was aware of the degree that funny money was funding his show, and whether he was cool with Dawood's aides writing his lines, but I let it pass. I was relieved. 'Whiskey and water and two cubes of ice.'

As he spun to face the bar, I asked Manav what the asshole's problem was.

Manav made a let-it-be face. We drank and buried our hatchets. The night got easier as more drink flowed in veins. I actually began to laugh. Then—the moment I was half dreading, half looking forward to. No not midnight, but the announcement that I read lives, the future. 'Dude, Anand here is a pro at reading faces and palms and what else, Anand?'

I smiled the smile of the modest psychic.

'So what does my face say?' this was a relatively pretty girl. She must be in some serial, I should have known which, since I was sure Fulscreme ran ads during it, but I couldn't bear to watch the soaps.

I should have said something like 'Your face is an essay in perfection' or something complimentary, it was a party, but you had to be honest with the psychic gods. When asked for my professional opinion, I just can't be flippant. 'Some other time, the light's no good.'

'We can switch on some lights,' she offered.

I was trying to remember why I had been so desperate for a New Year's Eve party. For some reason I was feeling very blank, it must have been Hari Laroia's cheap booze numbing my brain. 'You must negotiate harder for more pay,' I gave her the most obvious advice I could.

She took it. Thank the lord.

'Yes, these GGPK guys are real assholes,' she muttered, taking a swallow from her glass.

'What about me?' That was our friendly troublemaker again, back with my drink.

'You are going to spend all night reading ingredients of beauty products,' I said taking the glass and mouthing a 'Thanks'.

I laughed. The others laughed. The troublemaker grinned grudgingly. It was a decent comeback and an end to the silly requests. Just as things looked like they were going to settle, there was a tap on my shoulder. It was the host's partner, the ever gracious Prajna, with a 'jn'.

'So you're finally reading futures. What about me?'

The others took this as a cue to become spectators.

'I'm sure you get your answers from your sessions,' I answered. She was winding me up and I wasn't going to give her the satisfaction.

'I do, but what do you see?' she asked, insistent.

I see a graceless bitch. 'I see nothing right now,' I said. I had come to party, not duel.

'I thought so,' she said almost triumphantly.

I see your boyfriend arse-fucking someone else while you pretend to connect with the higher forces, but then you'd rather pick on a guest. I let her have her cheap victory. She offered me a prediction of her own, no doubt still trying to get a reaction from me. 'I don't see you working on Fulscreme for very long.'

Well, I wasn't masking my disgruntlement.

'In fact this year will be very turbulent,' she continued.

No shit, Nostradamus. Fulscreme was in danger of falling from number three. That would be my job on the line.

'You're quite the psychic,' I offered.

'We all are.' I had meant to be sarcastic but she didn't catch it. Fortunately, it diverted the attention from me.

'Prajna, tell me, what do you see in...'

I took that as a cue to slip away. This was the crappiest in a long history of crappy New Year's Eve parties and it was still ten minutes to midnight. I had to find someone to flirt with or have a non-hostile conversation with. I couldn't even drunk-dial Mitali tonight, the lines would probably all be jammed.

'Hey, you're Anando, right?' Finally a friendly-looking guy. He looked very Punjabi, fair, wide-jawed, hair sprouting from his collar, but he had a good open face and was the only cheerful guy I had seen in a while.

'Yep,' I said.

'It's Bhaskar, I was in FMS too, a batch junior,' he said.

'Hey man, how're you doing? You look so different without your beard,' I said.

'Man, the jhola days are gone. You kinda look corpo yourself,' he responded.

'Oh, it's good to meet a Delhi guy. This place has some oddballs,' I said, plainly relieved.

He laughed. 'Yeah man, Bombay's not as cool as they

make it out to be. People are less cosmopolitan than you think.'

I agreed with him.

He continued, 'In fact they're quite tight-assed. I'm having real trouble finding a place. I'm single, or non-veg, or wrong religion, or too good-looking. Haha.'

I laughed at that, I'd been one of the luckier ones. 'Really? I found a place in two weeks flat. Which broker are you using?'

'Lots of guys. Just haven't found a place that I like,' he replied.

'Right. Where's work?' I asked, offering my two bits of real estate consulting and few months of Bombay expertise.

'Andheri.'

'And where're you staying now?'

'The office guesthouse, but they're asking me to move,' he said.

Maybe it was the drink, or the relief of finding a friendly face at the party from hell, or maybe because there was some Delhi and alma mater bonding, the words spilled out of my mouth uncontrolled. 'You know what, I have an extra room that I'm not really using. I mean I got it in case my parents visited or something, I just use it to dump the extra stuff. You can use it till you find a place.'

'Wow, that's cool. You sure?' He was thrilled.

'Yeah, it's cool.' I said, playing cool by taking a swig of my drink.

'Thanks, man.'

'It's okay, man. You used to be studious, I hope you haven't turned into a serial killer or something.'

'No, not yet, though there's this one girl here who I could totally kill.'

'Lemme guess, it's Pra…'

'…jna,' he finished.

We both laughed.

'What is her problem?' he asked still laughing.

'I think she hates guests or something,' I hazarded.

'I mean it's a New Year's party, people pile on.' So that was his run-in story. Similar.

'I know.'

We both clinked our glasses to that.

It was so good to be agreeing with someone after all the conversations I'd had till then, I could have kissed Bhaskar at midnight. 2004 had been no Casablanca, but it felt like it could well be the start of a beautiful new friendship. 2005 came with a totally out of sync communal countdown. Some people were still at two, just before others shouted 'Happy New Year'. Prajna kissed Hari Laroia with the intensity of a horny female praying mantis. Bhaskar and I exchanged numbers and wished each other. I messaged Mitali an hour later. She replied as instantly as the cellphone service providers would allow.

It was a succinct, 'Ditto stranger.'

The rest of the night was better. I was happy to see the end of 2004.

A month later Bhaskar had still not found a flat he liked. He wasn't searching too hard either. It was some relief to have someone else to split the handling of the maids and shit, so it wasn't all bad, but I would have to drop the bomb on him sometime soon. I waited till a few days before Valentine's Day to bring it up with him. I was back from work, it was Friday and I was pissed that he was taking things so easy. He hadn't even bought groceries since he'd moved in and taken over the other loo with all his things. Bhaskar, you bastard, you'd caught me at a weak moment.

'Hey, Andy, how was work?'

'All right.'

'Can I fix you tea or something?'

What the fuck? This was totally off-character. He wanted something.

'No man, I'm good. Listen I've…'

'…Dude, I got something to say,' he cut me.

Fuck, here it was.

'Dude, I've…umm, you know, it's been a while that I've, umm, you know been with someone.'

What the heck, he was making a pass at me. Stingy homo.

He continued 'So…you know.'

'No, man, I don't,' I said as emphatically as I could to indicate my heterosexuality. I backed away from him. Dumping my laptop bag with a greater heave than necessary. Trying to put some aggressive body language into it. Being male. Or maybe that was the wrong strategy.

He said, 'There's this girl I've been sorta lining up. I'm going to meet her tonight.'

Behnchod, that was a relief.

'I really think I'm going to convert soon. So I might need to use your room,' he finished his pitch. For a second I thought he was changing religions, but with Bhaskar, everything was about sex.

'What?'

'Dude, my room's too small and it's just a mattress,' he explained.

Your room. You asshole, you don't pay rent or anything. 'Man, I've got stuff in my room. Why don't you go somewhere else?' I said.

'Man, there's no time,' he said.

'Fucker you've had more than a month, you could have gotten your own flat, with a bed and all.' I had to tell him.

'About that. There is nothing I like here, man. It's not like Delhi...'

Now he was trying to fucking grind me where I was weak.

'...besides, this is good, it's like college again. We can share rent and split things...save ourselves some money,' he said with the gleam in his eyes of someone who'd got it all figured.

'Bhaskar, man you don't pay for anything.' I'd had all I could take, he was probably earning more than I was.

'Dude, that was because I was looking, now I think this system works better.' He'd worked it all out in his head, I could tell.

'I don't know, man...'

'Hey, let's discuss this tomorrow, I gotta run for my date.'

Slimy shit. He began making the typical getting ready moves, taking out a shirt, uncreasing his pants. Bastard.

'You know it's been so long, my balls are all juicy and shit.'

I was not interested. I had dinner to heat and his room to make habitable.

'Why don't you jerk off?' I said, as a parting shot.

'It's not the same, fucker. Also I think you come differently when you jerk off versus when you do it. It's like you save your alpha semen for a woman,' he said, backing into the loo.

'Right.'

'You want a joint?' he offered.

I was surprised. Did I look like I needed one?

'Man, I always smoke one before a date, it makes me less desperate.' He pulled out a joint from the medicine chest in the loo and lit it.

'No, I'll pass.'

'You're a good guy, Andy...' Long drag. '...I'll ask Candice if she has any friends. These Christian chicks are easy to bag. It's their dresses and shit. You can't feel horny in a salwar kameez, but with your thighs rubbing against each other all day. Ooh yeah.' Half the joint turned to ash while he spouted his wisdom. 'All that stuff they hear about sinning. They want to sin, man. They want you to get them to confession. Haha.'

So now I had a flatmate. A juicy-balled, marijuana-smoking, bigoted, Christian-tail-seeking flatmate.

It got better. Despite Bhaskar's theorems, his doobies—as he called his joints—and the bedsheets I had to put for a wash. He paid half the rent. Which I guess was a little tax-free bonus for putting up with his shit. He shopped for groceries or dialled them in every third or fourth time, and it was a bit like college. The roommate you could tolerate only on alternate days. The sexist jokes, the easy availability of porn, the lingering smell of someone else's sweat, the disappearance of your soap or deo or aftershave or boxers even. He had good taste in music though. That was a huge plus since I had no taste. I mean I've always just listened to what was playing on radio or someone else's computer or ambient stuff. He would choose what album or genre he wanted to hear and then play that for a few hours, or he would play his guitar. Which he did quite a decent job of when he wasn't smoked up. When he was, he just wanted to play the blues. Which would have been all right, if he hadn't wanted to sing along as well. His poetry was atrocious.

'I was born too late, to a nigger mom (make that Brahmin UP-ite mother)
(Guitar thrum)
She spat me out, like a piece of gum
(Guitar thrum)
She din' want me, no one wan'ed me
(Guitar thrum)
I was one lonely son of a gun. (Or Punjabi dad)
(Violent guitar thrum)
So I got the blues. Yeah baby I got the blues. Yeah.'
(And frankly it was infectious.)

He had turned 403 Neelima Apartments into a boy's hostel. On the flip side, it did keep some of the more disturbing psychic forces at bay. While living alone I had been seeing moving shadows and flashes of colour in the corners. Something or things were trying to attract my attention in the only way they knew how. By making a racket on the edge of my awareness. You can't see these energies in broad daylight or tubelight if you look straight at them. While I knew that I shouldn't really be scared or anything, I really wasn't ready to meet Shroud Man or his ilk again. I didn't want to be Haley Joel Osment and run errands for the dead/undead/otherwise disembodied or indeed be their shrink. Fulscreme was bad enough.

Once Bhaskar moved in, all that stopped. Perhaps they were allergic to the Bhaskar blues.

Despite his pluses, there was one gnawing problem with him. There was no way I could risk getting Mitali in a room with him. He was too horny, crazy, sexist and he played the guitar. The two of them together had the makings of an alchemical reaction I couldn't predict. Even though Mitali hadn't visited even once since I got properly settled in. Still.

On the nights Bhaskar had his girlfriends over, it was too noisy to sleep. There was nothing to do other than browsing new age spirituality on the web. Reading the articles, the comments, the discussions on various themes, it was comforting to know that there were others like me. It was great to read about the sort of gifts others had. However, aside of the people running the site, most people's gifts seemed to cause them a great degree of pain. I, on the other hand, only had to suffer Bhaskar.

His girlfriends, perhaps embarrassed by the whole business, made sure they avoided me, coming and going when I was asleep or away. All except one.

It was the usual night. Bhaskar at it in his room, me sleepless in front of the computer, researching. Something about New Year's Eve didn't feel right and it wasn't just Prajna's bad manners, she had more than just a strange vibe, so I was looking for reasons why. I was so immersed in finding what it could be that when I heard, 'So you're interested in the occult?' I nearly jumped out of my seat. I was reading about spirits and a voice practically in my ear, seemed, well, paranormal.

I looked up and saw a girl, dressed in one of Bhaskar's shirts, but it could have been mine. She was tiny, she looked like she only made it halfway up the door and the shirt nearly covered her knees.

'Kuku,' she said.

'Cuckoo?' I asked, a little zapped. Wasn't it a little brazen on her part to comment on my sanity?

'No, no,' she said stretching out her hand, 'I'm Sarah, everyone calls me Kuku.'

'Hi, Kuku.'

'Hey! You're Andy aren't you?'

'Anando, yeah.'

'What were you reading?'

'Oh just stuff.' I didn't want to have to discuss any more than necessary. I wasn't even sure why we were having this conversation. I didn't want her to see what I was reading and have her roll her eyes at me. Possibly judge me for being cuckoo, for sure.

'No, tell me, I see you were on Spiritweb,' she said coming closer and peering at the computer. Her face finally caught the light and I saw she was lovely. As in model lovely. If she had been taller she could have walked on any ramp. Bhaskar had powers that bore investigating. 'Why're you reading on psychic power absorption?' she said, quite happy to read over my shoulder. She was damn sure of herself, in just a shirt.

'Umm...I...no reason, just curious, if it can be done.'

'Of course it can be,' she announced. 'Are you interested in doing it or are you a victim?'

'Say again,' I said.

'Has someone sucked your power? Have you met a psychic vampire?' she asked.

'Ummm…'

'Have you met someone you felt powerless in front of?'

'Now that you say…,' I said thinking about the charms of Prajna. Vampire. Whoa. I never knew there could be psychic vampires, it made sense though, energy may be easier to suck than blood.

'May I ask how you know all this? I haven't met too many people who're into the alternate stuff.'

'Oh, I'm a witch,' she said matter-of-factly. 'Wiccan.'

'Ah.' No wonder everyone called her Kuku.

'Were your powers absorbed by someone recently?'

'I'm not sure. Perhaps,' I said.

'Let me guess, she touched your right hand, almost accidentally. It is a she, right?'

Shoot. Yes indeed, Prajna had brushed my right hand while getting her drink and later she had put her hand on my right arm for no reason. I had found it flirtatious at the time.

'Why right hand?'

'You are new to this, right? This is pretty old stuff.'

I tilted my head, not agreeing or disagreeing, not wanting to compete. So she knew something I didn't. I was interested. She looked interesting. Pretty but also interesting, after all how many self-pronounced witches do you meet?

'Well, it's old knowledge, the right gives off, the left draws in. You know this, right? In paintings or sculptures of gods and goddesses, it's there, represented by painters and stoneworkers.' She struck the pose of a goddess. Holding her right palm up in a blessing and the left palm downwards, and tilting her hips as if she was doing Bharatnatyam. 'It should be obvious, no? The right hand is usually used to give energy. The left hand to absorb energy. Which is why the gods bless with the right, and hold the left down, to absorb energy. Some people say to absorb your negative energy.'

She seemed like she wanted to go on, so I let her have the chair and squatted on the mattress. She had my attention. It was distracting though, what with her bare legs and nipples poking out through the shirt. A shirt I had worn till a month ago. Not to mention, her looks. But the psychic could overpower the physical, so I concentrated. She covered the ground on protecting oneself from psychic attacks. Meanwhile, I replayed the night of New Year's Eve in my head.

Prajna had touched my palm, apparently accidentally, engaged me in some put-downs, which I had to respond to, played my ego while she absorbed my powers and then passed them off as her own, to the great delight of Bombay's Emmy winners. The vampire. Bitch.

'...and that's also why the dervishes dance like that, so that the energy flows through them,' Kuku finished.

'Thanks, Kuku. That was great. Really.'

She smiled drawing her knees together.

'I really did learn a lot.'

'So next time you meet your vampire, keep your right hand in your pocket,' she said getting up.

I wasn't quite sure if that was a barb or advice, it would have been quite embarrassing if she thought I was aroused while she was educating me. On the other hand...

'You might want to come to one of our meetings...It's not what people think.'

I didn't know if that was a come-on or a genuine invitation. I was tempted, but thinking back, Prajna had had no problem in disarming me, I wasn't sure I could take on a coven of witches. Even if they were cute, heck specially if they were cute. Cuteness may be their snare. Also, it would be wrong to go after Kuku. Flatmates had codes and I didn't want a retaliatory strike on Mitali. Bhaskar had more up his sleeve or trousers than he let on. I declined, as politely as one could a half-naked witch. There was much work to be done on bumping up my psychic abilities.

So from that night on I busied myself with Wiccan lore, Reiki, creating auras of protection and meditations for psychic strengthening. I acted on Kuku's advice and held my left hand up and right hand down while meditating. I was cautious shaking hands with anyone who offered their left hand to my outstretched right, in fact I avoided shaking hands as far as possible.

I meditated more. I was determined never again to be the 98-pound psychic weakling and have auras kicked in my face. I imagined myself bathed in all colours of light. I read. I discovered human energy patterns and thus what it meant to be created in a divine form. I discovered crystal power. Energy spots on the planet. Vortexes that suck you into multi-dimensional travel. I pored over religious texts. I learnt about the twisted power of invocations, spells and exorcisms. I could've started a pretty successful cult with a set of principles gleaned from recurrent refrains on the Internet. All I had to do was spout in Old English or Pali or something and I could be the new messiah. The next L Ron Hubbard.

Changes were happening. At work I was calmer, more tolerant of the sales guys and my own competitive team, people smiled more and more when they met me.

More profound changes however were happening within. My brain was rewiring. I know that because my dreams were chaotic. Jumpy like MTV promos. I remember this crazy dream where I am wading through a pool of milk or perhaps Fulscreme, while arms reach out to pull me in. I panic, trying to wade away, when up ahead Prajna, dressed only in a white shirt, beckons for me to come to her. Something about her seems inviting yet dangerous, Prajna turns into Mitali as I wade towards her. Then I feel a tug, and there is Kuku tugging at my left hand. When I look back Mitali has turned into Bhaskar.

I woke up in a sweat. There were more of the same, getting progressively more symbolic. After these crazy nights there was a period for a few nights that I didn't dream at all, or if I did, I don't remember. Then one night I fell asleep during a meditation and had a very strange dream. I call it a dream because I don't know what else to call it.

I was walking upstream along a river, the path strewn with rounded stones. It must have been close to the hills or in a valley because there were gigantic shadows in the distance. It was nighttime with very little moonlight, so I only had a sense of the shadows, I couldn't really see that far. As I walked, the little light that there was, disappeared, and I only had a sense of walking on in darkness. I could hear the river flow next to me, rushing over rapids. Then it felt like there was no path to walk on anymore. I tried to see if there was any way, hoping for some light. As can only happen in dreams, the ground before me became visible. The path I was on, had ended at bushes. When I looked more closely at the bushes, there seemed to be a way forward, overgrown though it was with river weed. I moved the bushes aside and looked. The path led to a gaping hole in the ground. When I walked towards it, I saw that there were stairs leading down. Large old stairs, carved out of rock, their sides rounded by the years. Since in a dream you don't have quite the same fear of unknown passages, I walked down. It was dark, very dark but light from some secret source illuminated the way. Dream lighting. The stairs led to a tunnel. The tunnel wound its way deep underground. It felt as though I was walking under the river. Perhaps I could hear the river, a distant roar above, but it's more likely that I just felt that I was under the river. The tunnel wound this way and that and then suddenly there was a faint light. A little, then as I walked towards it, it grew. I was at a door. When I stepped out it was dark again but not to the same degree.

I was in a room. A room that seemed familiar. I looked around and noticed someone lying in a bed under a thin bed-sheet. Someone surrounded by books. A form that looked familiar. I tried to make out the face of the person sleeping and slowly it began to take shape. I could make out that it was worried. So very worried. Worried for the test it had to take the next day and the repercussion of that single test on the rest of its life. I felt bad for it. The sleeping form began to change, to take more definite shape, it began to look more like a boy. A boy I had met before. A boy who looked a lot like I did, when I was in class twelve. Then suddenly the eyes of the boy snapped opened. I strained, I wanted to get a better look at him. I wanted to be sure he was me. Then I realised I had a cowl over my head that was obstructing my vision. I couldn't get my hands to remove the cowl. It stayed there, but I wanted to communicate. I wanted to tell him, it would be okay. That the exam meant nothing, that life gave more chances. Many, many more chances. I opened my mouth to speak, only no words came out, I raised my arm to point to his books, to tell him that these weren't all that important, that life would work out just fine, then I felt a force pulling at me from the tunnel behind. And then the room disappeared. My eyes opened. When the room took shape I was at 403 Neelima Apartments. I was awake.

I was Shroudy. I had reached into the past or seen the future depending on how you saw it. Through a dream. Obviously that was a line of communication or dimensional travel that existed. How wonderful. What other things could meditation reveal, I wondered. It felt like something had been triggered. A magical unclicking. Like the rewiring was complete. That now I could visit if I chose, a world that always existed parallel to one's own. That now, after a long time my psychic powers were once again beginning to grow. I felt stronger, ready to take on psychic vampires, covens and any others who wanted to pit their Theta waves against mine.

Twelve

~~~~~~

Like a disciplined psychic athlete, I devoted every night to some sort of spiritual exercise. The days turned to weeks, then into months. The heat gave way to rolling clouds and a wet cold breeze, and then to pitter-patter and heavy rain. Had I taken any exam in theology, I'm sure I would have passed, but alas, I had had no other noteworthy experience, made no connection with another dimension. I had made no connection with Mitali for a while either. So after what seemed like centuries, I called. I think I was upset that she had moved in with Danny, but with all the New Age revelations, meditations and work, I had allowed her to fade into the background. It was silly to have forgotten the reason for moving to Bombay in the first place. She answered after five rings and sounded glum.

'Hey, it's been a while and you haven't come home and seen it with furniture. Not that there's much, but it's not bare,' I said after the opening pc.

'I've been busy, Andy,' she said, using her work voice.

'With what, MC?'

'This and that. I'll tell you when we meet. Set a date.'

Uncharacteristically decisive on her part, it must be the effect of the work voice.

'Tomorrow?' I asked.

'For god's sake, Andy, tomorrow is Tuesday.'

'Are you in the mood for drinking?'

'Yes,' she snapped.

'Well then drink tomorrow.'

'And be hungover at work the day after?'

'You don't have to drink that much surely,' I chided.

'I do,' she said.

'Okay, let's meet early then. What time will you get done with work?'

'Sixish. But I may be chasing a story, so I might be near home anyway.'

'So let's say Bandraish around six then,' I said.

That gave us enough options, plus it was a short walk for her, and close enough for me to get back and have enough time for a quick meditation before sleeping. Even with the rain and potholed ole Bombay.

Tuesday morning I was at office in a good mood, twiddling my thumbs, browsing the net, stroking my beard. I had started growing it a little after the Shroudy vision/dream and it now completely covered all the bald spots on my chin. It was nice to have a beard at RG. I was the only one. Everyone was clean-shaven, or at best wearing a well-trimmed corporate moustache. This was my little rebellion. A subtle sign that I would never be one of them. I would do my duty to Fulscreme but I wouldn't go potty writing concepts for product or brand extensions. Nor do the mandatory give n' take with R&D guys and Legal. That was for those who belonged to the system. Those who wanted to clothe, feed, wash with and apply on every citizen of India a gloriously over-claimed RG product. The Empire's Clone Army. Well, I wasn't a part of it and the beard was my fist in the air.

While I did some spreadsheets on volume and sales, my mind wasn't in it. My presentation wasn't due until Friday and it was more entertaining to see how much more people revealed of themselves on Orkut. The stiff office persona all dressed up on the RG Intranet, compared to the cool social one partying hard. The drunken photographs and the silly wall posts. You could figure out who had a crush on whom so easily. Who was needy and whose boyfriend was going to dump them. I thought our office Intranet was bad, this took the freaking cake.

Just before lunchtime, Mitali called. 'Hey, I'm at Vakola, is there a secret place you keep your keys or something?'

'Why're you at Vakola? We were supposed to meet at Bandra, in about six hours from now,' I asked, pleased that she was at my flat, excited almost.

'I had a fight with Danny and I don't want to see his face or stay at his place.' There was embarrassment, almost a note of apology in her voice somewhere. My heart beat a little faster. This was my chance, except my keys were dangling by my side and not half buried under a potted plant.

'No, I don't keep my keys anyplace special, they're with me.'

'What about your roomie?' she asked.

'He has his own room and his own key.'

'Well how fast can you get here?' she was very demanding for someone who had barely kept in touch all these months.

'Ummm...I can't leave right away...if you can kill some time, I should be able to leave by about three. So be there by three-thirty.'

'Okay, I'll see. Hurry.'

It had been pitter-pattering all day. So to be there by three-thirty, I calculated that I would have to leave by about a quarter to three. I had to figure out some excuse for my boss. He wouldn't be pleased. What with the beard and whatnot. But heck, this was what I had been waiting for. For Mitali to stay with me. I was going to kick Bhaskar out and show her that I was the one for her. For that I had to get home quickly.

I told my boss that my family had sent me a package through a family friend and the gentleman in question was leaving by the evening flight, so I had to go catch up with him. There was nothing he could say, he waved his hand imperiously. A go-on, get-lost wave. I mean you don't expect a Brand Director to tell petty lies. I finished lunch, bought some supplies for the house from our ground floor shop. Just in case we ate at home or in case Mitali felt like cooking or something.

But things, when they have to, never go according to plan. There were urgent mails that needed responding to, my juniors wanted to bounce some ideas off me, and the Creative Director of the agency called to complain about how we'd handled one of his ideas. I really wanted to hang up, but that would not do. There was a new code of etiquette on handling suppliers, which we had to adhere to, or be pulled up for. You could lose a promotion or a few percentage points of your increment. So I put up with his whining for half an hour.

It was about three-thirty by the time I got around to leaving. The rain was coming down hard. I felt guilty for making Mitali wait for longer than agreed upon. I got into my car and zipped off, saluting the guard at the gate. I prayed that I should make good speed, but the rain was pretty damn incessant and there were pools of water everywhere. As I turned onto the highway I received a greater shock. There was a huge jam. I cursed my luck, the fates, the powers. They were out to bugger up the one evening I had gotten with Mitali in so long. An evening when she perhaps was vulnerable, needing the shoulder of her long-trusted friend, an evening when she may discover that her trusted friend was just right for her, that he was also a great lover. Instead, I was stuck in traffic that was moving fifteen feet every ten minutes or so.

I called her and her phone rang but there was no response. What the heck was she doing to kill time? Dancing in the rain? Meanwhile the cars were using only one-third of the highway. There was water all around and the rain, if anything, was coming down harder. I sat at the wheel frying slowly with impotent anger. I hit the steering wheel in frustration. I called my juniors to talk about work and vent. They informed me that HR had declared an early holiday on account of the rain and asked people to leave before the train tracks got flooded.

So much for lying about picking up a package. I dialled Mitali again, but couldn't get through. After about half an hour things got much worse. The sky was dark and the rain coming down harder. I saw more cars now stalled by the side of the road than before. This was not good. Then suddenly there were major splashes and I saw a bunch of people pass me by riding an elephant. Now that was an out-of-the box solution to the jam. A pity, I didn't have the number of dial-an-elephant-cab. By now water had started seeping into the floor of the car, and all the junk was floating up. Old petrol bills, a pencil, some plastic parts, biscuit crumbs and what must be rat's droppings. It was five-thirty.

Then my cellphone stopped receiving a signal, the engine started spluttering. I couldn't remember my father's instructions. Should I be keeping the engine on low rev so that it didn't flood or on high rev so that the exhaust didn't flood. I thought about Karna from the Mahabharata who also forgot all his learning when he needed it most. I thought that I too may die with my shoulder against the back wheels of my dinky Maruti, as some errant Arjun in a Totyota Qualis ran me down.

The lane to the extreme left was waterlogged but empty, I thought the risk worth taking, but no sooner had I swerved towards it than my car began to drift and I saw another Maruti float by, so I immediately veered back to the extreme right lane ignoring all the honks of protest from the back. Meanwhile I was loop-dialling Mitali's phone.

About half an hour later I got an opportunity to take the exit to the domestic airport and I took it. There was no point trying to get home in the car now. There was too much water and the car was too light to be safe in. So I turned in and found a tight spot between two Indica cabs.

I had to switch off the engine and push the car into some sort of a postioning. It was jutting out and I thought I should try and do better, but when I looked around I saw that it didn't really matter. There were cars stalled all around, some in the middle of the road. Before getting out, I put my wallet, keys and phone in a plastic packet, shoved the entire thing inside my trouser pocket, and stuffed my handkerchief on top of it all to jam it in place. Then I began wading through the knee-deep water.

This was looking bad, really bad. How is it I hadn't been alerted to this earlier? Was nature beyond the reach of my gifts? Or perhaps I was acting on psychic instinct by leaving earlier, just that idiot Creative Director had wasted valuable minutes. There were many like me wading through the water. People held hands and formed chains so that they didn't slip into open manholes or fall into potholes. Some had fashioned walking sticks out of branches, which they were sticking into the water ahead of them.

I overtook groups of people, wading, using my arms in swimming strokes, to move faster. I was in a desperate hurry to get home. Mitali, I was pretty sure, didn't know how to swim. Worse, she would be the type to venture out and be brave. I didn't even want to imagine what it would be like if she was stranded somewhere.

On entering Vakola, I discovered that the water was chest high and flowing in all kinds of swirling currents. It was going to be damn dangerous, but I had to get home to Mitali. She would be totally stuck without me. Shit, dead rats, plastic packets, and all kinds of creepy crawly things wrapped themselves around me, as I swam, waded, bounced and prayed my way home. The only mantra I mouthed in the last five hundred metres or so was 'Please-please keep Mitali safe. Please-please keep Mitali safe.' I know it didn't have the balance or power of my earlier mantras but there was no time to construct a well-balanced one, I hoped the intense emotions made up for the lack of magic.

Things brushed passed me, swam with me and filled my trousers, shirt and underwear but I kept the mantra going.

A dead cow. Please-please keep Mitali safe.

A floating sari. Please-please keep Mitali safe.

A shoe, a bicycle tyre, a pot. Please-please keep Mitali safe.

Shit. Floating shit. Black stuff. Please God, whatever you may have against me, please-please keep Mitali safe.

The water had reached my neck. It was dark. The lights were out, I had to make my way by what little I could see. Fortunately the water around our building was no worse than waist deep, and there were no apartments on the ground floor. I walked up the stairs praying that I would find Mitali sitting at the stairs, in front of my door, twiddling her thumbs. She wasn't there.

The phone network was down. The electricity was gone. I was in a blue funk. I didn't know what to do. There was no way I could go looking for her, I didn't know where to start. I asked the watchman if a girl had come to my flat. He answered that a girl had come looking for my flat around lunch time, but she had left soon after. Yes, she must have gone and sat at some restaurant and cooled off. Where did she go after?

Dammit Mitali, where are you? God oh god, please-please keep Mitali safe.

I didn't know what else to do, so I bathed, changed, and sat down in meditation. I would have to try and reach her telepathically. There was no good panicking. I inhaled deeply, tried to calm my mind, and concentrated on her. Tried reaching her. Exhorted the face I saw so clearly in my head to call me as soon as she could.

Around midnight my phone rang. It was Bhaskar.

'Dude, are you safe?'

'Yes, I'm home. Where are you?' I replied.

'I'm in office, we had to come back, there was no way to get home. You know, I'm reading on the Internet, our area is hit bad, man. You sure you okay?'

'Yeah, there's water outside but the flat is fine,' I said.

'Right, you might be stuck in the flat for some days, man. The entire area is flooded,' he added, not sadistic, just breaking the facts.

'Listen do you have any news of my pal Mitali? Did she contact you?' I asked him, clutching at straws.

'No dude, why would she do that?'

Damn you Mitali, where the heck are you? He hung up, and I called Mitali. This time the call went through.

After a few rings she answered.

'Aanu, are you all right?' she said, almost shouting, with what may have been both concern and relief.

'Dammit, Mitali, where the heck are you, I've been so worried, so bloody worried.' I was crying. I was so relieved to hear her voice.

'I'm fine, Aanu, I tried reaching you...the networks were all down.'

'Where are you?' I asked.

'I'm at umm...my place...Danny's, where else?'

'I thought...you fought...that you didn't want to see him again.'

'I did...then he called, he apologised...he was very sweet, we met and we made peace,' she said.

It hurt. I don't know whether it was for the fact that she had gone back to him, or because I had walked through shit and floodwaters to get to her.

'You're okay, that's great. I was really worried,' I said holding back more tears.

'I'm sorry you were worried, I tried to call and tell you I was going back home, I really did.'

'It's cool,' I said, choking, and hung up before I started bawling.

I cried angrily for a long time. I felt small. I felt stupid. I felt heartbroken for the nth time. I couldn't believe anyone had the power to hurt me this bad. I was angry at the gods, I was angry that they hadn't thought to tell me that I was praying without reason and that she was safe in Danny's arms and not drifting in the floodwaters of Vakola. I was angry at the weather, with the Destinies, the Furies, I was angry with myself but mostly I was hurting with the pain of having my heart blown out of me.

Sometime during the night I was hungry so I ate a packet of biscuits. Then since I was unable to sleep, I sat cross-legged and decided to have a mental confrontation with the powers that be. I controlled my breathing, I focused my mind. The tears stopped, there was a passable calm. I shoved Mitali's face out of my thoughts. I put a lid on my anger. Inhaling through one nostril to a count of six, holding to a count of twelve, exhaling from the other to a count of three. In five minutes all I could hear was the sound of my breathing. Like the sea that had surged during the day.

Then there was a voice in my head. 'Hi.'

'Hi, who is this?' I asked.

'It's me.'

It could be me talking to myself, I mean I've done that before, but this time it felt different.

'Who are you?'

'It's me, Uncle.'

'Uncle?'

'Yes, you would have been, wouldn't you?'

Was this the voice of my unborn niece or nephew?

'Why are you talking to me? Do you have something to say?'

'No, you were just so sad, I thought I'd cheer you up.'

I wasn't sure I was cheered, I was spooked but there was also a sense of achievement, I had finally figured channelling. 'Is there anything you want to tell me then?' I asked.

'No...' a pause and then '...do you have questions?'

'Are you real?'

'Yes and no. Depends what you think real is.'

'Is that it? Aren't you just a voice in my head?'

'Where else would I be a voice?'

'So why did you die before even being born?'

'That was the extent of my karma.'

'Then why did my sister, Didi, suffer so?'

'That was her karma, her path. This is the path she chose.'

'What about my karma?'

'You're living it, you will live and react to the script you have chosen for yourself.'

'Who are you?'

'I'm the voice in your head.'

'Yes, but who are you?'

'Does it matter, are you feeling better?'

'Yes.'

'Well then, it worked, didn't it?'

It did.

We spoke for about an hour after. I'm not sure I learnt much that was new to me, but the answers came so quickly and were so precise that I'm sure it wasn't me talking to myself. It felt like another voice. A happier voice in my head. A sorted voice. I allowed it to calm me, I asked it all sorts of questions. It was happy to answer.

A few days later the waters receded and life came back to normal. Slowly. Vakola and the city was a wreck. A garbage heap. I had to get the car towed to the Maruti workshop, and there it stayed for about three weeks.

After my little channelling session on the night of the flood, my mood lightened. I tried to think less of Mitali's betrayal. I read more. The Bible, the Koran, the Gita. I had read the Gita before, of course, but I wanted to read it again. I filled my head with the words of God's people and waited to hear from God directly. I had suffered and I had been transformed by it. When was he going to send an archangel? Or speak to me from a bush. I tried to imagine what medium he would use. In this age, perhaps a phone call, email or message in a random site. Perhaps he was old school, and would appear in a shaft of light. I read and I waited.

Work was tougher to do, after the night of July 26th when the skies opened on Bombay. Every job on Fulscreme felt more unreal, unimportant, unnecessary. Still, I had my beard. I tugged at it. I wasn't angry with RG the company, just in disagreement with everything they stood for. When I got the sign from above, I would leave and if it was in my karma, I would expose them for their hollow practices. But for now I would wait. Surely the message was any day in coming now, I mean, I now had all the abilities that any of my family had. It had to lead somewhere.

Thirteen

At work, I was stroking my beard, pulling at the shorter hairs to coax them to catch up, straightening the tangles, when my landline rang. It had to be Mr Praveen Kumar, head, North India sales, and now the new head of our retail store—Apnamart, calling no doubt to complain about something. He was never happy with Fulscreme— there just wasn't enough Fulscreme where there was a demand for it. Namely the small towns up north, where people were too deluded or too stingy to buy the number one and two moisturisers. Or there was too much of it in the west, where they didn't care for it.

It was Green Park. They never called this early. Ma's small voice on the phone. She was apologetic, almost. Oh Ma, I weep at how humble you are, how little you think of yourself, despite your manifest spiritual ability.

'Sorry to call you in the morning, but we've had to move Thamma to the hospital.'

'Why, what happened?'

'She slipped and fell in the loo. She was in quite a lot of pain after that, in fact all night she couldn't sleep, so this morning we moved her to St Ignatius.'

'Oh. Is she okay, is she better? Do you want me to come?' I asked, because well, they were growing old and hospitals can be shitty. The guilt of ignoring Thamma sat heavily within, I wanted to do something.

'She's had a fall, she's how she can be. No, you stay, your work's important,' Ma said. If only you knew Ma, if only you knew. 'No, I can come,' I said. I was ready to up and leave. It would beat facing Praveen Kumar and his satanic tribe.

'No, it's fine, Aanu, we can manage. We'll let you know if you're needed,' she said, I could hear Baba prompting her from the dining table, where he must have been sitting drinking his tea. I wanted to go home.

Before I could argue any further they hung up. I sat there a while cradling the phone, pretending to be on a call, in case some shit came asking about his fortune in the morning. It's awful to be homesick. It's worse when you can't even be there when they need you, when you can't be a half-decent son or grandson, and they believe you're doing something important. When all you're doing is landing up at your desk. I kept the receiver down finally and tried concentrating on the distribution figures for Fulscreme. It was column after column of meaningless numbers.

The day passed with some emails from Mr Praveen Kumar's team and the usual shit. A beard-stroking day. I had stopped telling coffee route fortunes. I was sure that leaked my spiritual energy. The reason I was not evolving to what I was meant to be.

Didi called late at night. 'Li'l brother how are you?' She sounded quite cheerful despite Thamma's fall and whatnot.

'I'm as well as can be. How are you? How are things?' I answered.

'So on the Thamma front, she's in less pain, since they've got her on painkillers.'

'That's good I guess.'

'She was asking about you, actually, quite a bit. You were always her favourite.' She cackled a little at that. I guess it was to indicate that she wasn't jealous or that she was half-serious about it, or whatever emotions the less favourite grandchild is healthily expected to have.

'Didi. Come on, tell me. Should I come?'

She laughed good-naturedly, Didi could tell I was feeling guilty, 'No, you stay. Work.'

I stayed silent. Everyone thought my work was so important, maybe I should really take it more seriously.

She continued quite merrily, 'Oh, I don't know whether it's the painkillers or shock or what, but she's breaking into poetry, now and then. I wish I could record it.'

What? Poetry? Thamma? There was something odd.

'Did you tell the doctors about it?' I asked, concerned.

'What's to tell, Aanu? It's normal poetry. It's just that we've never seen that side of her.'

'Right. Well keep me posted. All well with you?' I asked.

'Yes. Okay, gotta run now. Have to go help Ma with the hospital food and night shift and all that. You take care li'l brother.' They were all being so affectionate and thoughtful about me. I wasn't the one who had fallen, it was Thamma. I felt guilty for not being there with her. I mean after all Thamma had done for me. I had tried to be dutiful, I had asked the folks if I should come, I had been insistent even, they'd asked me not to.

But poetry?

God spoke in verse did he not? The holy books will have us believe he did. Was this the sign I'd been looking for? Should I be at Thamma's bedside taking dictation? Why oh why were God's signs so complicated to read. Couldn't he just speak to me from a bush, or via an angel or through an unlisted number? I didn't sleep much that night, trying to work out what God was trying to tell me. I went browsing, hopping from one New Age site to another, just clicking on random links, hoping that with serendipity, I'd come to a message from God, but naah, there was no such thing.

The next thing I knew it was nine a.m. and I was not out of bed. I was late getting in at work and bleary-eyed. My boss didn't like it. I could see that from his expression when I walked in, so I made some excuse about my grandmother's health. The story gained credibility as I got a call from home during the telling of it.

'Aanu?' It was Baba.

'Hi Baba, what's the news?' I said playing the concerned grandson to my boss, butting the glass door open, excusing myself with the give-me-five-minutes palm.

'Aanu, the doctors are saying your grandmother had a stroke.'

'What?'

He continued, 'Yeah, looking at her age and her high blood pressure, they're worried about how serious it may be…she's also a little numb in her legs…they're not quite working. They're not sure whether that's the stroke's doing or from the fall.'

'Oh God!' What kind of sign were you sending me?

'She's been asking where you are. Seems to have forgotten that you went to Bombay...you don't have to come right away,' he finished.

My family, they were all so nice. You don't have to do this or do that. You can just be. I wanted to be with my Thamma, it would have been easier if they had asked me to come. Now it was up to my judgement of the situation. Which I had to judge without knowing just how serious Thamma's condition was. Why couldn't they, like Praveen Kumar and the Apnamart guys, just fix a day for a meeting? I would meet the Apnamart characters for much less than someone having a stroke, but no, my family was so undemanding, I had to decide when to go, when to apply for leave, when to decide that my personal life tipped the scales over.

I left work early that day and went to the nearest mall, I didn't feel like going home and hearing Bhaskar's theories on everything. I thought it may cheer me up. Retail therapy it's called, isn't it? I wasn't going to buy anything, I just wanted to be surrounded by people. By India's great aspiring classes. Aspiring for 9.2 per cent per annum growth or whatever GDP story they had bought into. The malls truly captured our collective aspiration. It was all windows and little shopping. A nation coveting. What were Hannibal Lecter's words, 'We covet what we see, Clarice, what we see every day.' Or something to that effect.

I was coveting shoes and handbags, Dr Lecter. I was coveting fast food. I was coveting the ergonomic chair my boss sat on. I was coveting Apnamart growth plans. I was coveting sales girls who'd never worn T-shirts before they took up their current jobs. I was coveting sandwich chefs, who'd never eaten a sandwich they'd prepared. I was coveting Happy Hours between three p.m. and seven p.m. My phone rang. It was Didi.

'So you better come,' she said flatly. Finally an order.

'Why what happened?' I asked, I was upset they'd taken so long to call me.

'So, you know, Thamma's poetry is getting quite interesting. I didn't know she knew so much Urdu. I'd like to note it down and translate it, or figure out where she got it from, but I can't keep pace.'

'You need me to come take notes?' I asked.

'No, you fool. This can't be normal. Get here while she's still somewhat normal. We don't know what part of her brain the stroke has hit.' This was much more like the Didi I knew. 'This Urdu thing may be because some part of her brain has been affected.'

I was ready to fly down that minute but I said instead, 'Fine, I'll see how quickly I can come, will need a few days to wrap things up, get tickets and stuff.'

'All right, but come fast,' she said, before hanging up.

I was standing outside an electronic store when the call ended. I walked in for no reason. I picked up a dictaphone. It seemed like the reason I walked in, but I couldn't be sure. The next day I gave my boss the dope about my grandmother's ill health. That was more to make him feel crappy about doubting my excuse the previous day, than a reason for taking leave. I made calls to the Apnamart guys, sent off a spate of emails. Gave Bhaskar a lecture on running the flat. Gave the juniors something of a handover. Then booked a ticket for Friday evening. If I had taken off earlier, they would have deducted Saturday and Sunday as leave, it was pragmatic, if not dutiful. I somehow made it through work the next two days and then left for Delhi. A Kingfisher flight, quite hip and all, with wannabe models as stewardesses, all red skirts, lipstick and glamour, the world of air travel was too good to take, and somewhat suggestive of alcohol. I was ready for a drink myself, but it wasn't an international flight and I couldn't be drinking while the rest of my family was doing hospital duty.

Saturday morning I drove with Baba to the hospital to relieve Didi, who'd done the night shift. Ashok was coming to pick her up, I think, or maybe Baba would drop her home. Baba looked quite rattled, uncomfortable to be going to the hospital. I was sure it was because in the hospital, he had no choice but to confront the smell of death surrounding him. It must be goddamned overwhelming.

So I said to lighten the mood, 'Do you still smell death? It must be terrible at a hospital.'

'No.' Categorical.

'You don't smell it anymore? When did that happen?' I asked.

'I don't know, I don't smell it anymore,' he said, clearly reluctant to talk about it. He'd never really had a chat with me about this. As far as I could remember we'd never really had an adult to adult chat on anything important.

'Whoa,' I said. Big news, something had happened here.

He looked out of the window all angst-ridden, while I concentrated on the buses in the morning school rush.

'I'm not sure what I smelt.' He said that looking out, his mind somewhere distant, his voice tinged not with doubt, but something else, sadness perhaps.

Baba, you doubter, you. After all the drama in my childhood years. He had done something, some kriya. You don't get rid of gifts just like that. There was something he wasn't telling me. Well, I had time, we were going to be in the hospital for a while. He'd get around to telling me, by and by.

Somehow we walked to the room without being challenged by hospital security. I had heard St Ignatius was strict with visitors. Baba handed me the visitor pass, and walked past the security with an air of self-absorption. Clearly not that strict.

Thamma had a nice airy room, you had to give that to St Ignatius. They had great rooms, no wonder they had such a good reputation. I had expected more tubes and monitors, but there was just one IV stand and that too didn't seem attached to her. A monitor, two wires leading out from it, which were attached to electrodes on her head and heart. Thamma had little plastic tubes sticking out of the veins on the back of her hands. They're called cannulae, as I learnt later. The monitor beeped periodically, birds chirped outside. Didi welcomed me with a tired smile. Not a patch on the smile on Thamma's face, when she opened her eyes and realised she had visitors.

'Hello and welcome,' she said in English, not Bengali. That was pretty odd. Had the stroke invigorated her language neurons?

'Hello, Thamma,' I replied in English too. 'Look what I got you.' I held out the dictaphone for her to see.

She went back to Bengali when she asked me what it was and how she was supposed to operate it, with all the tubes running in and out of her arms. I told her I would operate it, that I had brought it to record her poetry.

She immediately rattled off a couplet, welcoming me to her world:

Na milna, dil pe bojh rakh ke, is tarah
Mulaqaat ho aisi, to bicchadna qubool hai.

Whoa, that was quicker than I could turn the power on in the dictaphone and press record. It was a digital gadget. No tapes and stuff, a high-end dictaphone. Still not fast enough.

Let me translate:

Don't meet me with such a heavy heart
If meetings are like this, then departing is better.

(The Urdu is more poetic than my translation.)

Her Urdu, for someone who had never spoken it, nor was a particularly avid watcher of the 50s Hindi movies was impressive. Even if she was quoting something she'd heard or read, the accent wasn't Bengali. I would get the next one, I promised.

'Good luck with that. I'll see you in the evening,' Didi said, guessing my plans as I fiddled with the dictaphone.

'It's cool,' I said, noticing for the first time how tired Didi looked, 'I can spend the night here. You rest.'

'We'll see, she can be quite a handful.'

With that Didi dialled Ashok and left. Baba left a little later.

Thamma was a handful. She threw tantrums with the nurses, refusing to do as they told, she spat out her food, she was childish at times, aloof and unresponsive at others. She was a totally different person from the Thamma I knew. Why hadn't they given me some indication of the actual effect of her stroke? By nine-thirty at night, the dictaphone was lying unused and I was lying on the sofa, totally spent. Even though all I had done was call the nurses in, and sometimes help them move Thamma from side to side, watch over her and just react to what she did or said. I couldn't believe it was this exhausting. Didi came in. Somehow, the Sens had managed to procure an extra visitor pass. That helped our relay system.

'I'm okay to stay,' I feigned. I sat around for about two minutes to show that I meant it.

'Will you hurry up with your drama and get a move on, Ashok is waiting downstairs.'

I got up.

'It's really all right, Aanu, I'm used to doing the night shift. Anyway once she's asleep, I meditate. It's fine.'

I gave Thamma's hand a squeeze, then dragged my feet walking out of the room. As soon as I was out of Didi's line of sight, I rushed downstairs to get a lift with Ashok. Catching an auto at that time would have been painful and I was too pooped to get into a negotiation battle. I didn't even know what the multiplier for the current rates was.

Sure enough, Ashok was waiting at the exit. We chit-chatted on the drive back. Doing the driver's duty had made Ashok more conversational than I remembered. He seemed to be in good form. Doing well at work. Good in most ways except one. Once this thing was over, they might look to adopt, he told me. After all, Thamma was a floor above the maternity ward.

On reaching home, I ate a quick dinner with Ma, who was as quiet as Ashok had been chatty and then I hit the sack. I slept till lunch time the next day. Baba went to do the day shift without me. Ma was sympathetic. She said the first day was rough and then one got used to the schedule. I asked Ma what the latest update on Thamma was. She informed me that Didi said the doctors wanted to keep her for a few more days for observation, they weren't terribly thrilled by Thamma's Urdu recitation.

I stayed at home, thinking I would catch up with some of the Delhi gang, but felt guilty for socialising while the rest of my family made tiffin or argued with the nurses. Then with nothing left to do, I called Didi and told her I would do the night shift.

At around half past nine in the evening I took an auto to St Ignatius. Baba was relieved to see me, he said she'd been a terror during the day. I could believe him. She was dozing, snoring even. She must have expended all her stroke-induced energy during the day.

I sat on the hospital sofa noticing for the first time how much it resembled a railway bunk. The dark blue leather roughly the same width. Wide enough to sit on without your legs dangling, and if you spread the bedsheet, long enough to sleep on. I looked at the bedroll thinking I should spread it, get ready for the night, but I wasn't sleepy just yet. So I drew up the chair next to Thamma and sat looking at her. At the woman who ran the family and who had had such a profound influence on my life.

She lay with her mouth open. Breathing in deeply, her chest rising and then collapsing like a faulty accordion. The nurses, since I couldn't see Baba doing it, had tied her hair into two small pony-tails. She looked like a kindergarten kid with progeria. I felt a huge wave of sadness well up. I found it hard to believe that modern medicine couldn't find a way of curing her. It was just a stroke, they were common. Surely they had blood-thinners, clot-dissolvers, circulation-boosters, dissolving glues, stents, whatever, to fix this kind of thing.

Who was I kidding? Western medicine, pah! It was just so limited. What was its history compared to that of civilisation? Of recorded medicinal systems even? Any system that ignored other systems that had come before it because of hubris or a so-called scientific temper, had to be guilty of some contradiction. What did they know about what it meant to be human? Their knowledge was based on cadavers, of a generalised opinion of the body and organs. Any idiot could tell you that we're not all the same body. To treat a generalised body is like treating the dead circuit on a computer. At most they could abstract what a working body's organs should be doing, but did they really know what they *did*? Why do we fall prey to one disease and not the other when faced with the same viruses? Why are some people prone to some kinds of diseases? Why can you hack off some parts and expect things to be much the same but not what seem like equivalent parts? They might understand organs, but not what it meant to be a human. In a world manifestly dual-natured, how could they treat just the matter? They shouldn't just have been on the lookout for blood clots in the brain, they should have been tracing the energy medians in Thamma's body. If they were even vaguely interested in healing, the energy that coursed through the human body was very visible.

You can trace the energy medians by the way the cells change in pattern, the way the hair grows and is aligned on the skin. The ways the circulatory system curves and bends. The way the muscles are formed. You can sense it in the path the breath takes, the way food digests. Why do we have hair in our armpits? They think it must be to do with pheromones. You would have a better answer if you looked at the Chinese drawings on lines of force. They intersect under the arm. The hair is insulation. But heck, no it's better to consider them as pheromone dissipators. They should have checked all the blockages, not just the one in the brain, because a block in one place, increases the resistance of the flow, and thus it's bound to cause a short-circuit somewhere else, but no, they failed to appreciate how balanced the body is. Pretenders treating the material body, when it's just so obvious that what runs the body isn't matter.

I moved my palms slowly about two inches above Thamma's arms. Trying to sense just where the blockages were. Feeling with my mind for the flow of her energy. I moved my palms in circles over her abdomen, trying to ease the flow of the energy at her core. I cupped my hand over her forehead trying to pass energy on to her brain. I couldn't massage the energy meridians that ran through her back without waking her, but I willed them to flow.

I probed with my mind, feeling for bottlenecks in her medians. I could sense one in her shoulder, one near her heart, two on the legs just above the back of the knee and two in her head. Deep in her brain.

Thamma I will cure you. Let that be my thanks to you.

I continued, hands moving in circles, in expanding and

then contracting spirals. Clockwise for one half of the body, anti for the other half. Synchronising each revolution with her breath, mind probing, will focusing on the energy, urging it to flow unblocked. Soon my breathing was synchronised with Thamma's and my hands to the rise and fall of her chest.

I realised it was morning when the nurses walked in with the morning dose of medication. I was fast asleep on the sofa. Healing was tiring.

Thamma woke, grumbled to the nurses, beamed at me sitting on the sofa. Then I left the room while the nurses cleaned her and did other things that nurses do. Didi came soon after.

'So how was it?' she asked.

'Not bad at all. She slept through the night quite peacefully,' I replied, honestly.

'Wow. Even in this state she's picking favourites. She hasn't slept through the night once when I've done the nights.'

I smiled. I was her favourite after all, no contest, no point denying it.

I slept through the day and went back in the night. Didi spoke in hushed tones when I walked into the room.

'Did something happen last night?'

I shook my head.

'Except for one very childlike fit, she's been dozing through most of the day.'

Hmm, I thought. Something had worked. Or not.

'Also no Urdu couplets. Not even when the nurse dropped her bedpan,' she said.

I nodded taking that in, that could be good or bad.

'Well then be prepared for a terrible night. She's bound to be awake soon and full of energy. God help you.' Saying that she left.

I sat and watched Thamma for a while. Her laboured, ragged breathing. The monitor beeping its regular beep. The screen showing the jump at the start of the systolic and the half jump at the start of the diastolic. Erratic like the distracted scribbles of a junior-schooler. It all looked a lot like the day before, but I must have done her some good to give her a day of rest. I would continue with the healing tonight. Let St Ignatius take the credit if they had to.

I walked over to her, shut my eyes and began. I let my palms move two to four inches over her body, feeling for the energy medians. Feeling for the lines of force. When I found one, I would run my palm with the flow of energy. Stopping at bottlenecks to ease them. Much as you would do with any pipe or drain. If your pipes are clean, you can be as healthy as a god.

I kept working. I forgot myself. I was just moving my hands through little streams of energy. Willing them to come clean, willing Thamma to get well. Willing the clots to dissolve, the energy medians to dilate, the forces to flow. After about half an hour of this I think I heard Thamma stirring.

Then suddenly her eyes snapped open.

'Anando!' She looked at me, 'What are you doing?'

I must have looked like a bad magician or music conductor or pervert, with my arms outstretched, hovering on top of her body. Perspiring, tired. 'Er…trying to help you,' I mumbled.

'There's no need of that. I'm quite all right.' She looked like she thought I'd been up to no good. Then she kicked at the bedsheet that covered her. Either it was the energy my healing had unleashed that had heated her up or she wanted to check whether she'd been touched.

I backed off to go sit on the sofa, but she snapped, 'No, don't sit, I have something to tell you and I can't shout.' She must have decided that I was her respectful grandson, and couldn't have been feeling her up. Or whatever.

I stood at the side of her bed, feeling guilty. Sitting would have made her have to crane her neck. Guilty because I guess I was trying something alternative, and it felt illegal.

'You must not marry right away, Anando, even if you have a girl.' It was as though we were in the middle of discussing my love life and she'd taken a break to get a sip of water, and then continued.

'What? Thamma...I...' So she did think I was up to something sexual.

'Yes, you have so much potential,' she said, her voice dropping.

I leaned closer to hear how she'd reached the conclusions she had.

'You remind me so much of Bubai. Your Kaka.'

Kaku was nearly all-good, so it was a relief, she didn't think I was some pervert.

'I'm not going to marry a Muslim, Thamma, don't worry, I have...'

'Don't be stupid, Anando. You all misunderstand me, my reasons. I wasn't against Abhijeet marrying a Muslim. I was against him marrying at all,' she said, and then paused to let it sink in. I bit my lip trying to figure out where she was going with that. She continued, 'It's not that I like the Muslims, good heavens no, I saw what they were capable of after Partition, but I'm not against them. They have their faith and we have ours.'

'Then what...' I started.

'Oh, but he was so gifted. There's so much he could have done. Instead he let it dissipate by marrying.'

'I see...' I didn't.

'Do you?' she said, sharply. It was the same tone she used when speaking to my mother, or other people who didn't see the world her way.

'Well then, don't dissipate away. Use what you have been given. This family is touched by God, you are touched by God, use that. Become the best you can.'

I nodded. There was no point speaking to have her cut you down before you completed a sentence. Besides I had to think this through. She looked so demanding, I wanted to rise to my potential, God knows I did, the signs just hadn't come. If they came and coincided with Mitali's affections, well then I would be in a pretty difficult position.

'Abhijeet could have done a lot, been someone of importance in the world, but he sacrificed what he could have been for what he thought was love. I ask you, is he happy now?'

That, I thought, was an unfair question to ask anyone.

I nodded again, an ambiguous nod. The nod of a devoted indulgent grandson, neither agreeing nor being so impolite as to disagree with an ailing grandparent.

'Look at you nodding like a fool,' she said with grandparental hauteur.

Then she glared at me, I could feel her trying to turn on her X-ray vision.

'I understand Thamma, I won't marry right away.' Mitali needed much convincing, it would take several months, years even. 'And I will try to be better, be what you think I should be.'

Her gaze softened. She said nothing for a while, just looked, either gauging my potential or perhaps it was affection. 'Ha, maybe I was wrong about you after all.' She seemed calmer, she moved her palm to cover mine. 'Bend over,' she demanded and as I did, she kissed my forehead. This was more affection than I had received from her all my life. I was nearly moved to tears.

'Well, you'll do what you're supposed to, I suppose. Now I have to sleep,' she announced. And then as if a switch had been flicked, she dozed off.

I stood there for a while, unbelieving. She had been childish and spouting Urdu poetry all these days, for a day she just sleeps, then suddenly she wakes and speaks cogently on why she disapproved of my uncle's marriage and advises me to not dissipate and be the best that I could be.

A lot of things to consider, but I could only think of one thing—was this my first miracle?

I looked at her dozing peacefully, her breathing seemed more regular, less laboured and it was hypnotic, I might have dozed off myself if I didn't feel so charged. Was this the sign that I had asked for?

It was a great morning when it came. Sunny and cool. Octobers in Delhi could surprise you. I was looking out of the window, following the seemingly random flight patterns of the birds, when the nurses came. They made the usual apologetic noises for me to leave the room and I left. I went to the canteen downstairs, since it would take at least fifteen minutes for them to finish their morning duties.

I got myself a vegetable patty and sweet dispenser-tea. It was a stale patty and sweet, sweet tea but it felt good. Thamma had risen and spoken just like she used to. Like the woman we all knew she was. Like the one who controlled her life and that of everyone else in her ambit. She was no longer spouting Urdu poetry or acting like a five-year-old. I had healed her. Perhaps some day I would write a paper on medicine. I took another bite of stale potatoes and peas and looked at all the harassed, tired, bedraggled faces around me. There was so much I could offer them, there was so much good I could do, my heart wanted to reach out and help them all so bad, I thought it might break free of my chest. I noticed that my phone had buzzed. It was on silent, I must have done that when I came in for the night shift. Didi was trying to reach me.

'Whr r u? Come 2 d room.'

She must have come in for the morning shift early and was irked to not find me manning the post. Or the doctors had discovered the progress in Thamma's health and wanted to know just how I'd managed. They wouldn't ask me straight up, they'd think it was all their drugs and IV bottles, but when they did come around, I could point them in the right direction. Ask them to study the basic precepts of Chinese medicine, Reiki and Ayurveda. It would be hard for them to accept a different way, but you can't argue with results. Their way was flawed.

I sauntered up. Just outside the room, Didi saw me and got off the phone.

'Where the heck have you been?' she snapped.

'I was just getting something to eat, Didi, I mean what's with the…'

'Thamma's had another stroke. The doctor suspects it happened in her sleep, but wants to know if anything odd happened last night.'

The doctor on duty was standing next to Thamma making notes on his binder, I walked in and explained that she had woken and spoken to me, and seemed quite normal, her old self when she did. I left out the part about my uncle's marriage and my healing. The doctor nodded and made some notes.

'Well Mr Sen, her speaking to you 'normally' given her condition these last few weeks, was not normal,' he admonished in a calm, almost soothing voice.

I nodded. I could see Didi shaking her head.

'That must have been the result of the stroke. Or she may have had it soon after. We will be moving her to the ICU, and will have to run some tests, I'm paging Dr Bhatia, the head of neurology,' he finished.

'Okay,' I said and sat down, I wasn't sure I'd heard him clearly with the blood thrumming in my ears. Had he said ICU? Neurology?

Didi conferred with him, while I just looked at Thamma's prone form. Within half an hour Thamma was plugged into at least three different machines and two tubes in the intensive care unit. I was allowed in for about a minute because I insisted on seeing her and then I was asked to leave.

Didi and I sat on the benches outside the ICU and waited. Then since nothing seemed to be happening, we went and had chai in the canteen. I was pretty dog-tired by then.

Didi made some stern eye contact across the formica-topped table and asked, 'Did anything weird happen?'

I told her about what Thamma had said about Kaku's marriage.

'Hmm…interesting. Anything else? What prompted her to talk about Kaku's marriage?'

'Nothing. I was standing next to her. I was willing her to get better, then suddenly her eyes popped open, and she told me I reminded her of Kaku and asked me not to marry.'

'Willing her to get better?' The emphasis on the willing. Didi was a damned bloodhound.

'Yes willing, trying to heal her spiritually,' I said.

'Just willing, huh?' she went on.

'Yup.'

We sat in silence for a minute.

'Well, I guess no harm could come of that,' she didn't say it like she meant it, but she was letting me off the hook. 'What else did she say, I'm interested.'

I told her verbatim as much as I could remember what she'd said.

'Ah, she was always so fond of you. I mean why would she care what I became, you're the grandson, you'll take the mighty name of the Sens forward. The Baidyas will conquer the world.'

Then she went quiet, I'm not sure why, but I guess the thought of taking the name forward may have triggered the memory of her miscarriage.

Her silence sat there between us. Everything that Didi

did that morning was making me anxious. She must have been doing this deliberately. To punish me for 'willing' Thamma to health. If I had a stroke at that moment, there would be no question who was responsible. For god's sakes, I had only been trying to help and there was no doubt that I'd made some headway. If this wasn't my first case of healing, I would have known when to stop and what to change.

Didi asked me to go home and bathe and rest, but I didn't want to go. I suppose it was guilt or concern. Later in the day we visited Thamma in turns. She was conscious but back to being childish, except that half her face didn't move. She was bawling one moment, giggling and gurgling the next and had trouble recognising us. She mistook the nurse for Didi and me for her husband.

When he finally came after all his surgeries and private patients, Dr Bhatia didn't look happy. He said a proper diagnosis was only possible after the test results came in, but he sort of hinted that it was damn serious. Later, when he had the results he asked us to call in the rest of the family.

We did. There wasn't much of a family to call.

Kaku came soon, mercifully without his wife. He stayed in Bombay, so he was a flight away. I knew that but I hadn't contacted him in all my months in Bombay. I was just following family protocol. It was good to finally meet him and see that he had the Sen look, the roundness of face and largeness of forehead, despite Thamma's insistence that he was not a Sen anymore.

Baby Pishi and Khuku Pishi, my father's cousins, came a few days later. They had spent quite a bit of their childhood under Thamma's care, due to the vagaries of their father's business. Their younger brother Sudipto, aka Tubu Kaku was a little more distant, growing up when his father's business was more stable and hence with little recollection of Thamma's care and kindness.

St Ignatius ran dozens of tests. The lab was so busy, we had to get some of them done from labs outside. In between hearing Baby Pishi's rather teary tales of how she was forever indebted to Kakima's kindness and Khuku Pishi's probing enquiries into my life, I managed to get some time with Kaku. We used his office car for the running around. He caught up on the histories of the Sens of Green Park and I on the Sen and Ansari of Worli, career choices, how Delhi had changed and felt different after you had lived in Bombay. While waiting for results at a swanky new pathological lab in Hauz Khas, I managed to extract his 'ghost story'.

I was spooked by it. There was no debating that Kaku had his dealings with ghosts. Thamma had found us similar, so what was I going to run into? Who was going to scratch me? I knew I must not be scared, gifts come with their dark side and if I had to meet a ghoul, I would. Though I didn't want to be dealing with the dead, or those in limbo, just yet. Some breathing exercises were called for.

After spending a week in the ICU, and being declared stable, Thamma was moved back into a private room. Baby Pishi and Khuku Pishi took this as a sign that she was getting better, said their teary byes and caught trains or flights back home. Or both, I remember trips to both the airport and the station to drop them off.

Kaku stayed on. He was seeing his mother after many years. Or he sensed something else. That night, I decided that I would do night duty again. Didi arched her eyebrows but let it be. Kaku spent the days with Thamma. He said he had much to talk to her about, apologise, explain. Thamma seemed happy with him. He was her favourite before I came on the scene, I guess he was back to being the favourite now that they were on talking terms again. Whenever I walked in for the night shift I saw him sitting by her side, her hand in his. He speaking softly, soothingly, she looking at him like an adoring child, her cheeks and pillowcase wet with tears. If only they had been less adamant, less ready to take such hard positions, she might not have had a stroke in the first place.

The third night that I spent there, I began to hear sounds. It's difficult to describe them, but it sounded like an army. Not a modern army, not even a medieval one, there was something ancient about it. There were bells, chanting, and the thump of footsoldiers, cavalry perhaps. The movement of heavy carts. It was distant. St Ignatius is in East of Kailash and if I was to estimate where the sounds were coming from, it seemed to be from the Yamuna or across the Yamuna, several kilometres away. I couldn't really hear the sounds in the morning, but as I sat alone with Thamma at night I could hear them, distant and muffled.

I asked the nurses if there was something up, but they just looked upset to be reminded that there was an outside world. So I tried figuring what it could be. I even asked a doctor whether he heard any distant sounds of bells, but seeing his reaction, I didn't probe. I didn't want to be admitted for tinnitus or something.

There was not much to do. I didn't really want to try healing. It was obviously potent, but I needed to learn more technique and I couldn't practice on Thamma. There was nothing to do at night but sleep, I guess. It's just that the sounds were there now through the night, faint but disturbing. There was something peculiar about them that I hadn't put my finger on.

I paced around the room thinking about everything that had happened, Thamma's instructions to me before her second stroke, or as a result of, what was I to believe in? Thamma's mini recovery then collapse, was that a little window her brain gave her to relay something important to me? Kaku's story, the world of the dead, so close to us, so ready to interfere. I left the bathroom light on, since I was seeing more moving shadows after hearing his stories and I wanted to be sure there was no trick of the light when I met my first spirit. I was considering everything that I had experienced the last few days, when I noticed the little picture of Shiva by the bedside table, that Kaku had left for Thamma. It was a typical calendar art illustration, with Shiva in three-fourths of a profile in what looked like a silver/chrome alloy frame. A rather dashing Shiva. Noble, handsome and somewhat dangerous. Thamma's favourite god. I knew from family history, that this was a much-loved representation of him, since it was a picture she had lovingly given Kaku when he went to the college hostel. I'm assuming it was to give him strength to face ragging, engineering and other challenges faced by Bengali men leaving their homes for the first time. Now he had brought it back. She had more serious challenges to face.

Shiva, the lord of the ganas.

I had finally figured what the sounds I had been hearing were. It was the sound of Shiva's army of ganas. I looked at Thamma, sleeping peacefully and realised they were coming for her. Slowly, taking their time. Announcing their intentions, as they ought to, when coming for the devout.

So now I could sense death coming. Cool. How had that happened? Just a progression of my gifts. Was this the beginning of seeing more spirits and other things? No, it felt like there was something else to it. I was excited, I had to figure it out. More pacing ensued.

What was it that Baba had said? He didn't smell death anymore which meant he'd willed his gift away. The only way to do that was to pass it on and who else but his son, his flesh and blood. Someone with biological rights to his inheritance. He would have to know that I was willing, I couldn't remember him asking me, perhaps he had in a roundabout way. He must have figured that since I already had gifts of my own, and was open to the psychic world, the forces above, channels and energies, I would be an easy receiver. It would have made it easier to transfer, but he must have done some serious willing and mantra-making of his own. Just when you think you know your family they surprise you. Trust you Baba, and well, thank you.

Indeed if this was the approach of death then I was hearing it, not smelling. Also not alarmed or knocked dysfunctional by it. Gifts transmute then, when they pass. That must be the case, or they must react with what I already had and change. How interesting, every day spent with Thamma had been a lesson.

If Baba had passed his gift on, then unfortunately, that could only mean that Thamma was dying. I could hardly announce that though, what good would that do? She had lived a full life and met the people who cared about her. I guess it was as good a time to go as any. We had to accept her passing, Baba's gift-transfer at least allowed me the time to say goodbye properly.

So I held Thamma's hand and wished her well. Another adventure awaited her on the other side, I prayed for her, that she would have the right guides and friendly souls to help her in her journey. Most of all I thanked her for her role in my life and for everything she had done for the family. I said all this softly, so as not to wake her, but loud enough to register in her subconscious. It was a few hours' walk at best on foot from the Yamuna, god knows when the ganas were scheduled to come. It was best to say farewell properly.

Two days later Thamma died.

Her breathing slowed and slowed till they had to take her to the ICU. There her heart stopped beating. I think she went as peacefully as you could in a hospital.

The ganas had walked slowly.

She was cremated old-style at the Nigambodh ghat by the banks of the Yamuna. I think she had left instructions not to be put through the newfangled electric crematoriums. I thought it would take longer, but it only took about three hours for her body to go. It's funny how a lifetime of thoughts, actions, memories takes only three hours to erase. Completely. What was left we gathered in a brass pot, which we took to Haridwar and emptied into the Ganga. I offered to drive to Garhmukhteshwar and

Shujoy Dutta

empty it into the Ganga canal there, but Baba had turned quite devout.

We went in two taxis to Haridwar. Didi, Ma and Baba in one, Kaku and I in the other. It was a quick affair, then we went straight to the ghats, identified the pandits who perform the ceremony, they did their little haggling, then there were some pandas to pay for all the things that needed to be bought and donated and then Baba walked into the river with the ashes. It barely took an hour.

It was a quiet drive while going, and a nearly quiet drive back. Somewhere near the new Muzzafarnagar bypass, Kaku asked me, 'Anando, you were asking about everyone's stories a few days ago. I think you were calling them the story of our gifts…'

'Yeah Kaku, it's just I'm in no mood to…'

'Did you work it out?'

'Work what out? I was just…'

'Did you ever wonder…or ask your Thamma, what her gift was?' he asked.

No, that thought hadn't struck me. I don't know why.

He went on, without a comment from me. 'She was a remarkable woman, it's not just any woman who can bring up three sons without much help, but I believe her greatest gift was persuasion,' he said.

'Persuasion?'

'Yes,' he stated. He let it stay there for a bit as the sugarcane fields blurred by.

'She could be very convincing, but it took on an altogether different form, a potency when Baba left,' he said looking out of the window.

'Yeah, Dadu leaving to become a sadhu must have affected her deeply,' I said, urging him to go on.

'Do you still believe that?' Kaku enquired with a little edge in his tone.

'That he left to become a sadhu or that he became one? That's what Thamma told me.'

'Yes, I know…' he seemed saddened by that.

'Thamma was always worried about the men in the family leaving, that they never returned home, that the family was touched by God, and it affected everyone differently,' I explained. I wanted to make Thamma's side of the story clear, I owed her that.

'That's why you think we all have gifts, we're touched by God?' he sort of half asked and half stated, as we both turned to look at each other.

'Yes,' I said.

'I'm not sure they're gifts Anando…they're not gifts at all.'

'What? Why do you say that Kaku?'

'Your Dadu contacted me, this must have been when Dada died in the war.'

'What? Why didn't you tell anyone?' This was a bloody bomb.

'He was living with his mistress,' pat came the answer.

'Oh.' This got better. Or worse. Something inside me began to feel loose.

'He had left home to be with her. I guess he got bored with domesticity. With three boys and having to bear the burden of his other brother's children every now and then,' Kaku said.

My head was swimming in some sort of viscous slow-moving fluid. I couldn't believe this. Dadu, I had always been led to believe, was a most spiritual man.

230 *Shujoy Dutta*

More so, as he'd gone from being a dandy to becoming a sadhu.

Kaku continued, 'Ma became a little strange after that. Insisting that we were all special, protected. She was always on the lookout for abilities in all of us. I was established as the one who could see spirits. Your Baba was older, but she made it out to be like he had visions. She made a big deal about the dreams that he had. I think she managed to convince him over time. You said something about being able to smell death right?'

I nodded.

'Even Chhorda, who was the practical one, who perhaps understood more than he let on, was taken by it. He became more daring than he was, he took on more risks. I think that's why he joined the army as well...

'Your Dadu met me when they brought Chhorda's remains home. He apologised for everything, even asked me to stay with him for a few days, saying that Rabiaji— that was his mistresses's name—had always been very fond of me. But I was too angry to listen to him. I told him he was dead to us, I think he spoke to your Baba too, but I can't be sure, you'll have to ask him.'

I doubted that I was going to bring it up. My ticket was booked for the next day. But it was more the other flotsam that was surfacing inside my head.

'I did tell Ma, your Thamma, about it, but she was convinced I had lost my mind from the grief of Chhorda's death. She knew, I believe from the start, but never accepted it. It hurt her. And by then she had this make-believe world where we were all so special. The only thing that nearly broke her is when I told her that I was in love with Sabira...' he said.

'What? Why? She told me...'

'Because your grandfather's mistress was Muslim too. A poetess, quite well known in Delhi at the time. She was the petni that I saw. All the times I saw her, she must have been visiting Baba. The day I saw her outside the shed in the rain, I'm sure now that she was wearing dark glasses to hide her face. Now that I think about it, given all Chhorda's stories, he must have known too. Hah. Ma must have learnt all that Urdu poetry, to see what your Dadu found attractive or to get him back, I don't know what. It's just sad. It's a sad sad business. The stroke was a long time in the making, I'm not surprised it was so severe.'

This was getting worse. Was Kaku the crazy one, or Thamma or was I?

'What did she tell you?' he asked me, looking out at the sugarcane fields.

'Nothing really, how she wasn't that upset that you married a Muslim,' I replied.

'Really? Good to know. Hard to believe really, but I wish she'd told me. Sabby would be happy to know,' he said, still looking out.

I left it at that. No point asking anything or messing with Kaku's mind, since I couldn't tell true from false at the moment. All I knew was that I was feeling nauseous. Either from motion-sickness or the revelations. Actually it wasn't nausea as much as this pain, slowly growing inside. Not a knock-you-out kind of pain, but something incisive and deep. Not a large flesh wound as much as something small and sharp being thrust in, like a pinprick to the heart.

He continued. 'I didn't know that you didn't know about your Dadu. He was a weak man. Despite that, your Thamma loved him. That's why she went on so many pilgrimages. It was partly for the pilgrimage, but also for the possibility that she would meet him at some dhaam. She had persuaded herself of it. Sad, to put yourself through so much for such a selfish man. Anyway, no point speaking ill of the dead; he went a few years ago. You need to be strong for your family now.'

'Yeah, Thamma's absence will be a huge hole in the flat,' I said, nodding.

'Not just her, I think the house is going,' he said.

'What?' Good lord, the flat, this couldn't be happening.

'Yeah, I'm surprised you don't know? Your Baba has it as collateral for the business, his partners pulled out last year, so the bank is eyeing the house.'

I wanted to get out of the car and retch.

We stopped at a roadside dhaba just before we hit the Meerut bypass and I used the water from a tubewell to wash my face. I had to jog the pump a few times for the water to flow long enough for me to hold my head under. It felt better but only a little. Why hadn't anyone told me? What was I being shielded for? I could've chipped in, what the heck was I earning for anyway? I was coming back, Fulscreme be dammed. I had to make sure we didn't lose the flat. Worst case scenario, at least arrange some place for them to stay. I was sure I could get a loan for a decent place in Gurgaon. It would be a hike for them, and far away from friends and all that was familiar, but it would be a roof. If only the nausea would pass and I could think clearly. I made a mental note of applying for sick leave when I came back for the shraadh. I had to sort this out. I had to be there for my parents.

When I asked Baba about the house, he asked me not to worry, that the bank was not going to get it, and what business was it of Kaku's advising me on what to do, when he had stopped being a part of the house.

I thought I would stay on, but I left for Bombay. The nausea was, if anything, getting worse. I would have to go see a doctor. It could be a depressed nerve or something, perhaps it was better to get some sulphur-dioxide-soaked sea air. The flight was crazy, there was tons of turbulence and I kept getting these memory flashes from childhood. Also the nausea was not passing, it was accompanied by an ache inside, like trapped gas, but my stomach was fine.

When I got to the apartment I found it disorderly and untidy. Bhaskar just couldn't be trusted to act like an adult. I cleaned the living room and my room, which clearly had been used for some physical activity. In putting away things I found Dadu's cuff links. I had mixed feelings about it, but Thamma had given them to me with all her love. So I promised myself that I would buy or get a shirt tailored that allowed me to wear those cuff links and look like a burra saab.

Back at work, there was no problem looking like I had come back from a serious tragedy. I did. My beard was scruffy and thanks to the nausea, I hadn't slept. As a result my eyes were puffy. Usually people pass the typical jibes about you taking three weeks off work, but on that day people greeted me with nods and sympathetic low voices.

I dealt with their faux sympathy and with the five hundred odd mails. Two hundred of which were from the Apnamart team. I would have done okay, reintegrated back into the RG fold, had people I didn't really know, not paused by my desk to give me the 'how're you holding up' nod on their way to coffee. Plus there was the nausea, which was turning into a bit of a headache. It got so bad, that I asked Shreya and Rupesh, with whom I had had a total of fifteen minutes of interaction in my life (they were on other teams but we shared the same boss) if they wanted a drink in the evening. I think they agreed out of sympathy and that put me off, even more.

We went to the office bar. Well it's the bar closest to office where people usually drop in for a bit before heading home. So there are always some RG people and usually some competitors to eavesdrop. We spoke about RG and our boss—the only common ground we had and then I proceeded to get massively drunk. I figured it would kill the headache, nausea and help me not recollect the last few days and other sundry shit that was popping in my head.

I remember speaking a lot to the two of them, telling them their futures but I can't be sure. I was drinking too fast and I can't remember whether I ate at all. I was upset with Thamma's death or with Kaku's revelations, I don't know. I drank and I didn't care what I was drinking. It was good to be with the two of them, they were easy, relaxed, I couldn't believe we hadn't hung out more. Rupesh was quite the elder brother type and Shreya was cute, but I was in love with Mitali. I can't remember if I hit on her though. I wanted to call Mitali, I think, but Rupesh stopped me from drunk-dialling. I think Shreya was insisting at the time to be dropped home. I can't remember very much after that. I think I caught a cab home, I can't be sure.

The next day, I walked in bleary-eyed to work around lunchtime. It wasn't a big deal, since I'd been bleary-eyed the day before too and everyone knew that I had come back from a personal loss. People would attribute it to the sorrow and not to drunkenness. They'd say the tragedy had hit me hard. It had. I reached my desk to see a post-it on my laptop.

'URGENT. Meet me when you get in.' Scribbled in a rushed hand, 'Urgent' underlined twice, the second underline had ripped the paper. It was my boss.

I would just tell him I was upset, sick and needed the drink yesterday since Rupesh and Shreya would have ratted on me anyway. I took a couple of deep breaths, checked my breath for alcohol against my palm, and walked into his room looking busy and ready with the apology. 'Sorry boss, things have been rough.' I said before he could spew any venom.

'Sit, Anando. Sit,' he said, calmly, playing some other game, or just in another phase of the game.

He looked serious, not angry, just serious. 'What's all this that I hear?' he asked paternally.

'I went out with Shreya and Rupesh, I got drunk, my grandmother's death was more painful than I realised I guess.' It was near enough to the truth. 'Why, what did Shreya and Rupesh say?'

'It's not Shreya and Rupesh, Anando, everyone has been saying things,' he said.

'You gotta be kidding me, Ashish.' I never really used his name, but then he was not that much older than me.

'Anando, do you remember what you said last night to everyone?' he asked, still very calm.

'Not all of it. No, I was very drunk as I told you,' I replied sharply, irritated that one night was being made a big deal of. I mean, come on give a guy a break.

'You announced to everyone, that you could tell their futures. When people asked, you said, 'I can see you making more unbelievable claims on behalf of your brands and fighting with legal over it.' He sat back and looked at me, awaiting an explanation.

'Ha, did I?'

'Now ordinarily, it could pass off as a joke, because whatever you may think personally about your job and the organisation, shouldn't matter, but Urmila Bisht was also in the bar, and she did not like it.'

No kidding. Urmila Bisht, our MD, was there. In such a low-key bar? Weird. Must have been poaching someone or something. 'Right,' I said.

'She asked HR to look you up, and they told her what they had told me before.'

I looked blank, waiting for him to explain.

'What is this shit about being psychic?' he fired, for the first time sounding irritated.

'Err…what?' It was embarrassing to admit to it at work. I mean I was, but it felt shady, illegal. Like admitting to being related to the mafia or something. It's not something you discuss with your boss, next they'll be asking why it wasn't on my CV.

He continued, without waiting for me to reply, 'I mean

initially we all thought you did it for a laugh. However, HR spotted that you were spending all your time on the Intranet, so basically people figured that you were reporting stuff that you read there.'

I gulped, my throat was dry. I could see myself sitting in front of him listening, but I was detaching.

'HR usually files the time you spend online and they found you spending a disproportionate amount of time on the Intranet.'

The snoopy assholes. 'What, really?' I asked.

'Yeah, then it became a joke. Someone would post something online and then ask you about their lives when they went to get a coffee, just to see how often you were checking their profile. You were fucking obsessed.'

The headache was intensifying with every pulse. I could feel the throb-throb of mounting pressure on the temples, at the back, on the top, on the insides. As if blood was going into the head, but unable to make its way out.

'You mean they were all just…'

'What is it that you told Anvita?' That was his wife. 'You told her, her dad was sick,' he said his voice rising.

'Is he?'

'Of course he is, I've been on the phone every day about it. Even sometimes during meetings. I couldn't believe that you would try to pass that off as being a psychic. I ignored this whole psychic, ESP crap the first few months, thinking you were lonely coming in from Delhi and it was something silly, a stunt to make friends with. But now it's become a big deal, with Mrs Bisht getting involved.'

'So what are you saying?' I asked.

'Get a hold on yourself for god's sakes. Stop acting so stupidly. Get some help.'

He wasn't firing me but he did say for god's sakes. I remember that. There was little to be gained by apologising or anything, so I went back to my desk. The headache was much worse. An un-hangover kind of headache. I went to the loo, I washed my face, splashed water. Poured water on my head, and it wouldn't go. So I went inside a stall and tried to relax, tried to shit out whatever toxins I had consumed the night before.

No shit. But the memory flashes were more vivid. I remembered reading people's profiles. I remembered telling people, almost verbatim the words I'd read on their pages. Sometimes things wouldn't come to me right away, I couldn't quite recall a factoid, so I would ask them to tell me their name, their date of birth, all the stuff you usually require for astrology or numerology. But that would help jog my memory, and before I knew it, I'd recollect what I had seen and would spew stuff about them.

I got sick. I retched all over the loo. It took some serious washing up. I managed somehow. The squirter is a useful invention. Got up and left the stall. Then I packed my desk and left for home, I couldn't bear to be at work. Everyone looked and smirked and whispered and ducked laughing. Assholes and their condescending glances. They had been playing me, god, they had all been playing me.

I collapsed on the sofa as soon as I got home. I felt exhausted physically but my mind was on overdrive. I tried calming myself down, but I couldn't stop the memory flashes. The many, many rememberings, all the neural links that were twisted and knotted were unravelling. Heck, I suddenly remembered everything. How it started, how it had progressed, everything.

Bulu Pishi, the one who said she was going abroad. That's how it had all started.

I was there in the living room reading, reading the book on palmistry, when the phone rang. Baba answered it. I remembered hearing his side of the conversation. He must have been speaking to Bulu Pishi's husband. It was, I figured, about coming back, about how the job was not working out. Baba didn't notice me and I didn't notice him, I was absorbed in my book. Or was I? I can see myself sitting there on the sofa, legs across one of the arms in my leopard print shorts. How is it that I can remember now what Baba said on the phone? Did Thamma know about it too? Did she put me up to it or was it innocent grandmotherly fondness?

'Then there's no point taking Ashima there now is it?' Baba had said, concerned.

It must have stuck in the back of my head somewhere.

The teacher at Shiksha, who asked me about her life. She'd made me the legit psychic at school but when she asked about herself, nothing had come to me, till I asked for her full name. Then I remembered the two teachers in the bus talking about Vani's operation. I was reading a book on I-Ching, in the seat, just behind them.

Her name, Vani Gupta. I told her what I'd heard, that she'd had an operation and it had been successful. She had drawn her hand away at that, scared at what I could tell from a cursory glance at her palm. I wasn't reading Ma'am, I was recalling.

Dear god, it was all coming back.

How I was helping Mr Gomes total the English papers in class nine. We were all there in the room, the top five of 9-A and I knew Manish was three marks ahead of me, we were all keeping tabs, we were a competitive lot. I changed the one on five in one of my answers in the paper, to a four on five. That put me ahead, I guess he got half a mark somewhere else.

It was a rush, a rush of memories. Some were deliberate actions on my part, some not. I didn't do it all to get attention, you must believe me. As the years went by I absorbed things perhaps subconsciously. Though it couldn't be entirely subconscious since I remember it all now.

I remembered reading that the Akshardham temple was having its opening ceremony. Those were the bells and sounds that drifted in, almost indistinctly to Thamma's room at St Ignatius. I heard them or maybe I thought I heard them, because I knew it was going on, just on the other side of the Yamuna, and the doctors and nurses had no time for it. Those were the two days before Thamma died. I had lied even to myself. I had pretended to myself that I heard the ganas, that Baba's gift had mutated as it passed on to me.

I remembered offering to carry the corrected test papers in Shiksha and then seeing how the Gifted section had scored. I remembered all the profile pages on the RG Intranet and Orkut and the other sites that I had visited. Lord, what was wrong with me?

As I discovered later, there is a word for this condition, it's called cryptomnesia. Forgetting where you saw or heard something, then thinking it's an original thought of yours.

So it appeared that the only gift I had was forgetting where I read or heard something.

I sat there on the bed in the dark as the memories came and the headache slowly passed. There were just two things to check and one person to check them with. I called Didi. She answered on the third ring.

'Hi, Aanu, tell me.' She sounded so happy.

'How're you doing, Didi?' I tried.

'I'm fine, Aanu, you sound low, has something happened?'

'No, just work. I called to check a couple of things.'

'Yeah, cool, fire away,' she said all upbeat, she must have been doing yoga.

'You remember your college days well don't you?' I started.

'Yeah, of course, it was college, who doesn't?'

'You remember you and Radhika and Urmi and a fourth girl, a friend of yours…'

'Pooja…'

'…came home and did a…'

'…a planchet session. Of course I do. It was so much fun,' she finished for me.

'Fun, was it?'

'Yeah, we were all out to spook Pooja who had been acting all high and mighty,' she said.

'So you were making it up?' I asked.

'Yes Aanu, Radhika and I had a tough time not laughing, trying to pull the coin and then manage the tripod this way and then that. It was so tough, we had to speak the letters we wanted instead of getting to it, because we just couldn't get the coin to stop at the right letter.' She laughed.

'Ah, and what about the spelling backwards?'

'We'd seen that in the horror film, you remember the one about the guy who comes back from the dead in the morgue.'

'No,' I said.

'Haha, yes that could be any horror film. It was in that film, the backward writing.'

'What about Nemo Tisca?' I asked, finally.

She laughed a full throaty laugh at that. 'Oh god, you remember that. You really have a great memory.'

I bit my lip. 'Yes.'

'Ha, I didn't know what name to come up with about who I'd marry. I think you were reading *Twenty Thousand Leagues Under the Sea*, so I think that's what triggered Nemo. It was to make it a little exotic. Then Radhika got into the act and came up with Tisca. She was a classmate of ours who Radhika thought had a crush on me. A lesbian thing was so cool then.' Didi was full of giggles.

'Ah.'

She sensed something was amiss. 'It was all a joke, little brother.'

'Still pretty good acting by you and Radhika.'

'Urmi too. She was totally convincing. Is that all you called for?' Didi asked.

'Just one more thing. You remember Prannoy Uncle had an accident don't you?'

'Ye...s,' she said dragging the word, and paused. 'But that's got nothing to do with the planchet.'

'Do you know how it happened?'

'I do.'

'How?' I had to know.

She was quiet for a bit, I couldn't tell if she was upset or what, then, 'After what he did to me, I went to his house and cut the brakes on his bike.'

'So he fell and lost sense in his hands or something.'

'Yes.'

'Okay, I just wanted to know.'

'Why're you asking this suddenly?' she asked.

'I just needed to know whether you had anything to do with it,' I replied.

She waited, I think she was trying to evaluate if I was judging her harshly or considering her criminal act worth reporting. 'I did. I should have told you or someone before. I feel terrible now.' The giggles were gone.

'It's all right, he deserved it. I gotta go now Didi.' And I hung up before she could ask me or react to anything.

I remembered then, Didi looking up the little navy blue telephone directory that Baba maintained and taking down an address. I remembered glancing at the page later, the only name that jumped out of it was Prannoy Mukherjee. I was reading a book on numerology at the time.

The cellphone rang, it was Didi. I let it ring. The headache had passed but something much worse was growing inside. It felt like the conversation with Kaku all over again. Only this time more dark shit was surfacing. Thamma's Gifts.

I needed tea. Bhaskar, the asshole, had used up all the milk. I picked up some money to go buy some. I must have not found milk right away, because I remember walking to the next shop down the street, and then the one on the main road and then towards the highway. After that I began wandering.

I remember wandering a lot. Wandering to the station. Then into a moving train. Then getting off at another station. Then on again. Then when the ticket collector caught me, off again. Then on again. Then in a compartment with lots of people, then on stations, then on roads, then the memories blur. I wandered a lot. My clothes tore, they became rags. My hair matted. My shoes gave way, and then my socks. The soles of my feet cracked, turned black and hard. What little money I had, I spent somewhere. I begged, I think. I must have looked the part with my unkempt matted mane and beard. I slept at stations, at bus stops, at temples, under flyovers, in the gardens of homes, under parked trucks. I stood in lines at temples which gave out blankets and mosques that fed the poor. I ate at gurudwaras, I sat outside churches for alms. I sat outside dhabas for leftovers. I wandered. I wandered. It must have been damn difficult to find milk.

Fourteen

I can't remember how much I walked, how many train rides I took, or which city or town I stayed in. I remember being hungry, thirsty, cold, hot, ill. I remember defecating in the open, on the side of the roads, on heaps of dirt, on railway tracks, by the banks of nallahs, in the grasses that grow on river banks. I remember picking food off the road, fighting with dogs, being chased by guards, being avoided by passersby, being shooed by cops. I don't remember anything mattering.

I stayed where I had some sort of roof and moved when I felt like or was driven away.

When I came to, I was at sitting on the banks of the Ganga, my back to a wall, at Har ki Pauri in Haridwar. I can't remember how I got there or why. I was in tatters and I was cold. It was early in the morning, just after sunrise and I hugged the tatters to my skin to keep the cold Himalayan wind out. But there was little there to hug. There was a saffron bundle lying close by. It had lain there unclaimed for quite a while. Whichever unfortunate sadhu it belonged to must have gone for a dip and gotten washed away or committed jal samadhi. I waited, watched, no one came for it.

After a while I got up, splashed myself with the river water. I was reeking. It was an unpleasant mixture of faeces, urine, dirt, rot, bodily secretions. Death, my father from an earlier life, would have said. So I got in. It was bone-chillingly cold. I couldn't feel my feet after the first few minutes, but I waded in. After standing waist-deep for a while, I finally took a dip. The cold knocked my breath out but I stayed under. It actually felt good after a while. It made the Himalayan wind feel pleasant when I got out. I had stopped smelling like an Indian Railways toilet.

I stepped out, wore the saffron dhoti and put the angavastram over my shoulders. The clothes smelt of camphor and sweat, but otherwise clean enough. I rested against one of the walls of the buildings that bordered the ghats and began to weep. I wept for myself. For being a bloody fool. For believing I was special, gifted, different. I wept for my Thamma, for her selfish husband. For the damage he'd done to her, and she in turn to us. I wept for the relay of damage. I wept for my family, my family that was touched by God, that discussed God at the breakfast table. I wept for the Sen men who never returned home. I wept for my unborn niece or nephew, my childless uncle, my homeless parents. I wept till I had no more tears, nothing to weep for.

Or because I was distracted by voices around me.

'Dude, he looks like one of those sadhu men, man, I'm sure he could score us some.'

I opened my eyes and saw a group of American students.

There were five of them. Three guys and two girls. Rutgers, it said on one of their sweatshirts.

'You've interrupted his dhyana, fool,' a girl said.

'Sorry to bother you,' the Rutgers boy said, speaking slowly, enunciating each word carefully, 'We were just looking for some ganja.' And he mimed the act of smoking with a chillum.

'You've come all this way to smoke dope?' I asked.

They literally took a step backwards.

'Jesus, he speaks English,' one of the girls exclaimed.

'Wow, do you have any?' the Rutgers boy asked, persistent.

'Of course I speak English, why shouldn't I, and no I don't have any marijuana,' I said curtly.

'Cool, we were just checking.'

'Your English is very good...how do you...' she left it dangling.

I was about to say that I was schooled in it, but then the skinniest of the boys answered for me, 'He's a yogi, man, they know all kinds of things.'

Indeed I did. Most of the time I didn't remember reading or hearing it.

'So you've come all the way from the US, to get high is it? Wouldn't it be cheaper to spend the airfare on dope back there?' I asked them.

'No, we're seeing India,' the more attractive of the girls said, 'but the grass is a plus.'

'That's good,' I said. 'As long as you didn't come here looking for God.' Yes, it's good to be honest.

'You making fun of us?' the lanky boy asked. 'Because man, we are spiritual. We want to connect, I mean we're not yogis, but we care.'

'So have you found God?' the Rutgers guy asked, cutting the lanky one and any response that I may have had to his bull.

'Have I found God?' Had I found God?

'Well, you could say, that God has found me. Or better still that after a lifetime, I have found myself.'

'Whoa, man…I mean, swamiji.' The Rutgers one no longer seemed interested in dope. 'So can you show us how we could do some meditation, like some of the breathing and stuff, do you know mantras, are you some sort of a guru?'

'I doubt that.'

They were disappointed, I think their thoughts returned to getting grass.

'Well, what do you think God is?' I asked, happy for their company, their insulation against the cold mountain wind.

'He's the all-powerful, all-loving one, man,' said one of the boys, I couldn't keep track.

'He's the creator,' another offered.

'Is he all-loving?' I asked. 'Does this world show any evidence of being all-loved?'

They got into a little discussion among themselves, squatting on the steps of the ghat. After a little debate they offered me their concerted opinion.

'God is in everything,' the Rutgers one said.

'Or is God everything?' I asked immediately.

They nodded.

'If God is indeed this world, and everything in it, imagine the world in its entirety, do you think it cares particularly about you?'

They had now lined up on the steps below me. I think they liked the discussion.

'No, the world doesn't care,' one of them said.

'And if you took into account, the solar system, the milky-way, all the stars in it, all the galaxies and all the space in between, dark matter, dark energy, what emotions do they have for you?'

'I'm not sure they have any.'

'Swamiji, you know a lot of physics, man.'

'But that's just the matter, maybe there is an intelligent being behind it,' the lanky guy spoke.

By now we had been joined by some early morning hangers-about. I guess where foreigners crowd around a bearded saffron-clad man in India, a crowd soon forms.

'Let me tell you about God,' I said. And I did. In English and Hindi.

Don't you wonder at how unformed minds are? How conditioned they are by popular religion and TV shows. How they've never really applied commonsense to the one entity that they should have. That they consider so central to their world view, repose faith in, and base their identity on. How half-formed are the questions. How gleeful they were that I uttered their blasphemies for them. That I liberated them of what they could not say and what they could not ask. I asked the questions and gave the answers. How sad that most people didn't discuss God at the breakfast table.

Around afternoon, a man in a dhoti and coat held up his hand as though he had an important point to make, or question to raise. I welcomed the interjection, it was high time they started using their own minds. He stood and looked around before speaking. It seemed like an important point.

'Baba needs some rest,' he said to the gathered folk.

Whoa, I had a manager.

'Yes, yes,' people agreed happily, perhaps I was being too preachy.

I looked a little more closely at my manager. An odd-looking man. Almost as tall as me, but wider. I mean seeing how thin I had become anyone was wider than me, but he was wider than I was when at my heaviest. He had a trimmed moustache, pock or acne marks on his cheeks. There was something asymmetrical about his face. In another life I might have thought he was psychic. No, he wasn't psychic but he had something cruel about his face. A man who knew how the world worked and liked manipulating it. Whatever was he doing in little Haridwar? He could have easily blended into the mafia in Bombay or the politics of Delhi.

'We can all meet after lunch,' he offered to the disappointed audience.

They all agreed, philosophy and religion make us hungry. No wonder the lunches at religious sermons are so hearty.

Banwari Lal, that's what his name was, introduced himself to me and invited me to his home. He offered me his hall to continue my pravachan, if that was all right with me. I didn't care. I was happy to have vented, but I was glad to stop.

He fed me well. It was a simple dal, rice, gobi aloo and

saag meal, but it was the best meal I'd ever had. So I ate. I must have taken three platefuls of rice at least. His cook grumbled but Banwari Lal insisted that I eat my fill. I knew there would be some trade-off for this meal, but I was far too hungry to enquire. I was also conscious of being hungry after a long time. Consequently, it was difficult to say no to food. I had missed so many meals and subsisted on so little. I had no trouble eating what little scraps were thrown my way, my appetite on the whole had not mattered, but now it had been reawakened. The meal was like a bewitchment, like the witch's house in Hansel and Gretel. I just could not stop. Nothing else seemed to matter.

Towards the end, when I was served kheer, nearly sated, I began to think of my family. They must have grieved, to have lost Thamma and then me. They must have gone to the police, checked with my workplace, my boss may have gotten into trouble for talking me into suicide or a depression, or he may have claimed I was unfit mentally. Then I began to think of Mitali. What she must have been doing. Had she grieved for me? Or was she still in Danny's arms, too happy to care. I imagined her sitting on his lap, laughing at something trivial. Her hair falling in straight lines and then curling across her shoulder. The little stud on her nose. Sparkling as she laughed. How clean the screw on the stub was of any snot. How she had half a smile when listening to something funny and how that smile stretched and lit up her face when she was really happy, filling her whole being. I saw the back of her neck, the folds of skin on the inside of her neck, the slope of her shoulders, the curve of her breasts, the narrowness of her waist, toned and yet not just muscle. I thought I felt her skin, soft to the touch, her legs, which I had seen so infrequently, and what I imagined was her mound, the parting between, and where I would like to be at the moment. I was sipping, slurping the kheer, but I could feel an erection come on.

Then probably appropriately or inappropriately Banwari Lal told his cook that spiritual heat manifests itself in prodigious appetite and that Babaji would be staying on, so he should go shopping for the necessary ingredients for dinner. I didn't realise my decisions were being made for me but I was grateful. I was in no mood to continue my sermon. I had no interest in helping these people with their spiritual quests. I didn't care what they thought of God, whether their lives were better or worse for it, I wanted to move on. It was just that I was so full, so sated and so sleepy that I agreed to stay on in Banwari Lal's haveli.

I was shown a room on the second floor. It seemed to be meant for guests of a certain sort. A white-walled room with a polished red oxide floor. Along one wall there was a single bed with a thin mattress and an off-white bed sheet covering it, a durrie on the floor next to it. On the opposite side there was a door to a small attached bathroom, but little else by way of wall hangings or furniture. There was a narrow double door with a mosquito netting to enter the room. A small barred window looked out onto the Ganga. I peered out. It was good to see the river, even though it was a very small stretch. It felt invigorating, like a homecoming but of a different sort.

I looked down to see how far up I was, and realised the

reason for the bars on the window. There was a little ledge, which if you were nimble enough, led to the terrace next door. We seemed only two and a half floors up from the street. Without the bars, a child or a mildly agile cat-burglar could come in and rob Banwari Lal of his treasures. I looked around the room again, the whitewash was patchy, the floor irregular in colour and with a pronounced slope, the air mouldy. It wasn't luxurious, but in the ten, twenty, forty or two hundred days that I had been wandering, I had lived in such poor conditions that I could not have been more comfortable in a five-star.

Banwari Lal's manservant, whose name I discovered later was Cheeku, announced to people outside that Baba would be resting after lunch and the next session would happen only in the evening, so that they too had time to eat and rest.

At a little before five, I was woken by Cheeku, and asked whether I would like tea or milk or some juice perhaps. I was still full from lunch, so I waved off the offer. I was promptly informed that the evening session was to start at five-thirty and go on till seven-thirty so that people could go home for dinner. I could have slept a lot more, but since I had partaken of his food and he had promised the pravachan would go on, I felt honour-bound to keep Banwari Lal's word. So I splashed water on my face and brought myself back to the world of the spiritually impoverished. At half past five I descended. I was garlanded with roses and marigolds, led to the hall, where about twenty-odd people were seated on a large, red and black striped tent-house-regular durrie. The men to one side and the women to another, just like any regular pravachan.

The foreigners were missing. They were either not invited or had found their dope and moved on. There was a low bed, a takht with a mattress covered with a white sheet in front of the people. The most comfortable seat in the house. I had two hours to kill and little idea of what more I could tell them about God that they didn't already know. It was going to be pretty uncomfortable.

One of the Sens had finally become a sadhu, I had become my grandmother's version of my grandfather. Perhaps it was karmic inheritance, either that or God had a cruel sense of humour. I did my pranams to them, informing them that they shouldn't be sitting at my feet, that I was their equal in these matters, that I was no one to guide them. This of course had the opposite effect. Everyone started bowing with rather excessive pranams and chanting 'Ram Ram' or 'Har Har Mahadev' or 'Hare Rama Hare Krishna'. I was pretty sure the crowd in the morning had been more secular. This felt somewhat right wing and overwhelmingly Hindu.

I began as I had in the morning, 'Why are you all here?' I asked, scanning their faces. Wondering what I should say next. They looked devout, but would their intelligence wake, would they see me for the fraud I was? I waited for an answer. I don't think the audience is asked why they're at any pravachan in India. 'Isn't it obvious,' they should have said, 'to hear you wax eloquent about God and other things.' Or they assumed it was a leading question, that I would furnish an answer soon enough, as I had in the morning. I couldn't believe how glib I had been in the morning. Was it the blonde girl who had stirred the words? Had the sight of the students sitting at my feet filled me with the potency of the one thing India could be a superpower at? Was I channelling some exalted entity? Had Barathenom come to my rescue?

After about thirty seconds of silence, it became obvious that I was expecting an answer, so they began to speak. Once the replies started coming, they went on for about a minute. 'To learn from you, to listen to you, to be in the presence of spirituality, for punya, for moksha.' This was a very demanding class.

'So what is it that I can tell you that you don't already know?' I asked.

There were fewer takers for this. The dominant requirement seemed to be to lead them or bring them back to the path of God.

'You all are on your path to God, how do you expect me to help you?' I continued being difficult, hedging my way on.

'Help us get there faster, we have gone astray, we aren't worthy, how can we appease God?'

I'm summarising of course, it wasn't as coherent as that.

I picked up on the last bit. 'How does appeasing God help your lives?'

'God will be kind, he will take away our miseries, our lives will be more comfortable, we will come back on the path, we will earn punya.'

'So you want to live better lives. Why should God care about that? If God wanted you to live better lives surely some laddoos or fifty rupees won't be enough to convince him to make your lives better,' I said.

That got me started. There was something about appeasing God that really irritated me.

I lectured them on how they were essentially asking for material things, not God. And God wasn't idiotic or weak to fall for this. Also what concern of it was his, whether someone made more money than the other? That wasn't the sort of thing that affected him in the least. If they wanted to appease God, they had to understand what God was about. So I asked them, what possible interest could a God, or God Almighty have in any of them? If they had to be in a relationship with God they had to know what God was getting out of this. What was God getting out of this?

There was silence. Even Banwari Lal, who was standing at the back near the door with a half cynical smile, seemed interested at this point.

'Devotion,' someone offered.

'Devotees,' someone else corrected.

'Prayers?' It was a question.

'The sort of prayers you offer?' I asked back. 'Those sound like a wish list of a particularly spoilt child.'

There was more laughter at that than I had expected. How happy we were to be reminded of our pettiness, of our selfishness, of our limited lives, our limited intelligence, our limited virtue. But there was no running away now, I would have to answer the question I'd raised.

A line from a courtroom drama flashed in my head, 'Don't ask a question you can't answer.'

Then thousands of beaming faces of avtars, prophets and saints danced before my eyes, mocking me. Taunting me to go on, dig myself out of this.

'To understand what God gets out of all this, you have to ask yourself why did God create all this in the first place?' I gestured to the world at large. I waited.

'To understand God, you have to understand the first move.'

There was silence. There was an expectation of profundity.

'Let me put it another way, to understand God, you have to ask yourself, "Why would I create the universe?"' I said.

There was a murmur. Some people shut their eyes, I think trying to imagine why they, if empowered, would create the universe. Others seemed to be considering whether God's ways were too mysterious to evaluate, I could see some people weren't interested in creating anything new and so they couldn't really put that question to themselves. I could see others still just waiting for me to go on.

'If you were God, with everything that you imagine God to be, what could you possibly get out of creation?' I tried again, to see if they could summon some conceptual empathy.

There was an attentive silence now.

I had put this question to myself, it had occupied my thoughts on my late-night sessions reading up what the channellers, priests, theologists and saints had had to say, and I gave my audience the best answer that the Internet had provided me. 'Experience.' I used the Hindi word 'anubhav'.

I could see the prophets and the saints double up. Some of them gave me a high five. Others were wiping their eyes from laughing too hard.

You could tell that this was not the answer my audience expected. They looked blank, patiently waiting for an explanation.

'For someone who knows he is all powerful, all creative, all imagining, what is missing?' I waited, composing the answer in my head.

'The experience of it. The experience of how great and magnificent he is,' I stated.

'This is what God expects from every aspect of his creation, namely us. To feel how great he is. Since we're all just aspects of him, he urges many of us to arrive at a godliness of our own. So that he experiences the path of attaining godliness. So that a million, billion, uncountable parts of him, walk the path to becoming whole again. And thus he experiences what it is to become him, slowly, over the course of many experiences, many existences, a trillion times trillion times over. If you put yourself in God's shoes, you'll see that God is much like you in what he wants. You weren't wrong to offer God sweets and food, God is a child.'

There was silence and then noise. Some people held back tears, others wept but with what seemed like realisation or joy. I couldn't tell from their twisted expressions. Still others bowed low to me. Banwari Lal, who had sat down somewhere in the middle of my lecture, got up looking very pleased. I didn't know then, but he was collecting donations on my behalf. Not that I cared, we're all in this for selfish reasons. From the top down.

Once things calmed a bit, someone, either on cue from Banwari Lal or just because he was moved, started singing a kirtan and I joined in with everyone. From the smiles and tears on faces you could tell that it had been a cathartic and moving experience for many.

I was a hit.

Later Banwari Lal served a very pleasant dinner and I lay down on the hard bed, happy. Congratulating myself on my unnatural eloquence and the smooth way I had managed my sermon. Sermons. I felt good for giving these people some spiritual dope and while it worried me that I would run out of matter, I mean there's only that much you can learn from the Internet, on the whole, it had been a pretty good day. From nearly starving and dying of the cold, to being a swamiji with a following. My grandmother had been right. We were a family touched by God.

The days passed. I preached, people sang, people bowed, people prayed and people paid Banwari Lal. However, as news got around, my happiness waned. Being a guru was no easy business. They weren't happy with just my sermons, everyone wanted more. They wanted me to come to their homes for private sessions, they wanted me to bless them, their children. Their friend's children. Banwari Lal, of course threw a fit if any family suggested I should stay with them. He made a big shindig of being the first bhakt, of bringing Baba to the world, and speaking on my behalf. That I was only staying on because of his saatvik arrangements, that I would be in great pain if subjected to an impure environment, and may head back to the high mountains I had come from. Were they willing to risk losing Baba?

This went on for a few weeks, but having to fight off the constant pleas and arguments wore him down to the point where he relented, somewhat. I was allowed to eat at other people's places, or maybe he was cutting costs.

Cheeku however, was always with me wherever I went. As a bodyguard, but also as I began to suspect, a jailer.

So with this new arrangement in place I was out every day, blessing children, advising, healing. Mostly commonsense, pop psychology, simple hygiene, quasi-vaastu, educated guesses and the little astrology one can pull off based on the details people revealed.

I was really riding my luck thin, but still the Thursday evening pravachan at Banwari Lal's became something of a local event. Soon there were too many people for the hall. But then there's never a problem getting a hall for a sadhu to spout endlessly on in Haridwar. The action shifted to the prayer hall at a dharamshala close by. People donated clothes and food, and I'm sure donated generously to the box that Banwari Lal passed around. He was doing remarkably well on his initial investment.

This sort of thing couldn't last very long. After all, how many breakfast conversations worth of God did I have. How much new information had the great channelled entity Metaquetron and his friends revealed? Okay, add the hours of Internet browsing while Bhaskar bonked. I had been doing this for weeks, sooner or later I would dry up and they would all see me for the fraud I was.

I began to worry seriously when the local drunk, Mitthoo, started attending my sessions. 'Dhongi,' he had shouted from the back before he was led out. I was afraid this would start a trend. Another time, he tried to throw leftover food at me, shouting, 'Eat this, you used to eat this when you sat with me at the station.'

I must have shared a meal with him. I had shared a meal with all the poor in this city and many others besides.

I hadn't bothered to notice who sat next to me at a langar or who slept near me on a platform. He shouldn't have either, but he did. The hooch he drank was clearly not strong enough. The stuff that passes off as alcohol these days.

I didn't want to be the Babaji about town, but I didn't want to be found out. People in north Haridwar thought I'd come down from the mountains and had stopped at the ghats on my way. They didn't realise I was the beggar from the railway station and the free food lines, who'd been stopped from moving on.

I was trapped in a saffron jail. God works in funny ways. You have to ask yourself if God was a stand-up comic, what would his routine be? How would he set up a punch-line? I've seen a few acts in my life. They repeat a punch-line three times—till just repeating it, is the joke.

Anando Sen becomes Swami Satyanand. He'd said it, now it was a matter of repeating it. Try it out yourself, you may see the humour in it.

A shopkeeper, I forget his name, insisted I come to his shop to bless it. I agreed or let's just say Banwari Lal agreed. This time, thanks to Mitthoo's antics I was accompanied by Cheeku and two other boys from Baba Satyanand Bhakt Sangh, or whatever goon programme Banwari Lal ran in my name.

We went to his shop. It was on the main road in the Har ki Pauri area. The road that leads from the station up towards the mountain. We walked up the road from Banwari Lal's home. I passed the police station and the havaldars outside nodded at me. Whether that was because they recognised me from my pravachans or from checking their escaped murderer, conman databases or something, I don't know. I'm sure Banwari Lal had had me checked. He may have gotten taken in by my rhetoric on occasion, but he was no fool. I was his golden goose and he a sharp businessman. Of what I could tell of his business, he dealt mainly in me, rice and grains, but he must have had other investments. Ever since I had moved to his house he had begun to do much better. Due in no small part to the sons of the devout that he had rounded up to become sevaks for Baba or strongmen, who did a good job of intimidating the local competition.

So with Banawari Lal's reluctant permission, we went to this shopkeeper's shop. I entered followed by my three sangh boys. Looking at the absolute disarray it should have been obvious to anyone who entered the man's shop, that he had no interest in running one. It was meant to be the standard Haridwar fare. Jap maalas, little steel tridents, copper and wooden vessels and ladles and the like. Religious trinkets and baubles, pilgrimage souvenirs, but it was a godforsaken mess. There was no organisation, no arrangement, no attempt to maintain the façade of a shop. I couldn't see any tourist or even the most ardent jap maala enthusiast step into the man's shop. Perhaps a junk dealer but that was the extent of his clientele.

'You want me to bless your shop?' I asked, not impolitely, not with condescension, just to get my facts straight. He may have called me to clean it and put it in order.

'Ji, Swamiji,' he replied, looking suitably devout.

'Are you sure you want to run a shop?' I asked him.

He said, 'It was my inheritance, Swamiji, I must keep it going for the sake of my late father.'

'What would you rather do?' I asked.

'I would rather be a singer, Swamiji. If you remember me from your kirtans, every Thursday.'

Now that he said so, I did. Not a bad voice but certainly not playback material. 'Then you need to do some sadhana,' I said, looking at the chaos around me.

'I know Swamiji, but I can't run a shop and do riyaaz,' he said, pain or something like it shimmering behind glazed eyes.

If I were to bless that shop and it were to shut down, my spiritual equity would take a major beating. Mitthoo's brigade would grow. So I shut my eyes and desperately jogged my memory. It must have looked like I was meditating, invoking higher powers to bless his shop. I gave him a name and number and told him to call these people right away and tell them he had a large shop, give them the details of square footage, tell them what area the shop was in and that they would work out the rest. It helped that I ducked so many of Praveen Kumar's calls. In the process of calling back his team at Apnamart, the number had stuck in my head. I asked him to follow his heart and blessed him hurriedly. It was cheesy, and made me feel very stupid, but I did it. Had Mitthoo shouted anything at me then I would have cried with a sense of release and accepted that I was a fake, wholeheartedly.

The shopkeeper, ah, the name comes back, Nishit Goel, must have followed my instructions because they opened an Apnamart outlet from his shop three weeks later. I may not have loved the guys, or supplied them with enough Fulscreme, but I knew that they had stiff expansion targets and Station Road in Haridwar was a great spot for them.

Nishit Goel came to Banwari Lal's on the next Thursday session with a big basket of fruits. He said the rent alone from Apnamart was more than he made in two months as a shopkeeper. Which was not hard to believe. So he was going to try and become a singer in Bombay or audition for the next singing show on TV or something. He was happy. The Baba Bhakt Sangh boys were ecstatic, throwing their red scarves in the air, calling it the result of my blessings. If I was God's prophet, then capitalism was his religion.

Anando Sen becomes Baba Satyanand. Repeat number one.

Things were going well for Babaji, except that my sermons were getting repetitive and Banwari Lal was constantly at odds with other devotees. To see things his way, he was in a curious position. He was sure that I was just a good speaker. He also suspected, I'm sure, that I was wanted by the police. But he couldn't be sure what I was guilty of exactly. I think he was hoping for some sort of bounty he could cash me in for, once he'd milked my spiritual equity dry. He was just waiting for the right time. I think he started going to the local Internet café to see if he could dig up dope on me.

Then one day out of the blue, while walking down to the ghats for a bath, Mitthoo attacked me.

It was a normal day till then. I had risen, crapped, done some manjan with neem, since toothpaste was considered too materialistic. Crapped again to make room for Banwari Lal's breakfast. Then made my way for my morning dip to the river. Three of the sangh boys accompanied me. I stood at the banks, my hands folded in prayer, while they squatted. They were barely awake, I'm sure the sangh partied well, but they dare not miss their duties, Banwari Lal would see to that.

I continued my usual pretence of invoking the high heavens, by looking roughly north, in the direction of the hills. I don't know what I was thinking about that particular day, Mitali or my parents, perhaps, I can't say. Perhaps just thinking of how it would all end. Tarred, covered in feathers and sent out of town or maybe shaved and paraded all around town astride a donkey, who knew. In this particular regard, I was sure Banwari Lal would be very imaginative. I guess I was distracted and the sangh boys were sleepy or discussing conquests, so none of us realised till Mitthoo was literally ten feet away.

He rushed at me brandishing a nearly empty bottle, it must have been bad hooch or something.

'Death to pretenders!' I translate, the Hindi was even more glorious.

I raised my hand in defence, I didn't want to bear the brunt of the bottle on my face. I mean I'm no looker, but plastic surgery for babas, naah.

Then just as I expected my lights to go out I saw him tripping at the edge of one of the steps at the ghat and fall. The bottle broke and he cut himself. Before I could do anything the sangh boys had gotten to him. I asked them not to rough him up, but he was out cold anyway.

Some of the devotees who were eyewitnesses to the event, reported later on, that I held up my hand and Mitthoo fell. I had held up my arm in self-defence, his falling was his own thing but it became a freaking miracle. Swamiji could repel danger, throw off people from a distance, by raising an arm, or in some instances with just a gaze.

Anando Sen becomes Baba Satyanand. Repeat number two.

This latest incident was reason enough for Banwari Lal to place me under house arrest, I was getting too popular. He limited how many people could see me. He began to charge for private sessions. He limited my walks to half an hour in the morning to the ghats and half an hour in the evening. At both times I was escorted by the sangh boys and devotees were discouraged from seeking advice or blessings. The kirtans were cut down, as were the sermons. They shut me up in the room at night and Cheeku slept right in front of my door. I couldn't get out of the room without tripping over his ass. It was a prison, complete with the bars on my window. All I had to do now was start marking the days on the wall with my nails or shit.

I had to get out. I had to stop living this illusion, anyway. I had to figure out a way to get away from Banwari Lal and out of Haridwar. I had to get back to my family, but I had no money and no other means and frankly even if I did manage to slip away, I didn't have the stomach to slum it out again and beg my way to Delhi. The next day I told Banwari Lal that I wanted to leave and he threw a tantrum. 'Babaji, I've done so much for you how can you leave now?' he asked me with the mock-hurt of a Brothers Grimm step-parent.

'I must go. I can't stay attached to any place or the material world,' I tried.

'Babaji, we both need each other,' he said, his lips curling evilly and his eyebrows coming together.

'How is that?' I asked.

'Do I need to explain this to a sage as exalted as you?' he asked, smirking his evil grin.

'I think you should.' I genuinely wanted him to explain.

'Well, Babaji, I need you till the elections. And you need me for the success of your little charade.'

'Do I?' I asked louder than I had intended. Maintaining composure and volume would have been more Baba-like.

'Yes, without me, you would still be begging on the ghats, but look at you now.' He waved at all the empty baskets that were no doubt full of fruits and other goodies when they had arrived.

I didn't know what to say to him. He was right. I didn't know that he was in politics but I guess it made sense. Create a religious leader, get enough followers, then either use his blessings to rise to popularity and power, or expose him for a sham and come to popularity and power.

Well played, Banwari Lal, I thought I was the star of this show, but it should have been obvious to me that it was always you. I had to figure out a way of leaving his show, but I needed to throw off my guards and I needed regular clothes.

❦

Like all demonic palaces, there were some huge positives to Banwari Lal's prison. I got locked indoors pretty much at sunset. Post dinner, there was little to do but sleep. That meant that I would get up at dawn, curse Thamma, curse God, and then with nothing left to do, I would do some yoga and freehand exercises till the others woke, opened the doors of my jail and got me my breakfast. Banwari Lal was good enough to not stint on food. So the muscles started growing back.

It was a longer wait for breakfast one day, and I was looking out of the window, holding the bars when I discovered that one of the bars felt loose. So I examined them more closely. I hadn't noticed before, but two bars had been filed at the edges, but not enough to pry them loose. So I wasn't Banwari Lal's first prisoner. I wondered what had happened to my predecessor. Or predecessors. It was worrying. If someone had been desperate enough to file at the bars, who knew what tortures Banwari Lal could dream up.

That day and for the next few days, I used whatever cutlery was provided to me to file away at the bars. That meant gobbling breakfast and filing away before they came to get the empty plate. I hoped they wouldn't notice their spoons and knives becoming blunted and out of shape, but it was the only plan I could think of.

In ten days, I pulled at the bars and found that I could remove both.

On the morning of the eleventh, I woke earlier than usual. I pulled out the bars and placed them against the wall, under the window and then edged out carefully till I was sure of my balance on the ledge. Then I turned around gingerly, reached in and replaced the bars. If they burst in and found me missing, it would buy me some time, if they thought I'd worked another miracle. I had to be careful shimmying sideways across the ledge onto the neighbouring terrace, it was narrower than it looked. Then it was a matter of climbing the three-foot wall, which as I discovered had crumbling mortar and loose bricks that nearly resulted in my death. It was quite easy after that. The terrace had an unlocked door. I had to just walk down the stairs and out into the world. I ran out of the lane towards the main road, but just in time I saw two of my Bhakt Sangh guards dozing at the head of the lane. Banwari Lal was clearly not taking chances. I wasn't keen on taking any cither. If they woke as I sauntered by, it would be a miracle explaining what I was up to and that would be that. So I walked the other way, in the general direction of the the ghats. If I found any tourists, I was still in saffron, I could beg for some money, then get a train ticket and be off.

I made it to the ghats and walked in the shadows as far as I could towards the station. I must have walked fifty yards, when I saw someone teetering by the water. An early morning bather. He was singing. As I got closer I saw that it was Mitthoo, after his all night binge. The idiot was going to fall into the water. I pressed myself against the wall praying he didn't look my way, willing my body to meld with the shadows.

He raised his bottle high, he might have been taking aim or some such. Then he did something even a true psychic could not have foreseen. He slipped and fell into the water. He tried to get up but his legs kept giving way. I saw him spluttering as he tried to reach for the safety chains that lined the ghats, but the current was a little too strong for his drunken attempts. God was disposing of my last disbeliever. I stood in the shadows wondering what to do. Then on a ridiculous impulse, I ran down the ghats, jumped into the water and swam out to where I saw him bubbling. It wasn't much of a swim but it was exhausting dragging him and swimming back to the ghat. I heaved and huffed and reached out for the safety chains, somehow caught hold of one with my free arm and then yanked us in. As soon as I found my feet I hauled Mitthoo up and out and onto the steps of the ghat a hundred metres or more downstream.

I flipped him over to empty his lungs of water as I remembered seeing in the first-aid films they had shown us at the RG induction. I pumped his chest a little, hoping it wouldn't come to mouth-to-mouth resuscitation. He reeked. Fortunately he belched out water on the fourth or fifth pump. Ganga water inside you as you died, it seemed a pretty good way to go. I wondered what had prompted my uncharacteristic bravado. After a few more pumps and what little CPR I knew, he started groaning and began to regain consciousness, but heck, the sky was lighting up in the east, and any escape looked doomed.

I looked to see if I could still make a dash, but there were enough people about to alert the sangh boys, I had to get back to my room. As I got up to go, Mitthoo opened his eyes, saw me, looked to say something, then shut his eyes again. I left him lying there, he would be fine, but I would get caught. There was too much light now and the sangh boys would be stirring awake. I couldn't risk getting caught on the streets, I would have to postpone my escape.

I forgot which lane I had used to get to the ghats, cursed myself, ran, tripped, took detours, got lost, and then finally found the lane which led to Banwari Lal's. I had to creep back into the neighbour's house and up the stairs. Climbing over the three-foot wall and onto the ledge was far trickier this way round, the loose bricks didn't help. As was getting back into the room. The bars refused to come loose, but with much panicked pushing, yielded. It didn't help that I was dripping wet and scared shitless about slipping and falling. Bearing in mind how long it had taken for me to get back, I was worried they'd open the door with breakfast and catch me sneaking in. I part lunged, part dived into the room, grateful that I hadn't slipped and fallen.

I was in. I could relax.

Then there was shouting downstairs. The chaotic arguing of many voices. Mitthoo, the asshole, had raised the alarm. Now there was no way of escaping Haridwar's next MLA. I pushed the bars back into place, hoping that no one would see that they had been filed at the edges.

Meanwhile there were footsteps on the stairs. I heard them wake Cheeku and then fiddle with the bolts on the door. There was nothing else to do, so I sat down in padmasana and shut my eyes. Hoping that a meditating sadhu would throw them off their intended violence. Banwari Lal and three or four others burst into the room. Mitthoo was with them.'He's right here, I told you he couldn't have saved you,' Banwari Lal shouted angrily at Mitthoo, who gaped at me. I was so nervous it was hard to keep myself from trembling, I didn't know what would come next. Would Banwari Lal resort to violence or would his rudely woken aggression drown out Mitthoo's story of my attempted escape?

'Swamiji, where have you been?' one of the sangh bodyguards asked.

'Why, I've been right here,' I replied in the calmest voice I could manage. I could feel the veins in my neck throbbing. Had my voice quavered with tension, had I given myself away?

They were all there looking at the room, the barred window and at Mitthoo and me. Then one of the bodyguards noticed that my clothes and I were soaked.

'Swamiji, you're wet,' he said, an edge in his voice.

This was it, game set match to Banwari Lal.

'See I told you he saved me,' Mitthoo continued.

They looked at me. I looked back at them. No one said anything for a few seconds.

'Swamiji, you reached out from here and pulled Mitthoo out?' one of the sangh boys asked.

'Is that why you're wet?' Another boy.

I shrugged. It's either that or I climbed out of your window and was trying to make my getaway when this drunk appealed to my more humane instincts.

Mitthoo fell into a pranam. 'I'm sorry Swamiji, I didn't realise your powers.' Mitthoo wept, he was still clearly very drunk. They all bowed, including Banwari Lal, who looked confused for the first time. Fortunately they left me soon after to change and eat breakfast on my own. It was getting very cold in those wet clothes. When I came down word must have spread because I could hear an excited crowd.

'That Mitthoo.'

'He was always doubting Swamiji.'

'Saints are all-forgiving.'

'They travel astrally.'

'This is a true miracle.'

'We're all blessed to be his followers.'

When I walked into Banwari Lal's hall there was a hushed silence. There were about thirty or forty people crowded into the room. In reverential synchronisation, they all bent down into a pranam. Then got up chanting, 'Jai Babaji, jai Baba Satyanand. Babaji cure me, Babaji bless our children.' I felt powerful. They were ready to be led. Ready to believe whatever words spouted from my mouth, from that day and for the rest of their miserable lives or mine.

Then it clicked into place. I had been in a flux ever since I left my flat in Bombay, heck, I had got back my senses but I had been in a flux in Haridwar too.

Anando Sen becomes Baba Satyanand. Repeat three.

The three repeats that would get you a laugh.

Oh the brilliance of it!

Baba Satyanand! How stupid of me, I should have seen it. Satyanand—truth and joy. Isn't irony supposed to be the highest form of humour. And what have you made me, God, falsehood and misery. How divine of you.

This is what I had wanted. This is all I had wanted. To be your prophet, to give people your word. But how godly of you to make me the counterfeit. At every stage you've made sure I was the antithesis, the lie, the pretender. And now you had your final punchline in your little joke. Why? All I ever did was love you, try to understand you, bring your way to the world. But you weren't going to have it, were you? That's just not, what's the word, funny enough. Well, who can go against your will? You used my grandmother, you used me for your silly ends. What were we, after all? The set-up lines before the big Haha. I didn't give up, I kept belief alive, in me, in you, even when you made my whole life a lapse of memory. All I did was to remove the clouds of superstition and irrationality that cloud petty minds, but all you had in store for me was more of your mocking. You could have spoken to me, you could have revealed yourself, you could have let me become what I wanted to be, you know I tried hard enough. I would have been a good messenger but I was probably a far better joke. Hahaha.

A wannabe godman enters a hall. Stop, stop my sides are splitting. Knock knock. Who's there? Aanu. Aanu the one who thought he was a prophet? Hysterical.

Damn you. Damn you. Damn you. You've had your laugh. Someone's got to get you to hurt.

Later that day I removed all the pictures of gods and goddesses from the house. I was angry, but for some reason all my devotees saw that as a sign from me to find the God within. At the next kirtan, as soon as the singers started singing 'Hare Krishna, Hare Rama,' I started singing 'Dard de dil, dard de jigar,' you know the hit song from *Karz*. I wasn't thinking, it just felt like the thing to do, to break up the kirtan. But they weren't having it. Reading spiritual meaning into it, I mean the song is about being a lover so you can interpret it as being in love with God, they all broke into their best Mohammad Rafi impersonations. I could see even Banwari Lal sing with gusto. If it wasn't so pathetic I would have laughed my sides out. But instead there was a pounding in my head.

The kirtan was an even bigger hit than it used to be, I

mean how can you go wrong with the music of Laxmikant Pyarelal. Thursday evenings had become antakshari nights. Haha, there was no corrupting the devout.

I began to stay in my room longer. So a few days later there was this big temple opening that I refused to attend. Everyone was upset. Till some dirty real estate money was traced to the donations by some enterprising journalist. As far as north Haridwar went, there was nothing that Baba Satyanand did that wasn't in concert with higher forces.

If I shouted they thought I was in rapture, if I cursed I was driving away demons, if I kicked someone they would get back their hearing or sight or virility or self-respect, if I stripped in public that was a sign to be free and unashamed, if I pushed food away that was instruction to care for the less fortunate, if I farted in soprano, I'm sure it rained somewhere drought-ridden in India.

I wanted to leave Banwari Lal's house to go back to my old life, but there were devotees everywhere. Praying, prostrating, weeping. The joke was just not dying down. I couldn't sleep for the anger, I couldn't breathe, I couldn't function. I don't know how time passed. I must have been thinking, plotting. I can't remember. Then I started exercising. I would exercise at least four hours a day, or till I collapsed from exhaustion, but I needed it. Otherwise, the constant divine mocking was too much to bear.

'Be careful what you ask for, you may get it.' It's that bullshit line from some wannabe deep movie or some pop preacher. All those days it played in my head in a loop.

All the things I had wanted—to be with Mitali, to win a gold medal in swimming, to do well in my board exams, for Fulscreme to be a success, to be a better son, grandson, palmist, astrologer, sage, this is what God had chosen to give me. And in this fashion. Freaking sadist.

It's not like I hadn't been insulted before, selling Fulscreme was asking for it every day, but there are well-established forms of getting back. You forward a virus-ridden email, spit in the coffee, say something damaging that you've read off their Intranet profile at the lunch table, you can even rehearse the perfect put-down and just wait for the right moment. It's not like people hadn't laughed at me before, I've been the joke, I've laughed at myself and I've also made mental note to forward, spit, reveal or put-down. But what do you do when your entire life is the joke, the insult? What should one do, when one's notion of self is at odds with the Universe's? How should the joke treat the comic? Why should I accept God's version of my life? No, no. I had been hurt, all meaning, all sense of self had been emptied from me, and I would have it back. I would take whatever bullshit miracle God organised, whichever deluded soul he sent to get cured, whatever else he dreamed up to laugh at my hollowness, but I would find a way to sting him back. What is it that they say, 'Who the gods want to destroy they make mad.' That's what he was after. That much was clear from all the games he was playing. They should rewrite the shloka to 'What the gods want to enjoy, they drive to hollowness, to misery, to a lack of meaning and then madness.' Well, I wasn't letting go of my sanity till I got my revenge. God had hurt me, mocked me, emptied me. This life would come to nought, be a forgotten punchline if I didn't hurt him back. So I exercised. Purged my system and plotted. God had all of creation to use against me, but I had myself. Baba Satyanand would become Anando again. Anando would have the last laugh.

When I had finally worked out the first stage of my plan I went down to the floor that Banwari Lal lived on, and informed him that I was leaving for the mountains, for agyatvaas. He was cautious after all the miracles, so he didn't chance my powers. But he requested that Cheeku accompany me. And said that he would be very grateful if I would be back in time for the election next year. I agreed. I would have to give Cheeku the slip. I asked him for money for my trip, as his guru dakshina. He said that he would give Cheeku the requisite amount. The bastard, even a miracle-working sadhu wasn't to be trusted. I agreed.

The next day I asked Cheeku to buy us train tickets to Dehradun, from where I suggested we would go further north, and to not tell anyone. He got the tickets and I'm pretty sure he told Banwari Lal, who organised some woollens for Cheeku and me.

Then on a Sunday, we got ready, ate, brought down what little we were carrying—which was a small bundle of the clothes I had acquired and an attaché for Cheeku. Cheeku, from his mood, was obviously pretty pissed off to be going to the mountains. Who knew the reason for his loyalty to Banwari Lal? Maybe Banwari Lal had some leverage on him too.

We left early for the station, since I said we'd walk. It was a tearful farewell for Cheeku. I should have told him

not to grieve so much. It wouldn't be that long. Banwari
Lal prostrated himself in front of me and asked me to
forgive his lapses. Confusing character. I really hadn't
figured him out. His wife and children did the same. The
members of the sangh who were present all did elaborate
pranams. The sangh boys wanted to accompany me to the
station, but I wouldn't have it. I informed them that the
whole point of agyatvaas is to not be recognised and that
they would jeopardise my pilgrimage. With my newfound
spiritual powers, no one was challenging my authority.
They did follow at a respectful distance though. There
was no point trying to lose Cheeku in the morning throng,
since he had the money and the boys were sure to catch
me.

I had however, spent all night devising my plan. Just
before we got to the fork of the road, one of which led to
the bridge over the canal and to Shankracharya Chowk
and the other to the station, I stopped. I announced to
Cheeku, as if it had suddenly struck me, 'We can't start a
holy trip without taking a dip in the Ganga.'

Cheeku looked bewildered, not knowing what to do.
It was too far to signal to the sangh boys for advice,
besides he would reveal that we were being followed, and
who knew the outcome of spiritual wrath. He must have
imagined himself being burnt to a crisp.

So he argued that we would miss the train, but I told
him it would take us only ten minutes and that we had
plenty of time. So back we walked towards the ghats. I
could see the sangh boys take a sharp turn as well. They
weren't taking chances. They were probably booked on
the same train.

At the ghats, considering the hour, there were a fair number of bathers. I asked Cheeku to take his dips first explaining that I would have to say a prayer first. He did as instructed but remained alert to me running away. I watched him take the dips, then instructed him to say as much of the mantra, 'Om namah bhagavate vasudevaya' as he could underwater. The second time he took a dip, I reached into his trousers and removed the plastic packet that had the money. On his third dip I slipped it into my langot. As he got out of the water I tied the knot tight, to be sure there was no way the money could slip out or be washed away. Then once Cheeku was done, he stood on the steps of the ghat while I waded in. I guess he wasn't quite sure what I was going to do.

I had started hyperventilating the moment he had gotten into the water. I took the first dip mouthing the mantra for him to see. The next dip I walked in a little deeper and kicked off. I stayed as far as possible underwater. I would have to surface, to see where I was going, I didn't want to knock myself out on the pillars of the bridge but I breast- stroked for as long as I could underwater.

I bobbed once, checked my location then went under and swam with all my might. I hoped that Cheeku had not spotted me in all the bodies between us or believed it was another miracle and not an escape. Knowing Cheeku, he would have raised an alarm even if he thought it was a miracle. Actually especially if he thought it was a miracle and the sangh boys and Banwari Lal would investigate.

My breath ran out and I had to swim in plain sight to the opposite shore. It wasn't easy, it had been years since the pool at Shiksha. Also pools don't have currents and eddies, I would never have managed in the monsoon months. But fortunately the water level was much lower than it had been and the current less treacherous, so I survived. I was panting hard when I got out and my arms and legs felt leaden, but I had about five minutes or so before Cheeku and the sangh boys spotted me. So I picked up the first lungi I could and made off with it, before the bather noticed. I had to move quickly before Banwari Lal and his companions got into action. I might have been paranoid but I couldn't risk getting caught or spotted. I hiked up the lungi South Indian style and jogged to Kankhal which is to the south, along one of the canals. It was a five-hundred-metre jog to the market and I was completely out of breath. I dived in panting into the first barber shop that I found. I asked him for a shave and a haircut. In a checked lungi I must have looked like an unkempt carpenter or something and not a baba. Or so I hoped.

Half an hour later, I went to an underwear store and then a clothes shop. I changed at the back of the store, since they didn't have a trial room. I looked at myself in the little mirror, it was shocking to see the transformation. It would be very hard to recognise me as Swami Satyanand, but not impossible.

I walked back up the road I had jogged down less than half an hour back, to where it met the highway, trying to change my body language. I tried a swagger, that didn't work, so I just walked fast.

Some sangh boys on their motorbikes were riding slowly along the highway. Some from Dam Kothi at the fork in the canal towards Rishikesh and some others towards the road to Delhi. They seemed to be checking the canal for a body, or footprints, there must have been others checking at the ghats. I nearly broke into a prayer, but I checked myself.

They didn't look twice at me. I hailed the first bus that was headed towards Delhi and got in.

Bye bye Swami Satyanand.

Fifteen

The bus I was in went only to Muzaffarnagar. I had to catch another one to Delhi. Then with the last bit of cash I had left, the 501 bus from the Inter State Bus Terminus and off at the Free Church at Green Park. From there it was a short walk to first floor, X-35. The only place I thought of as home. There was a little notice on the door informing me that the State Bank of India was now in possession of the flat. That any mail for the Sens should be forwarded to 1242, Wimbledon Heights, Sector 22, Gurgaon. There was no way I could get to Gurgaon free, so I walked to Greater Kailash, to Didi's.

The sun had set by the time I got there but I barely registered the walk. My mind was full of thoughts. Stage One went off glitch-free, now it was time for Stage Two. I had to channel the devil, invoke Beelzebub, demons, commit blasphemy, anything.

Our matter and essence who art every-bloody-where
Thou gavest us your son, your prophets, your sages, your name
For many millennia you've played your little game
Now that you've enjoyed your little joke

Your divinity needs a godforsaken poke
And I'll be damned if I don't find a way.

Why was Lucifer cast out of heaven? Because he had threatened to be a god in his own right. He'd got it all wrong. If you had to take God down, you had to try and be the Ungod.

I rang the bell, Didi opened the door, saw me, stood there looking at me till recognition dawned, then she hugged me and broke down crying.

'Where have you been...we were so worried...they never found a body, so we never gave up hope...but it was tough...I'm going to call Ma and Baba right now...God, I thought you had killed yourself...the police asked me so many times about your last phone call...that idiot friend of yours, Bhaskar...your boss called...I asked Bhaskar to take your stuff...why Aanu why...was there girl trouble...your boss mentioned something...how could you do this to us...when you didn't come for Thamma's shraadh...obviously the cops didn't try hard enough...we had no pictures of you with a beard...' she babbled on between sobs.

It went on for a while till she stopped and looked up for an explanation. It was my cue to speak. I told her I'd had a major setback at work, that I wasn't who I had imagined I was. That I was depressed, very depressed, I didn't really know or care about anything, not even myself, I wandered, when I got out of it I worked with a local trader in Haridwar to earn money to come back. She didn't press me for more details, nor ask what caused the depression, she just said, 'You could have just gone to an ATM and withdrawn money.'

'I had no cards and had forgotten my PINs,' I lied.

'You could have called, we would have sent the money,' she said.

'I'm not sure I was completely recovered till a few days ago. By then I had earned the money,' I told her.

There was not much more to probe. She accepted that I had been in a depressed catatonic flux of some sort. So she called Ma and Baba, prepared them for a shock and then handed me the phone. I spoke to them, they wept and asked much the same questions that Didi had. It was sad to have to do it on the phone, still it was better than landing up in Gurgaon and giving them a thrombosis.

Ashok got kebabs from Saleem's to celebrate but I barely touched them. Being a sadhu for a few months had put me off meat.

The next morning I took a private cab to Gurgaon. It took forever since they had started building the metro, which had to be ready in time for the Commonwealth Games in 2010. Anyway, it didn't matter. It would have, if I was still employed at my previous job selling chips. Going by the jam at Ghitorni, I would have had to leave home at daybreak to get to work on time. I used the traffic jam to contemplate my course of action. Pick up from where I was the day before. Cars honked, people swore, hawkers peddled, but inside the Indica cab, it was quiet, still. Inside my head it was quieter, stiller. A meditative calm. A calm so deep, I could see the endgame.

a2-a4, the flank pawn begins to move.

A bishop sashays down, urging the pawn to vacate that square, prodding it to move down the flank.

a4-a5.

The pawn is met with another pawn coming at it, it can't move straight forward.

There is another pawn diagonally to its right. It can kill and move on. But what's this? There are other things in the distance. Lots of other things. Some very large threatening pieces. And hold on, is this new? The squares are coloured, alternately. If it were to kill it would get killed, things would be equal. But it would mean its own death. The pawn takes all this in suddenly. Thus far, all it had considered was marching forward, sidestepping left or right as the occasion demanded. Now it knew better. What should it do now?

What would you do, if you were the pawn that discovered the chess game?

My parents were so happy and sad at the same time, it nearly weakened my resolve for revenge. I did love them. Ma had cooked all my favourite dishes for me, and Didi must have told her that I hadn't touched the non-veg. So there was aloo-bodir rosha, kodai daal, baati chochori, and a chhanar jhaal that was a Sen special.

Baba asked many questions about what I had been up to, but Ma just wept and was happy to have me home. I was happy to see their flat. Though this was not home, it had a lot of the old stuff in it. It seemed habitable enough. They had managed a deal with the bank, sold the Green Park house, paid off the business debts and with the remaining money got this flat. It wasn't a bad deal, Baba said. A lot of retired people had moved to Gurgaon, so they had a social life here. They were even planning a big pujo in the sector. They had carved out some happiness for themselves here away from the ghost of Thamma.

Still I enquired about her things. They had kept some of her stuff along with my things in the guestroom. They asked me to check what I would like to keep, since there was less space compared to the Green Park flat. I complained that now it was just the two of them, versus all the people who stayed in Green Park, they could allow for some of my junk.

We were behaving almost like a normal family.

I went through Thamma's stuff and mine. I saw her old pictures. With her and Dadu, and then of her and her three sons, and then two sons, and then her two grandchildren. And then just her, with no great-grandchildren. Oh Thamma, what a funny hand we were dealt. The revenge was for you too. Rummaging through the little suitcase that had her stuff I found the dictaphone that I had bought for her, which I kept. There was also a little plastic box with all her medicines, which I kept too.

I had little interest in my things. I didn't need the books on palmistry, astrology or spirituality anymore. Or the yearbooks and class photographs. I found an invitation for a wedding that had happened many months ago. It was Ruma's. I would call her and congratulate her.

Over the next few days I contacted the bank, got hold of a debit card, spent time with my parents and my sister, I wanted the goodbye to be proper now, and I needed time to figure out a course of action. Plan.

A lot of the next few days had to be spent visiting the local police station, explaining where I had been and why. I left out the part about being a Baba, but I did mention working for Banwari Lal. There was little Banwari Lal could do now. I mean what would he want the blessings of a marketing executive for. Without my beard, my hair and my saffron clothes I was just Anando Sen. The rest of the time I went on walks. Around Sector 22 and around the little green patch in Wimbledon Heights working out just how the pawn could invert the game, how I could hurt God.

⁓

Thoughts from my meditations in Haridwar and Wimbledon Heights: The problem with taking revenge on God.

How can you actually hurt God? Can you? The problem is that being an infinitesimally small part of God, the odds are loaded against you. There are those that say any creation of God that you hurt will hurt God, but they're not talking revenge. Also, looking at the damage that nature can wreak on humans, deaths by the hundreds and thousands, there is no evidence to suggest that God does not enjoy pain. So a huge bomb, even if I could get my hands on it, was off.

What about a place of worship? That too made little sense. History had seen so many invaders destroy one temple or another. If history and memory were right, little of God's vengeance visited them. So I doubt God gets terribly put out by such stuff. I could damage the planet. But the planet was resilient and even if I did organise a nuclear winter, or worse still a Krypton-like explosion, what was the Earth compared to the scale of the Universe. The Universe itself was probably one of many. No, I had to think small. Not of scale but incisiveness. Think qualitatively. Not think of hitting at God's creation, but at God himself, at His very being. There was no way I could deliver a knockout punch, it had to be more like a pinprick to the heart.

It didn't have to be complex, if anything it needed God-like simplicity.

It took many rounds of the Wimbledon Heights park working it out, fine-tuning just what it would take. If you had to attack God, you had to hurt his essence. And what is God if not Love?

I needed the resolve to see it through because I didn't think God would like getting hurt. Who does? Being Omniscient and Omnipotent and Omnieverything, he would make it tricky for me. However, since I was a part of his creation, he had to play by his rules, that meant I got my Free Will.

Once my debit card was operational and my account unfrozen, I was ready. I got myself a ticket to Bombay, kept a little money for incidental expenses and transferred the rest to my parents' accounts. They needed the money, I didn't. The good thing about exacting one's revenge on God is that it was quite cheap.

What're you thinking? That I was going to kill my parents or something? Na, I loved them but not that much. They had and would suffer anyway. I went to Didi's for a day, told her I was going back to Bombay to get on with things and said a proper farewell. I even called Ashok at work and said my goodbyes.

When I had my head clear and all things worked out, I told my parents in the evening that I was leaving for

Bombay the next morning. They had expected it. I packed my things. Had a solemn meal and we went to sleep. I woke early to have my last tea with them. You can't say goodbye without having tea with your parents. It was so normal it almost made me cry. We discussed the headlines, the work ethic of Bombayites and the state of the nation. There was no mention of God. Then we said bye and I wiped off my tears. The taxi to the airport was surprisingly quick. After haggling with the taxi driver, in spite of having decided the fare beforehand, and grudgingly paying him fifty rupees extra for the Gurgaon Jat etiquette fund, I walked into Terminal 1B. The airport was a mess, what with the construction of a new terminal next door and leaky pipes and multiple air carriers competing with each other for every square inch of space. It was the sort of environment to make anyone lose his or her temper. I on the other hand, felt calm, cool. That's what happens when you have a plan in place.

You see the thing with God is that you can only hurt God if in some way you know that you're hurting the most precious part of you. What do you love most? As far as I was concerned, there were two things. Mitali and myself, in that order. I would have to eliminate both. There was no reason to suffer too much. My shitty life was proof that God is a sadist.

But do it, I would. It would be very difficult for me, since getting Mitali to love me had been my single point agenda for about a decade or more. It would be less difficult to do myself in. Others that I loved would be hurt too. Ma, Baba, Didi. That couldn't be helped, they were all a part of God, and knowing that I didn't want to hurt them anymore, only made me sure of how correct my plan was. It wouldn't do to hurt Mitali's boyfriend. Or maybe it would, if it was still Danny. There would be another one who would blame and thus hate God, and perhaps the hatred would spread.

Every part of me that didn't think it was the right plan was revolting against it, but that was just God playing with me. It would go, it would all go.

I rang the bell at the flat, it was the weekend so Bhaskar would be home at that hour. He opened the door. And blinked while his overworked and over-drugged processors finally click-whirled and worked out who was standing at the door. One could be forgiving, he was sleepy and the last time he'd seen me I had had a beard. Once he did recognise me, fortunately he had the grace to look shocked.

'Dude, I thought you were dead or something.'

Then when I asked him if I could enter, he opened the door fully, and let me in.

He looked vaguely embarrassed at having his stuff strewn all over the flat.

'Since there was no sign of you I've sort of taken over, but you can sleep here for a few days if you need to,' he offered generously.

He shouldn't have been embarrassed since he'd thought I was dead. I would have taken over the flat if he had disappeared, at some point in the past, I had meant to. 'I only need a few days.' I could have said the lease was still in my name, but that would have been needlessly petty.

He moved things around and made space in the smaller room, which used to be his and I opened my bag and took out my things. Some of my stuff was in cardboard cartons lined against the wall. I saw a few things from work. Good old Bhaskar, he hadn't really believed that I had died.

While I settled in he made us some disgusting over-boiled and commensurately over-sweetened tea.

'Bhaskar, you really have to learn how to be useful in the kitchen,' I laughed, touched that he had tried.

'Dude, we have a bai, and you're back.' Then of course, realising the implication of such a statement, 'But only for a few days, right?'

'Right.'

The next thing to do would be to find Mitali.

'By any chance do you have my cellphone?' I asked him, hoping. It would make life simpler.

'Oh about that, sorry dude, I gave it to Diana.'

'Diana?'

'I was banging her a few months ago, we've broken up now. Can't really ask her to return the phone. Sorry, I'll get you a phone, I may have my older phone lying somewhere.'

'Thanks, did you by any chance keep my SIM card?' I asked.

'No dude, why would I do that?' he asked, mortified at the suggestion.

'Just thought I'd check.'

Anyway it wasn't going to be so difficult to remember Mitali's number. I had dialled it many, many times. Once I got my fingers moving over the phone it would come back. Worst case, I would contact her at work.

Bhaskar walked back in to my room, brandishing an old, much-dented Nokia.

'So what happened man, where did you go?'

Bhaskar had finally woken up.

'Bhaskar, would you have my friend Mitali's number on your phone?'

'The hot one, I wish. I mean not to hurt you or anything, thought you guys were like cousins or something.' He was still rattled, working his way to his blasé composure, 'So you gonna tell me or what?'

'I travelled, spent some time in Haridwar, then went to Delhi and now I'm back,' I said.

'Whoa dude, you really did travel.' Then he enquired about the details and I gave him practically the same story that I had given Didi.

Bhaskar had kept my wallet, my cards and other paperwork in the boxes. The money from the wallet was missing but I may have taken it when I left to get milk.

I had to go to the police station at Andheri and close the case filed there, the cops in Gurgaon had insisted I do that at the earliest. So I did, I didn't want to be hauled in for questioning in the middle of my revenge. It took a while with all the affidavits, statements, proofs of identification and all the copies. I had to get a doctor's statement too, but there was no hurry. There was nothing the cops liked more than a closed case. I was sure they were going to be lenient. It took a few days, but it got sorted.

Then with my new SIM and Bhaskar's old phone I called Mitali. It took a few punches of the keys, some muscle and visual memory and a couple of wrong numbers, but finally I got through to her.

'Hello,' said the voice on the other end of the line.

'MC. Hi. It's me, Anando.'

She thought it was a prank and hung up without bothering to verify. I called back five minutes later. Then again seven minutes later. I had time on my side, it would take me another fifteen minutes or so of walking to get to her office. She finally answered.

'It is you, isn't it?' she said with less disbelief and more irritation.

'Yep.'

'You bastard, you had me so worried. What the fuck happened? Was there a girl?' she asked.

There has always been a girl, Mitali, but no it wasn't about a girl.

'No, don't worry, I'll explain when I meet you. Are you free tonight?' I asked her.

She accepted the dodge, 'Ummm...tonight I may be busy let me see if I can cancel. I'll call you in five, okay? Don't disappear again.' She spoke hurriedly and there were sounds of her tossing things around. She may have been checking her diary.

I laughed. 'I'm not going anywhere now.'

She was busy and couldn't cancel, so we fixed to meet the next evening for dinner at her place. She gave me the address, it wasn't Danny's.

I had expected to see her at the window of her office. If not completely visible then at least in silhouette, I would recognise her silhouette anywhere. But the windows were too reflective, so I sat outside and waited. When she left her office I followed her. She met a man for dinner near her place at Bandra. It wasn't Danny. She outgrew you too Danny, huh. I'm sad for you, I hope you do better with your music.

The dinner didn't seem that friendly, it seemed like a first date or at least the opening stages of one of her romances. God had spared Danny heartbreak. No, that was unlikely, God had just saved Danny excessive grieving.

That night I looked up the lethal dose for sleeping pills on Bhaskar's laptop at home. I also looked up other painless ways to kill, just in case the sleeping pills didn't work. Then out of reflex or something I looked up the channelling and spiritual sites. I don't know why. I can only say it was out of habit. When I sit in front of a monitor with the Internet browser on, I end up looking at what the angels, archangels, exalted spirits and long dead ancestors have to say. It seems the natural thing to do.

It was there, still the same. The same positive, feel-good, make a difference in a vague, light-being kinda way tripe. As friendly, loving and hopeful and vacant as they could be.

'Welcome friend, be aware that the Earth is shifting from the vibrations of the third dimension and speedily onto the fifth. A lot of you may have felt this shift already in your beings. While some of you have experienced visions and felt the loving energy stream down, others may have experienced emotional upheavals.'

You betcha.

'Don't worry, all this will pass and as we move closer to becoming light beings, you will discover new abilities.'

Like the ability to murder.

'Rejoice in this time, you who are here on Earth have been chosen to make a very significant contribution.'

Yes, I was aiming for significant.

'So go forth with positive energy and make a difference because you are one of the chosen few.'

I was going to. Soon.

I bid the Energies and the Earthlings well for the transition. It had obviously not dawned on them that turning into light beings meant giving up the corporeal body. Mass death on a planetary scale. Surely a reason to be optimistic, la-de-da and bathe in the stream of energy. More of the Almighty's loving plans for his beloved planet. Pity I wasn't going to be around to see them burning their way to the fifth dimension.

I slept, I woke. Milled about, did nothing for most of the day. Then in the evening I took my time getting ready for dinner. I wore the nicest shirt that Bhaskar had left for me in my boxes, the most fitting pair of jeans, the cleanest underwear. Sprayed on Bhaskar's aftershave and cologne. Polished my dark brown slip-ons, and took out two leaves of sleeping pills from Thamma's medicine box and ground them to powder. I took the rest just in case some had expired or were nearing expiry and thus less effective. Perhaps I should have carried a knife, but there was no way to carry an effective one on my person without it showing. She would hug me, and I might stab myself before I got started. That would give God some more laughs. Besides, I was pretty sure Mitali would have a functioning kitchen.

En route to Mitali's, I bought a bottle of wine. I trudged up three flights of stairs because the lift in her building wasn't working. Maybe she had downgraded now that she was single again. I couldn't find a bell for her apartment so I knocked.

She opened the door and stood there looking heart-stoppingly beautiful. God was in this game to win. She had a one-shoulder or is it called off-shoulder top on, of indeterminable colour. It wasn't moss or mustard or any of the colours I had learnt the names of. It wasn't in the green, grey or brown family. Her jeans were skin-fitted and Indigo blue. She seemed to be fitter than I remembered. Her hair fell in waves about her shoulders, and did I spy lipstick?

Once she had done absorbing my appearance and verifying that it wasn't some spirit, I handed her the bottle of wine and said, 'Hi, Mits, great to see you, too.'

'You bastard, hi. You've lost a lot of weight, you're looking almost handsome. What have you been up to?' she asked, taking the bottle and hugging me.

I was drowning in her perfume and losing my resolve. It had seemed so possible on all those walks around Wimbledon. The hug was a little longer than previous ones. I didn't want to let go, and for a fleeting moment, I felt that maybe neither did she.

She backed off. 'Okay, I've got a roast chicken in the oven, so why don't you pour us some wine and fill me in on this year that you've been gone.'

'It needs to be chilled a little.' I was worried she'd taste the pills in the warm wine. Or empty her glass complaining that I'd gotten her cheap vinegar instead of wine.

'Oh I've got one in the fridge, we can have yours later. Don't worry we've got time, it's Friday.'

She was upbeat. She walked back to her open kitchen and put on an apron. Then she rummaged around, while I took the bottle of white out of the fridge, found glasses, rinsed them, since they looked somewhat unwashed, dried them, found the corkscrew, struggled with it, dug out the cork, poured out the wine and popped the bottle back in the fridge.

I carried the two glasses to the living room. Then it was time to bring out the little paper pouch with the sleeping pills powder. I poured it into one glass stirring it in, as best as I could with my index finger.

Then I took the other in my hand and said, 'Cheers.'

She picked up her glass and said 'Chin-chin' and took a small sip. Then she walked back to the kitchen.

'Tastes a little funny no, I've never gone wrong with the Chilean wine before.'

'It tastes fine,' I said.

She walked back to the living room area, balancing a salad and chips and dip. While placing it on the table she knocked her glass down. 'Oh crap! I'm such a klutz.'

I winced. God was not so easily beaten. Then I noticed the sediment at the bottom and got up quickly to pick it up before she thought I was trying to give her a date rape drug or something.

'That's fine, we have plenty of time. It's Friday,' I said gallantly and winked. 'Time and wine.'

She brought a rag to wipe the spill and I took the glass and went back into the kitchen. While she was wiping down, I poured wine onto the sediment, stirring as soundlessly as possible with the back of a teaspoon. There wasn't that much left in the glass so either most of it had spilt out or dissolved. I couldn't take a chance, I would have to mix the other pills in. But how was I going to crush them?

'What are you doing tooling around there? You haven't even bothered to notice my plating.'

I had. It was pretty decent considering her cooking skills but I was absorbed in the dissolving pills business.

'I did, just looking around your kitchen,' I announced.

'What are you stirring?' she asked stressing the 'are' with some degree of amusement.

'Nothing, just airing the wine in your glass.'

'Don't be silly, come here, tell me about this year of disappearance. Oh, one sec, just take a peep in the oven to see the chicken's not burning.'

I was actually put off by the smell of the meat, but didn't have the heart to tell her. Which blueblooded Bengali in recorded history had turned vegetarian!

'It looks fine,' I said after a glance.

We clinked glasses again and I told her what had happened. There was no point lying to her now. She was going to die soon—well, irrespective, she deserved the truth. She listened attentively but broke into a hysterical fit, curling into a ball to laugh, when I told her I'd become a Baba.

'You know I've always known there was something very wrong with you,' she said spraying the wine out of her nose. 'Pour me another.'

I did. I found another glass and put two pills in it, poured wine into it, stirred it and then placed it in the fridge at the back.

'Will you stop airing the wine and get me a refill quickly? I wanna get tipsy quickly,' she laughed. Tittered actually.

'Coming up.'

'So you've realised you're not psychic,' she stated.

'Yep.'

'Had you checked with me, I could have told you this fifteen years ago and spared you lots of misery.' She snorted with laughter. Or chortled if that's more feminine. And she was very, fundamentally feminine in everything she did that evening. A good way to go, Mitali. At the peak of your beauty and laughing your head off.

We ate salad, had chips with dip, while she quizzed me on the details of my year, and I waited for the pills to take effect. In the middle the oven pinged, she brought the chicken out, let it rest, then served us each some pieces with some mushroom and red wine sauce. She had spent time on the Internet as well, preparing for this evening.

We ate. We drank. We ate some more. There was butterscotch icecream which she drizzled with muesli for dessert. I waited. She drank. I drank. Then she told me about her split with Danny. How he'd met some singer. That it had been heartbreaking for her, perhaps for the first, or may be the second time. That she was so lonely for so many months and needed to talk, needed comforting but I was nowhere to be found.

I apologised, and said I was here now.

She wiped two tears and proceeded to drink faster, which was alarming. Because I was worried the pills wouldn't dissolve fast enough. She asked about the sediments once but I replied that it must be the cork, or just dregs. I was hoping that the cocktail of wine and sleeping pills would kick in soon, but I couldn't be sure just how much she'd actually consumed since so little of the pills actually dissolved. She drank some more, I drank some more and then I realised we were sitting on the same sofa. Very close. Close enough to kiss, close enough to kill.

Then she felt sick, rushed to the loo and retched noisily.

Dammit. God had beaten me.

When she came back she sat down on the sofa, even closer, slowly gradually, she was leaning against me, and soon she was stretching her legs out on the sofa, ready to lie down.

'You're a fool Anando,' she said, her head falling onto my lap.

'Yes,' I agreed.

'I don't feel so well, Anando,' she mumbled drowsily.

Maybe God had not won after all.

'I think I'll just sleep for a bit, all right. Don't go anywhere,' she said.

'I'm not going anywhere.'

I wasn't. Not till she was fast asleep.

'You're so sweet,' she had begun slurring. 'You and I...we could have had something.'

God. You're a sadist. Or just a very accomplished player.

She slurred, 'Iff only...you hadn't been...shoo shtupid...all thoshe yearsh ago...and felt me up.'

'I was a hormone-ridden boy,' I offered.

'Yeah I know,' she finished. Her breathing deeper and slower. She was asleep, never to wake.

I let her doze there on my lap, looking at her. Her hair spread out like a black wave. Her glowing skin, the arch of her eyebrows, the curve of her neck. That little upthrust chin. Beautiful, beautiful Mitali. You did deserve better. Better than Danny and Jack and Tom and whoever the heck you had been with. Better than me. I'm sorry to have done this to you. I am partially consoled by the fact that if you do die, then you would have chosen me as your killer before you came down to this silly planet. So I guess we had or will have some debt to work off, upstairs or somewhere, since I was clearly going to hell. If not, then you can grieve for me. Though I do hope you die. Without you dying my revenge on God is scarcely meaningful.

I felt awful in the auto ride back to my place, well, Bhaskar's. I was crying uncontrollably. That was good. That meant God was hurting too. The auto driver ignored me for the most part but asked me whether I had had my heart broken.

I told him, 'Much worse, I've probably killed my love.'

The Hindi made it easy for him to think I was speaking figuratively.

'Women are not to be trusted,' he said with gravitas.

'And neither is God,' I added.

He laughed at that, a short bark of a laugh.

'You're really hurting aren't you?' he asked.

'I hope God is as well,' I said in anger and pain.

'I'm sure he is.'

What was this? Was this an admission? Was God speaking to me through the auto driver? I got off, paid him, looking at him all the time, while he dug out the change, waiting for some parting shot from God. But none came.

In the flat Bhaskar, for a change, seemed to be sleeping alone.

I went to the kitchen, popped all the remaining pills into a mug, crushed them with the back of a ladle, then poured some cola onto it and took a sip. It was the bittersweet of bad chemistry but what the heck.

Suicide as far as my reading on most religions go, is a crime against God. That's why I chose it. It was a fitting response to God. Not because I didn't want to live anymore, no, I could live out my life as a non-psychic, selling Fulscreme and other things, till I dropped dead some day. But it was a way of telling God, that I reject you, your grand design, your smaller design for this planet and your insignificantly tiny design for me. I have put my love to a sleep that I don't think she will wake from and now I shall do the same to myself. I can't be sure that you're hurt by this but it seems like the best, or more appropriately, the worst thing to do.

I wanted so much to serve you, to be with you to spread your word, but you, you wouldn't have it. Would it have been so hard to have spoken to me? Would it be so bad if I was only this tiny bit special?

No one spoke back. So with nothing better to do than wait, I switched on Bhaskar's computer and the modem. Next to the modem I found a rolled joint, well one couldn't die without having smoked some pot, no? So I lit up while waiting to connect to the Internet. There was an invite from Mitali to join something called Facebook. It seemed an invitation-only version of Orkut. Some other time Mitali, some other life. Then while taking drags of Bhaskar's joint and sipping the bitter cola slowly, I browsed the New Age spiritual sites, it would be good to read what those idiots had to say, at least I could end this life laughing at God.

The usual crap, I took a larger gulp. This was going to take time. Do expired sleeping pills work? So I shut my eyes, and memories of childhood started coming back.

This must be what it's like to have your life flash before your eyes. But it was slow, not a flash at all.

Oh, I hadn't left a suicide note. I looked around and noticed the dictaphone that I had bought for Thamma. I switched it on. I didn't think it would do to just say I blame God, so I started speaking into it. I recorded the memories as they came, the reasons I hate God so.

'My father could smell death...'

Now that I've explained myself, told you the whole story, it's time to drink up this vile brew. My mood has fluctuated and I'm sorry if you were deceived at the start. Or indeed at any point. I could have come out and told you what I had done, at the very beginning, but it would make no sense without the why. If you still feel deceived, I'm sorry, but frankly I don't care. Worse things have happened to people.

I've used 'you', because I didn't really know what I was going to do with this recording, I assumed a generalised listener, now I'm pretty sure that that will be you, Bhaskar or the cops. If it is you Bhaskar, then 'Sorry man, sorry for you having to deal with the mess and whatever opinions I proffered on you, but let's face it, you piled on. Treat this as the comeuppance.'

'If you're a cop, then please consider this my suicide note, no one is to blame for my death, aside of God. And yes, this is an admission of murder, that is, if Mitali dies.'

I feel terribly tired but not yet ready to sleep. It's nearly morning.

The Internet browser is open on something that looks like a channelled message from some high power.

'Dear friend. You are special and we love you. You must know that you are and have always been special. Nothing that this life throws at you, should change that. From a very young age you must have felt different, knowing that you were special. That is a very real feeling. We are all born with gifts, but some of our gifts have a larger role to play in the grand design. At present the Earth is of great significance to our plans with the Universe. Which is why we are watching it, and specially you with great interest, love and understanding. What you do may have great impact on things to come. So act with love and know that we are always there for you.'

What?

This was God speaking to me, right, and not just some intelligent copy from some web developer looking to trap insecure individuals? I mean he chose such funny ways to get through, all kinds of methods, all kinds of voices, channels sometimes you couldn't even be sure he was talking to you. I mean, look at the ways he employs, has employed. He does care, doesn't he? He agrees that I'm special, no? Why else, would this of all the pages be open now? I do have his love, don't I? I could go back and wake Mitali. She'd probably retched out most of the pill-powder anyway. I could call her and wake her, I could vomit out her lovely dinner and the pills with it. Tonight may never have been. I just have to get out of this chair and then out of the door. I need to get up, but I'm just so damn tired, I just need to shut my eyes and gather my strength. Why did he have to wait till so late? I could call Mitali, or an ambulance to go to her place. I must. Just have to sit out this feeling of being uncoordinated. If I lie down it may just pass. If God can reach out to me, he can ensure that I wake in five minutes. He can do that, I'm sure. Look at the lengths he went to, to teach me a lesson. I could start life anew with Mitali. It could be a life of love. A life with God. I just have to make sure I can keep my eyes open. Keep talking. I'm sorry I doubted your love, God. I just have to get up and move to the door, I could get to the loo and then later, I could explain it all to Mitali. It could all just be a prank. Just something God and I had going on. A repeated line, an inside joke, a little haha.

Acknowledgements

I started the story of Anando, his grandmother and family in 2007, and let it lie for many years till I finally wrote it in 2013, and spent the next two years trying to find an agent or a publisher. It's a story that has taken a while to get published and I have a lot of people to thank for it.

First for causal reasons alone is Mohan who, thanks to a serendipitous chance meeting, introduced me to Manas Saikia and Speaking Tiger. Then to Manas, Renuka Chatterjee, Ravi Singh and the entire Speaking Tiger team for being kind enough to pick a novice to publish within their first year of setting up. Double thanks really to Renuka, for thinking the novel was good enough to publish and then spending hours editing to make it good enough.

I owe a huge debt of gratitude to my sister, Sharupa Dutta who had constantly encouraged me to write, who has backed me, promoted this novel, made sure I was present in literary circles, and, well, been my literary manager for most of her life.

To Sandeep Mark Joseph, who put the bug of writing in me in college. I was just wandering through things, but he made sure I read the right books, wrote in the right columns, used the right words. Being a writer was your dream, man and I shamelessly adopted it.

To my parents, my other sister Indrani, my uncle, my aunts who have tolerated me through what they probably rightly believed were my nutty spells, and whose stories and anecdotes I have unscrupulously twisted to create some of the characters and incidents.

To my grandmother, who was my first promoter and fan. And, though no Thamma, a woman who had as profound an influence on the life of her grandson. I hope this makes her at least as proud, as the poetry in class six did. Thank you, Mummum.

To Palash, Rajyasree, Latika and Abhik who were the first guinea pigs, kind enough to read the scratchy first draft and kinder enough to tell me how I should blend in the scratches.

To my friends and well-wishers who were unstinting in their encouragement, even though they'd seen me produce nothing in my first two attempts at taking a break to write.

A big thank you to Lexicon for helping promote this novel.

To all the agents and editors who passed on the novel, but were kind enough to make suggestions. Thank you, a lot of your comments helped. And well, in retrospect, living through the cliché of getting rejection letters is now a notch in my post and something I can boast about.

And finally to the one person who has contributed and sacrificed most for this novel, my wife Rasika. You put up with my moods, you edited, you proof-checked, you ideated, and you worked so that I could sit at home whiling the day away pretending to write. Without your encouragement and good sense, this novel would still be a ten-by-ten spreadsheet and I a cranky wannabe writer. I can't thank you enough.

Thank you all, and thank you for reading this novel.